To: Adam,

Merry Christmas 2013 !

Love,
Mom + Dad

ALSO BY CHRISTOPHER BUNN

THE TORMAY TRILOGY
The Hawk and His Boy
The Shadow at the Gate
The Wicked Day

A Storm in Tormay: The Complete Tormay Trilogy

Short Stories
The Model Universe and Other Stories
The Mike Murphy Files and Other Stories
The Christmas Caper
Ice and Fire
The Girl Next Door
The Ocean Won't Burn

The Hawk and His Boy

by
Christopher Bunn

Book One of The Tormay Trilogy

The Hawk and His Boy, *The Shadow at the Gate*, and *The Wicked Day* are not stand-alone books, but are simply portions of the larger story of The Tormay Trilogy.

For Jessica

THE HAWK
AND HIS BOY

CHAPTER ONE
DOWN THE CHIMNEY

The man raised his fist again.

"No shirking," he said. "If you know what's good for you."

The boy dabbed at his cut lip and then touched the wall. His fingertips were greasy with blood. The alley they stood in was narrow, but the moon shone down from overhead, glimmering on the stones of the wall. The sweet scent of selia blossoms filled the air.

"Hurry up."

"I need to get a feel for it first," said the boy sullenly.

Only a fool would climb without trying to understand a wall first. No telling what would be there. Ward spells woven into the stones. Holds and ledges that were illusions, melting away once your weight was on them. He leaned his forehead against the wall and closed his eyes. The stones were still warm from the day's sunlight. And something else.

"The wall's warded," said the boy. "It's listening to us."

"So be silent."

The boy cinched the knapsack on his back tight and began to climb. He was the best of the Juggler's children. The tiniest edge of rock was a foothold or a handhold to him. If he had been given a wall reaching up to the sky, he could have climbed it. Even up to the stars.

He listened as he climbed. Wavering focus could result in injury or death. Eight feet above the ground, he heard the first whispers of the ward spells contracting, weaving themselves tighter and waiting for the intruder. He froze into silence. He thought of the emptiness of sky, where even the wind blows in silence. He recalled a memory of night, mute with stars and darkness. The wards relaxed, hearing the same silence inside the boy. They became still, waiting for a real intruder, someone of noisy flesh and blood, not this shadow of a boy.

He climbed higher. Perhaps there would be some coins for the night's work. Maybe the Juggler's temper would hold good for a few days. After all, surely this was an important job. More important than purses stolen in the markets, or rings slipped from the fingers of ladies strolling the promenades. How else to explain the presence of the Knife? He was not one to bother himself with the Juggler and his pack of children.

It was a high wall, but it wasn't a hard climb. After a few minutes, he reached the gutter and swung up over it. He crept up to the peak of the roof and peered over. An enclosed garden sprawled below. Moonlight shone on bushes and trees. From what the boy could observe, the house was built along the lines of a large rectangle—three stories in some places, four in others—with a tower that surmounted it all on the eastern end.

He took some rope from his knapsack, tied a loop around the chimney, and tossed the free end down to the alley below. It did not take long for the man to climb up. The boy eyed him as he crept over the side of the roof, hungry for any sign of weakness. But Ronan of Aum had not become the Knife of the Thieves Guild by being weak. The boy shivered and rubbed his palms down the sides of his pants.

Only a fool would have said no to the Knife. But the boy had almost refused when the Juggler had approached him earlier that afternoon. He had felt the *no* trembling in fear on the tip of his tongue. The Knife needs a boy to do a chimney job tonight, the Juggler had said. Up a wall, down a chimney, into a sleeping house. As easy as that. The boy knew he could not say no. Not with the Knife involved.

When did the Knife ever have need for one of the Juggler's children? They were cutpurses and pickpockets. They were the whispers and breezes that ran through the marketplaces and the bustling streets of the Highneck Rise district where the lords and ladies came to shop. They were the children that came home to the Juggler with pockets full of coins and the lace handkerchiefs of ladies and the odd key ring or two. Some were climbers, like the boy, but that was done more in fun than anything else. Lazy afternoons in back of the Goose and Gold when the Juggler was snoring drunk on his bed. Scaling the wall there, with only the stableman to shout at them every now and then.

The Knife. The boy had seen him once before. One of the older children had pointed him out, a tall man walking into the Goose and Gold. The Knife. *More blood on his blade than any man in Hearne. Slide up to you closer than your shadow. Slit your throat and be halfway to Dolan before you even knew you were dead. Steal the regent's eyes right out of his head.*

The boy watched the man creep up through the darkness, up and across the roof toward him. Not creep. Flow. It was as if the Knife was made out of liquid shadow. He flowed. And settled next to the boy against the chimney.

"The wards," said the boy. "They didn't hear you?"

A scornful smile crossed the man's face. He pulled the rope up after him.

"Do you remember everything I told you?" he said.

2

"Yes, sir," said the boy. How could he forget? The two of them had sat the boy down in a back room at the Goose and Gold and gone over every detail until he could have recited them in his sleep.

"In the room at the top." The Knife pointed at the tower rising from the far corner of the manor roof. "Remember, boy. Don't open the box. If you do, I'll cut your throat open so wide the wind'll whistle through it."

"I won't."

"Good." The Knife paused. "What's your name, boy?"

"Jute, sir," he said. "At least that's what they call me."

"Well, Jute. The night won't wait much longer."

The man tossed the free end of the rope down the chimney. Jute clambered up onto the chimney ledge and then lowered himself into the shaft. Narrow, but not impossible for someone as thin as he was. It was obvious no one had lit a fire below in months, for it was the end of summer now. Only a dusting of soot coated the walls.

Jute climbed down into darkness. Wary. Listening. Tense with the effort of both focusing and trying to ignore fear at the same time. He rested halfway down the chimney, with his back wedged against one wall and his feet pressed against the opposite. The moon peered down at him through the tiny square of sky far above.

Down again.

After a while, the moonlight failed, and he found himself in complete darkness. *The chimney must have jinked,* he thought. *Somehow it bent, and I didn't notice.* For a moment he found it difficult to breathe, but he shut his eyes tight and that made things better. Hand over hand on the rope, feet feeling for stones in the wall to aid his descent. Down he went, until the chimney widened out and his toes touched the ribs of an iron grate below him.

Jute listened for a while, his eyes closed. But there was nothing to hear, except for the snuffle of a mouse as it skittered along a wall somewhere off to his left. He opened his eyes. He blinked, for the room seemed as light as day after the darkness of the chimney, but it was only the moonlight streaming in through the windows. He tiptoed to the door in the far right corner of the room. Just where the Knife had said it would be. He pressed his ear against the door and listened. Nothing. Except something was behind the door, or somewhere in that direction, listening to him.

He froze. The back of his neck prickled. There was a difference between something—a warding spell, a person—listening for whatever it might hear, as opposed to something listening to him. This thing, whatever it was, was listening specifically to him. That meant it had already identified him.

He had attempted to explain the idea to Lena once, right before she had tried breaking into the bakery in Highneck Rise. Wards are listening spells, mostly. Wards listen all the time. To everything—the wind, the ticking of clocks, people, songbirds, other wards. But a ward can also choose to listen to individual sounds. "Like if you walk through the tavern," he had said. "I can pick out the sound of your feet from among the other sounds. I begin to listen specifically to you because I have identified your sound. Once a ward has identified a sound it listens to that sound for a while, according to whatever rules are woven into the ward spell. If the ward then decides the sound is a threat, then it activates."

Lena had nodded and, later that day, snuck off to Highneck Rise without telling him. The lock on the back door of the bakery hadn't been difficult, but a ward had activated as soon as she had crossed the threshold. Her face was still scarred from the burn.

Jute closed his eyes, listening. The thing somewhere past the door wasn't hostile. Curious, perhaps, and something else he couldn't identify. It was listening specifically to him. Sweat trickled down his back. A tiny voice in the back of his mind suggested turning and leaving. But he couldn't. Turning back meant climbing up the chimney to the man waiting on the roof.

Jute slipped through the door and into a dark hall. *Once inside the hall, the door at the far end and then up the stairs*, the Knife had said.

The door opened and stairs rose before him. They wound around and around, higher and higher. Moonlight filtered down windows cut in the stone walls, softening the darkness into shadow. He was higher than the rest of the manor now. Looking out, he could see the roof stretching away below him. He thought he could make out the dark blot of the Knife crouched beside the chimney.

Up the stairs, boy. Up the stairs and into a small room. That's where the box is.

The sensation of the thing listening to him strengthened. It knew him somehow. He was sure of it. The voice inside his mind suggested again the wisdom of fleeing, but turning away was not an option. The man waiting at the top of the chimney was reason enough, but another reason trembled to astonished life inside Jute. If truth be told, he was not even sure of his own name. To find someone—something—that knew him would be more valuable than the richest purse he had ever stolen.

The stairway curved one more time and came to a door. A warning whispered from the door: a ward woven into the iron handle. He could hear the spell wavering through the air in search of whatever drew near. Instantly, he willed himself into silence, thinking of the quiet moon in her empty sky. The ward subsided back into sleep.

The handle turned under his fingers, and he was inside. Moonlight shone through windows. The city sprawled around him in every direction.

4

Like stars in the night, lamplight gleamed through chinks in the shuttered windows of houses. Overhead, the stars gleamed like lamplight. But Jute had no eye for any of this.

On a table in the middle of the room sat a box.

Somewhere in that room. It isn't a large place, so it shouldn't be difficult to find the thing.

Of course not. There's nothing else here. Only a table, a chair, and a box.

It was the box that called soundlessly to him, so clearly that he turned in fright, thinking someone had spoken his name. Several thoughts floated through his head, reminding him of the Knife, of instructions, of the Juggler, but he quashed them down. His nose twitched like a dog's. The pull was strong. It certainly wasn't a ward. Ward spells never pulled at people—at least, not any ward he'd felt before. Wards pushed people. Pushed them hard in deadly ways. This was like someone tugging at his hand.

It'll be the length of your forearm. Made of black oak and fastened with a catch and hinges of silver. If that isn't enough for you, there's a carving on the top of it. A hawk's head staring at you, with the moon and the sun rising and setting behind him.

The hawk's head gazed at him from the box, the eyes frozen in an unblinking stare. The carving was so lifelike that it seemed the bird was only resting, ready to spread its wings and fly free.

If you open the thing, it'll be my knife in your gullet. Just stow it in your bag, and back up the chimney with you. Don't stop to think, boy. Best not to think.

That was the trouble.

He didn't stop to think. His hand reached out, and the catch flipped up. The lid sprang open. Lying on a cushion of threadbare velvet was a dagger. It was an ugly thing, black and battered. Set within the handle was a gemstone. The stone was cracked and blackened, as if it had been subjected to great heat. It was hard to tell, but Jute suspected it might once have been red.

He shivered. It was the dagger that was aware. A questioning, delicate touch feathered around the edges of his mind. Curiosity, and then something else. Satisfaction.

Jute sat back on his heels in astonishment. How could this thing—this dagger—have anything to do with him, know him?

If you open the thing, it'll be my knife in your gullet.

He touched the blade and snatched his hand away. A smear of blood stained the iron. Surely the edge looked as dull as a spoon! Scarlet welled from his finger. He sucked the salt of it into his mouth. The awareness brushing his thoughts vanished. There was nothing. Only an old, cheap-

5

looking dagger. The stone in the handle was probably just glass. And yet he could have sworn, right when he had felt the sting of the cut, someone had whispered in his ear.

If you open the thing, it'll be my knife in your gullet.

Sweat sprang from Jute's forehead, and he shivered. He shut the box. His hands shook. The hawk no longer looked lifelike. It was a crude carving at best. He stuffed the box into his knapsack. His teeth chattered.

What have I done?

Jute fled from the room. He ran through the doorway and down the dark stairs. Behind him, he felt a soundless wave of menace explode and roll down the steps after him as the ward triggered. He lunged forward. His heart thumped within his chest. Heat surged against his back. He ran so fast that his feet barely touched the stairs. Down and down, curving around and around, until he grew dizzier with each step he took. He risked a glance behind him, but there was only shadow and silence.

Jute crept back into the room with the fireplace. He took one despairing look around the room, but there was nothing to do except climb back up the chimney. The knapsack swung from his back, and the box inside seemed to grow heavier the higher he went. He had to rest for a moment, wedged between the chimney walls, for the dread inside him had welled up until his hands were too weak to hold his weight on the rope. But then his scalp prickled, for a whisper drifted down from above him.

"Jute. Come up, boy. Come up."

Trembling, Jute continued. The opening of the chimney came into view, first as a smudge of night, then widening into a square of sky speckled with stars. The shape of the man's head peered down. Jute could make out the black spots of the man's eyes.

"Do you have it?" said the man.

"Yes," said Jute, trying not to let his teeth chatter. His hands ached on the rope.

"Did you open it?" said the man.

"No!" said Jute, feeling the sweat bead cold on his skin.

"Hand it here."

"Let me come up first," said the boy.

"Hand it up."

The man leaned down into the well of the chimney, one arm extended. He snatched the box up and examined it in the moonlight.

"Well done," he said, turning back. "Come up, boy."

Jute pulled himself up to the edge and a blessed view of stars and the city sleeping around them. He could smell the selia blossom on the breeze. And then, almost carelessly, the man's hand touched his shoulder and Jute felt a sting that dulled into nothing.

6

Time slowed.

Numb.

A needle gleamed in the man's hand.

"Nothing personal, boy," said the man. "We all have our jobs to do."

And he pushed Jute.

Gently.

He fell.

Down and down.

Down into darkness. Which blossomed with bursts of light as his head struck the chimney walls. Stars in the night sky. His silent sky. And then nothing.

Nothing personal, boy.

The eastern horizon blushed into purple, even though sunrise was another hour away. The moon retreated over the sea to the west, gazing down on the city of Hearne with her silver eye. Another eye gazed down on Hearne. High in the sky soared a hawk. Nothing escaped his attention. The bird circled wider. The wind bore him up. A scream of defiance and exultation burst forth from his beak. He soared higher into the emptiness of the sky.

CHAPTER TWO
LEVORETH CALLAS

Far to the north, Levoreth woke up frowning, tangled in her bedsheets and the thoughts in her mind. She padded to the window. A breeze cooled her brow. Over the mountains in the east, the sky was streaked with rose paling to blue. Murmurs drifted up from the barn below—the stable hands pitching hay for the horses. A boy yawned his way across the courtyard, water slopping from the buckets he was carrying.

She sat down on the window settle and gazed out. She could see all the way down to the ford beyond the cornfields. The road crossed the river there and made its way southwest through the forests of Dolan, and further still, across the plains and, ultimately, to the city of Hearne.

Why was she thinking so much of Hearne these days?

It had been a long time since she had been south. It had been a long time since she had been anywhere. She frowned again. A thought tickled at the back of her mind and then was gone before she could reach for it.

She shrugged into a frock and went downstairs. The scent of bread met her as she walked across the hall and opened the kitchen door. An old woman was bent over the oven, poking with a paddle at several loaves of bread inside. She straightened up, her face red from the oven's heat.

"M'lady Levoreth—it's early for you to be up," said the old woman.

"Nonsense, Yora. The sun's nearly up and the hands are up, and I just saw Mirek ambling across the yard."

"The lazy good-for-nothing. It's a wonder he's awake. He's near as bad as his father who died of sleep, snoring away his life in the sun—M'lady! You'll burn yourself!" The girl had stooped down and pulled a loaf of bread from the oven with her hands. She grinned at Yora and ripped a hunk of bread free. It steamed in her grasp.

"It's quite done. And smells wonderful, too."

"M'lady! You shouldn't be doing such things!"

Levoreth went outside, chewing on her piece of bread. The sun edged up over the mountains. She squinted up into the light and then frowned down at her toes in the dirt.

The stable hands ducked their heads when she walked into the barn. Even the villagers were not as reverent as that with her uncle, Hennen

Callas, the duke of Dolan. But the stable hands held her in awe and would never let her forget it. It had been her own fault.

She had been careless one day, two years ago. It had been getting harder to remember, to be careful. But she had forgotten. Perhaps it had been the intoxication of a spring after a long, cold winter. She had hiked out to the upper pasture in search of the first lupines. The previous week to that day, the Farrows in their gaily painted caravans had rolled through Dolan, and Hennen Callas had bought three wild colts off of them. He had happily parted with a purse stuffed with gold, for the Farrows had an eye for horseflesh that was unsurpassed in all the duchies of Tormay. The colts had been turned out into the upper pasture to wait until Hennen had time to break them to bridle.

Not thinking, she had set the colts dancing around her—wheeling away and thundering back at a gallop to stop, quivering, in front of her, pushing their silken noses into her palms. Their minds thrilled against hers, jarring her with impressions of childish delight. She caught images of time blurring into light and back again, shot through with joy and gold and pounding hearts, and the vast spaces of the northern plains racing away beneath their flying hooves. Their thoughts trembled with the solemnity of her name.

Rejoice! Sun and speed and wind. Rejoice!

Something had made her turn. Three stable hands sat on the fence at the end of the pasture, their mouths gaping. They tumbled off the fence and ran off. The colts wheeled and danced around her. Sunlight shimmered in the air, and everywhere there was the perfume of sage and lupine and the freshness of the earth wakening to spring. Wakening for her.

That had been two years ago.

Levoreth swallowed the last bite of bread and whistled. All the horses in the barn stuck their heads out of their stalls and nickered at her. Whispers of horse-thought brushed against her mind: oats, sunlight, and canters through the grasses of the high fields. She smiled.

"You're all just as lazy as Mirek," she said. A roan stretched its neck out and breathed alfalfa on her.

She rode the roan down to the ford and reined him to a halt in the shallows of the river. Sunlight shone on the water sliding over stones. The road curved from the ford and stretched away into the forest. Deep within the forest it split into two roads: one road to the south, toward Harth and Hearne; the other west to Andolan, the ducal seat of Dolan. Hearne. It had been many years since she had been to that city. The thought tickled again at the back of her mind and she caught it this time.

Soon.

"Soon?" she said aloud.

You have slept long enough, Levoreth Callas. You have slept too long. Your time draws near. Not today. Not tomorrow. But perhaps the next. Or perhaps after that.

And she frowned up at the sky and then down at the light sparkling on the water rippling by. The voice was her own.

When she brought the roan to a clattering halt in the yard, Hennen Callas was striding down the manor steps. He was a tall man, with gray hair and kind brown eyes.

"Levoreth."

"Uncle," she said, dismounting and flipping the reins to a hovering groom.

"It has been quite a while, hmm." He stopped and blinked several times.

"Yes?" she said.

"I have it in mind," he said. "I have it in mind to . . ." He trailed off again and gazed across the yard. "Blast those boys. They haven't mucked the mares out yet."

"You were saying?" she said.

"What? Oh. As I was saying, I think it time we paid a visit to Botrell in Hearne."

"Hearne?"

"Been a few years since we've been down to the city," her uncle said, "and every trader coming north says Botrell has a mare, Riverrun's dam, been foaling the best hunters since Min the Morn first set hoof in Tormay."

"Which is an exaggeration," Levoreth said, "as Min the Morn supposedly lived over seven hundred years ago, and the tradition of formal hunting began less than two hundred years ago when your great-great-grandfather broke his neck riding out after wolves. So the story goes."

Hennen blinked. "But there's also the Autumn Fair. Everyone goes who's anybody. Even the royal court of Harth. Your aunt has her heart set on going this fall, and besides, you haven't been since you were a little girl." A puzzled expression crept over his weathered face. She waited and said nothing.

"What's more," he said, "I received a raven last week, with word from Botrell that the duke of Mizra will be attending the Fair this year."

"Yes?" she said, smiling at him. And then words failed her uncle, for he turned and beat a hasty retreat toward the safety of the barn.

CHAPTER THREE
EXPECTATIONS

The Knife strode through the dark streets of Hearne. Houses sleeping still, shuttered windows, bolted doors and gates—he was alone. The box was a comforting weight in the bag slung across his back. Shadows, but he'd be paid well for this night's work. Nearly enough gold to take him far away from this miserable city, up to the Flessoray Islands, off the coast of Harlech. Nearly enough. And there he could lose himself on one of the islands and never be known for who he was, never be found again.

Nearly enough gold.

Night was weakening fast into the dark blues of morning, and he cast the sky one disinterested glance. If he had paused to look more carefully, he might have seen a hawk flying far overhead. He came to the Goose and Gold. The inn was still shuttered against the night. He slipped down the alley that ran alongside the inn and knocked at a door. It popped open and revealed the face of the Juggler.

"Success?" said the fat man.

"As expected," said the Knife, moving past him into the room. The building was silent around them.

"And the boy?"

"Did his job well."

"He was the best I had," said the Juggler, trying to look sad. "I hope our patron takes my loss into account. I'm a poor man who loves his children. They're all I have."

"You will be rewarded," said the Knife. "Enough gold to keep you drunk for a year."

"Ah," said the fat man, rubbing his hands together.

"You will also forget this night. It never happened. If even a whisper of this is heard anywhere from Harth to Harlech, I'll come for you. Understand?"

"Of course." The fat man smiled shakily. "I would never dream of—"

"Don't even dream of it. I'm not fond of killing children. You, however, would be a different matter altogether."

They walked downstairs into the basement of the inn. At the far end of the room were the oak barrels where the innkeeper kept his wine and ale. The barrels were taller than a man and a good fifteen feet in diameter.

11

When he came to the last barrel, the Knife felt along its side until his fingers encountered a tiny catch. The side of the barrel swung out on well-oiled hinges. It was empty. Inside was an opening in the floor. The Knife climbed in and lowered himself down through the shaft. He paused.

"Tell your other children, those children you love so well, that the boy stumbled across a ward. A fire ward or something like that."

"Yes, yes." The Juggler nodded. "The sort that leaves nothing but ashes."

"We can't have them asking questions."

"I'll beat them if they do." And the Juggler smirked.

The other eyed him distastefully and then disappeared down the shaft. The Juggler closed the barrel door behind him. He waited, listening until the faint noises within faded into silence, and then, rubbing his hands together, he padded back up the stairs.

CHAPTER FOUR
WAKING UP

The boy Jute woke by degrees. First, he was only aware of pain—a dull sort that came in waves. He was not sure he had a body any longer. Pain was all he was, an ache that was everywhere. An ache that bloomed into fire.

He gasped. And then he heard a voice.

"There, you see? He's coming to."

Another voice rumbled an answer, but Jute could not make out what it said. He became aware of his body, lying heavy and useless on a mattress.

"He's been out long enough," said the first voice. "We'll get some answers now. Try that philter of yours again. Maybe that'll bring him around properly."

Recollection seeped back into Jute's mind. Images drifted through his mind. The Knife, like a shadow against the moonlit sky, reaching down for him. And then the prick of the needle and the long fall back down the chimney, into a well of darkness. But there had been something before that. He had opened the box. The black dagger. He had cut his finger on its edge.

A bitter odor tickled at his nose. He sneezed and opened his eyes. He was in a room lit by a candle burning on a table near the door. The light blurred in his eyes. Blinking, he tried to focus. He was aware of a figure seated next to him beside the bed. Another man stood at the foot of the bed. The man leaned forward, and the candlelight cast his features into shadowed relief. A hooked nose and a narrow skull gave him the appearance of a bird of prey stooping over its kill.

"Of all the houses in Hearne," said the man. His eyes glittered. "This is the one you should not have broken into. You'd have been safer robbing the regent's castle."

The pain flared down into Jute's bones with a sickening rush. His jaw clenched, grinding his teeth together. A spasm arched him off the bed, and his hand flailed off to the side, grabbing desperately. A warm hand grasped his. The pain subsided as quickly as it had sprung up.

"You're going to kill him, Nio," said the other voice.

"I'll snap him like a stick!" The hawk-faced man glared at the other seated next to the bed. "The box is gone, Severan! It's gone!"

"He's just a boy," said the older man. "I'm sure he wouldn't mind answering a few questions. Would you, boy?"

"No," said Jute, blinking away the tears blurring his sight. But then the candlelight winked out and he sank back down into blessed darkness.

The darkness was warm and complete. The warmth seeped into his bones. The pain receded. He was not sure whether he was awake or dreaming this darkness. Something rustled nearby and then settled into silence—a patient, waiting sort of silence.

Jute coughed experimentally. The silence deepened. He was relieved, however, for he knew that whoever was there was friendly. Someone different from the first two men. How he knew this, he wasn't sure. But there was a comfortable feel to the darkness, not unlike someone drowsing by the bed of a sick friend on the mend.

"Excuse me," said Jute.

"I was wondering when you would speak."

"Do I know you?" said Jute. "Your voice sounds familiar."

"Once or twice," said the voice. It spoke in an odd, old-fashioned sort of way. "In dreams. Mostly when you were small."

"Do you know who I am?" Jute asked, his voice eager.

"For a surety," said the other. "It is because I knew you that I've spoken to you."

"Who are you?" said the boy.

There was a pause, and then the voice chuckled. "Enough time for that later. We shall find our explanations when we must, but no sooner. If I were you, I would not say a word about opening the box. To anyone. You're in a difficult enough spot as it is."

"I didn't mean to open it," said Jute.

"Perhaps," said the voice. "There's usually a difference between what one means to do and what one is meant to do. At any rate, this Nio fellow will not be interested in whether or not you meant to open the box. What will interest him is whether you did. Tell him anything except that."

Someone shook his arm then, and he opened his eyes. Jute found himself blinking in the candlelight of the room. The thin-faced man, Nio, was gone, but the old man was still sitting by his bed.

"Could you stomach some food, boy?"

The old man had brought with him bread and a bowl of stew on a tray. Jute ate, and the man watched in silence. He was dressed in grubby clothes that hung loosely on his gaunt frame. His eyes were brown as polished walnut wood.

"What's your name, boy?" he asked.

"Jute, sir. At least, that's what I've been told." He mopped up the last bit of stew with some bread and eyed the old man nervously.

"Well, Jute," the old man said, "It's a name as good enough as another. As for myself, my name is Severan. You seem rather young for robbing houses. Work for the Thieves Guild, don't you?"

"Er, yes," said Jute. "Sort of." He plucked nervously at his blanket.

"Ah," said Severan. "You run with the Juggler's children?"

"Yes," said Jute, startled by him knowing.

The man nodded. "Even dusty old artifacts like me know a thing or two about this city. Guild or no Guild, they can't help you in this house. If Nio deals with you as he'd like, you'll be wishing you broke your neck falling down the chimney. He put a lot of stock in that old box, even though he couldn't figure out how to open it. He swore it held something valuable. Something unusual. Not sure if I ever believed it myself, but, no matter. He's angry, lad. Extremely angry. It never does to cross his sort."

"He's not—" Jute said, faltering as he remembered the fury in the other man's eyes. "Is he here?"

"He isn't here," said the old man. "You're in luck of a sort this evening. He hardly ever leaves this house these days so intent is he on his studies. Reading, researching, that sort of thing. For the moment, though, he's gone. Listen, Jute—you'd do well to tell me what you know. There'll be no harm coming to you if you tell me everything that happened two nights ago."

"Two nights ago?" said the boy in disbelief.

"Aye." Severan reached out and touched Jute's head. "You got a knock there, falling down the chimney. Strange that a clever lad like yourself would miss his step climbing a chimney. Perhaps you were pushed, eh? Perhaps your friend waiting for you at the top?"

Jute's eyes widened. The needle in Ronan's hand gleamed in his mind, gleaming in the moonlight. The old man sat back with a gloomy smile.

"Who can you trust, Jute?"

The candlelight dimmed down, like a golden eye winking at him from the shadows. The room blurred around the boy, and then there was only darkness.

CHAPTER FIVE
DISCUSSIONS DURING SUPPER

The duchess of Dolan had been born Melanor Ayn, only daughter of Rodret Ayn, whose family had held the western foothills of the Morn Mountains for the dukes of Dolan ever since Dolan Callas had built the town of Andolan.

The story Hennen always told Levoreth was that he had been hunting deer in the foothills when a stag led him to the country lodge of Rodret Ayn. A young woman had been hanging out the washing on a line, and she had paused, pegs in her mouth and a damp shift in her arms, when he had ridden up. Love at first sight for both of them, Hennen always solemnly intoned.

Melanor Callas's story, however, was different.

"That idiot tried to set his horse at the holly hedge bordering the garden. Of course the horse balked at the prickles and pitched him over onto his head. Knocked him cold, and blood everywhere. I ruined a good tablecloth wrapping up that knucklehead of his. Wouldn't be the last time, mind you. Fever took him for two whole days, raving out of his mind. When he came to, the first thing he did was propose to me in a most unsuitable way. I refused him, of course, until he had spoken to my father. It's best to keep a man waiting, my dear."

Prompted by meaningful glances from the duchess at supper, the duke broached the subject again. He looked down the table at Levoreth and cleared his throat. She ignored him and concentrated on Yora's mushroom and potato casserole. The steam rose up from her plate and tickled her nose. She chewed thoughtfully. Garlic, crushed pepper, dill.

"Your aunt and I've been talking," said Hennen, refilling his glass out of precaution. "She feels, as do I, that you're old enough now to—"

"Thyme," said Levoreth.

"Um—well, time is a consideration, of course. The fact is, you do so splendidly overseeing this house whenever your aunt is in Andolan." He gulped some wine.

"Fennel," said Levoreth. "But it's not fresh."

"What?" said the Duke.

"She's doing her trick again," said his wife. "Figuring out the herbs Yora used in the casserole. Levoreth, don't be difficult. What your uncle has been

16

referring to with such delicacy is that it's high time you were married." The duchess glanced at her husband, but he was applying himself industriously to his casserole. "Surely you've thought it yourself, my dear. How old are you now? Seventeen, eighteen? Don't tell me you're nineteen!" Melanor waved her hand. "I can never remember such things. No matter. Your age isn't important. What's important is that you're a grown woman. And not just any woman—you're lovely, sensible . . ."

"And bake excellent apple pies," said the duke.

". . . and can run a household without even raising your voice. I don't know how you do it, Levoreth. The maids mind you more than they do me."

"All the stable hands live in adoring fear of her," said Hennen. "Some of the tales they come up with, you'd think they'd been at the hard cider. Just the other day, that idiot Mirek had the nerve to tell me I shouldn't be riding the roan, as it's Levoreth's favorite. I threw him into the pigsty for his impertinence. Melanor, my dear, do you know the spotted sow?"

"No," said his wife. "We aren't acquainted."

"She bit Mirek. Twice on his hind end, before he could make it over the fence. I've never seen the boy move that fast, but that sow was moving faster." The duke shook his head. "Imagine that."

"I fail to see your point."

"The point is, my dear, you'd think a boy would run faster than an old pig."

"Hennen," said the duchess, "have some more casserole."

"Oh, all right," said the duke.

"Levoreth?"

"Yes, aunt?" said Levoreth.

"Would you at least consider accompanying us to Hearne for the Fair?"

"And miss the autumn here? The walnuts won't be picked in time and they'll rot with mildew. The stable hands will pine away for me and forget to muck out the horses. They're useless on their own. What's the Fair to me? Cooped up in Hearne and having to put up with dreary balls and teas and oily princes and lords slobbering all over my hand and telling me how beautiful I am while trying to calculate how much dowry I'd be bringing to their bed."

"Really, my dear," said her aunt.

"What's more," said Levoreth, "Botrell will ogle me shamelessly."

"Botrell'll do no such thing!" said the duke, pounding his fist on the table. "I'll horsewhip him in front of his own guests!"

"Nonsense," said Levoreth. "He's the regent of Hearne. He can do whatever he wants at his silly Fair."

"But if you don't go you won't meet Brond Gifernes!" said the duchess, and then her hand flew to her mouth in alarm.

"Brond Gifernes?" asked Levoreth. "The duke of Mizra?"

For once, Melanor Callas was at a loss for words. She was saved, however, by the door swinging open. Yora entered, bearing a platter of blueberry turnovers.

"Something for afters, m'lord?" asked Yora.

"Thank you, Yora," said the duke. He selected a turnover and bit into it. They remained silent while Yora cleared the dishes. The door closed again behind her.

"You were saying something about the Duke of Mizra," said Levoreth.

"Yes, Mizra!" said the duke, spraying crumbs onto the table. "No reason why we can't say things about the Duke of Mizra every now and then. Why, just the other day, I was talking with the miller down in the village and . . ."

"Uncle."

"Well, the fact is I received a raven from him last week."

"And?"

"And he's asked for your hand in marriage, and why not, I say! You couldn't do much better. He's a duke and you're the niece of a duke, and all the traders say he's got more gold than all the noble houses of Harth put together!" The duke banged his fist again on the table for emphasis and then ruined the effect by looking longingly at the door.

"My dear," said the duchess. "I know this comes as a bit of a shock, but do consider it. At least come to Hearne with us and meet the fellow. There's no harm in that."

"I'll think about it," said Levoreth. "Excuse me." She rose to leave the table. As she walked up the stairs, she heard the duke whisper behind her, "Shadows, why does she always make me feel like a little boy?!"

"That's because," said his wife, but then her voice faded and Levoreth did not hear the rest.

She sat on the settle of her window. The moon was rising. The voice whispered again in her head.

You have slept overly long. It is time to wake.

And she knew the voice was her own. It had been so many years. Years of living quietly in the sleepy backwoods of Dolan, days blurring into months and years and lifetimes, all slipping by her. Strange, how time had passed. It was as if she had been asleep for years, drowsing through the days. It was time to wake.

Perhaps for the last time. One last autumn—I can feel it—but not here in this place I've come to love so well, but in Hearne at the center of the duchies. The center of Tormay. At least, what man thinks is the center. For there is no center. Only the four stillpoints. The silence of the depths of the sea. The silence of the wind in an empty sky. The silence of a motionless flame. And the silence of the earth.

My beloved earth. I could sink into this loam and sleep forever. Down below root and leaf, below the spine of the mountain range and the stretch of the plains. I could sleep away the centuries instead of refashioning myself into one Levoreth after another. But this one—poor girl—this Levoreth is the last one I shall be. I can feel it in my bones. I've grown weary.

The moonlight painted the forest silver, etched with shadows. Levoreth let her thoughts drift out across the yard, through the fields and into the trees. She felt a fox trot by, his tongue lolling over sharp teeth, thoughts of chickens in his head. The oaks were mumbling about root rot and the band of noisy crows that had settled into the east forest fringes. A trader slept by the coals of his campfire, far down the woods road, snoring under his cart. His old horse dozed nearby, but her thought woke the animal and it nickered in question, scenting the air for her. She quieted the horse, and it contentedly went back to sleep.

I'm tired. Tired, irritable, and forgetful. I've forgotten so many things. How odd. I can't remember ever having been in the duchy of Mizra.

She turned from the window and gazed around her room. Fresh flowers in the vase next to her bed. A smile crossed her face. Yora looked after her jealously, as if she were the daughter the old woman had never had.

Sometimes I can barely remember who I am.

In the morning, Levoreth walked down the stairs and found the duchess knitting in the sitting room that looked out into the garden. A cat slept in her lap, paws wrapped around a ball of yarn.

"I'll go with you and Uncle to Hearne," said Levoreth.

Her aunt glanced up. The cat woke and jumped down. It rubbed its head against Levoreth's ankles. She scratched behind the cat's ears and it purred in adoration.

"Besides," said Levoreth, "who'll keep you company when Uncle is off talking horses with Botrell and every other half-witted noble?"

"You'll never get married with that attitude." But her aunt smiled. "You only have to meet this duke of Mizra fellow. For all we know, he might be missing his teeth."

The cat nipped Levoreth's finger out of affection and then strolled away. It flopped down in a pool of sunlight and promptly fell asleep.

"To be honest, Levoreth," said the duchess, "I was beginning to think you'd never leave this place—hiding away here like a hermit with no one at all around. Why, you've been here for two years and never once come back to Andolan. The only time we see you is when Hennen drags me out here so he can inspect new colts."

"I was tired of Andolan," said Levoreth. She turned away.

"Anyway," said her aunt, not hearing her. "I'll tell Hennen. He'll be pleased.

CHAPTER SIX
MURDER BY NIGHT

The night lay over the valley. A blanket of darkness was draped over the hills and ravines and stands of pine, over the sleeping houses of the hamlet nestled below the ford. Smoke drifted up from their chimneys. A stream glimmered its way through the valley, down from the mountains and into the larger Rennet valley and the River Rennet itself, which ran for leagues until it reached the far-off city of Hearne and the sea. The air smelled of pine and the scent of heather wafting down from the plain of Scarpe, which stretched away from the top of the rise to the north.

But there was another smell as well. Only the most sensitive of human noses could have noted it, and even then they would have not recognized the scent, thinking it perhaps the whiff of a dead animal, rotting in the thickets that covered the valley slope.

In the valley below, a dog barked, calling a warning to the sleeping villagers. There was fear and anger in the sound.

Wake! Wake! Danger approaches! Wake from your sleep, oh my masters!

But there was no response. No lights flaring in windows, no doors flung open to bloom with firelight and life.

Wake! Wake!

The dog fell silent.

The moon hid behind a cloud. The darkness deepened. It was the third hour after midnight, when the tide of blood is at its lowest ebb, when the soul sinks so low in slumber that the sleeper drifts near to death. The third hour after midnight is the time when dreams and nightmares gain form; the scratching at the door, the tapping at the window, and the stealthy step in the hallway come close to reality.

In the home of the miller, Fen awoke with a gasp. She was nine years old and the miller's youngest child. She had slept poorly for the past three days. Nightmares crowded her sleep, but they faded whenever she woke up so that she could remember nothing except fear and the horrible sensation of something watching her just out of the corner of her eye. She was more sensitive to such things than others. Even as a little girl, she had known things, such as where the ducks hid their eggs in the rushes, or whether there would be ice on the river in the morning, or the fact that milk turned to butter faster and sweeter if you said its true name as you churned: *butere*. No one had ever told her that word. She just knew it, somehow, gazing down at the milk. Her grandmother on her mother's side was a bit of a hedgewitch in her own small way. She wondered about her youngest granddaughter but never spoke of what she thought.

Fen sat up in bed, trembling. Beside her, her sister Magwin stirred in her sleep. Magwin was fifteen and would be married next spring. She never had nightmares. Fen tiptoed to the window and looked out. It was dark outside, but the few stars visible in the sky gave enough light for her to make out the vague, looming shape of the barn and the mill beyond on the bank of the stream.

What had woken her this time? Another nightmare, but something else as well. Something else. A sound. The dog had been barking. That was it. Poor Hafall, cooped up in the barn every night. But he wasn't barking anymore. Silence. Probably smelled the foxes that lived up in the brambles. The foxes were sniffing around the yard, no doubt, hungry for chickens.

Except—the barn door was open.

She did not see it at first, for the building was only a big blot of shadow. But for one instant, the moon peered out from behind her cloud and illumined the open door and the well of shadow within the door. The moon vanished again, and the barnyard plunged back into darkness.

Hafall will be out, she thought. *The foxes will be in. Killing the chickens. Blood on white feathers. Someone forgot to shut the door.*

Fear swept over her until it was all she could do to just stand there, shivering. She thought of her bed and Magwin breathing gently there, but then she turned and trudged out of the room, feeling her way through the darkness of the house. She was her father's daughter, and while he was a kind man, he stood for no weakness from his children.

It was cold outside. Her breath steamed in the air. The night was hushed with a silence, unbroken by anything except the murmur of the stream. The barn loomed up before her.

"Hafall?" she said. "Here, boy." Fen whistled softly, like her father had taught her—two fingers angled together between her lips. But there was no response. No sheepdog running up to lick her face and push his damp nose into her palm. Only silence. The girl stepped through the doorway of the barn and immediately stopped. Her toes felt a warm stickiness. She looked down. The dog lay at her feet. Trembling, Fen knelt.

"Hafall?"

His fur was matted and clumped with blood, but she stroked his coat anyway. A gaping hole had been torn in his throat. She touched his face, the muzzle brindled with gray and the floppy ears that had been attuned to so many years of the miller's children, watching over them with his brown eyes and patiently enduring all the indignations they had lovingly heaped upon him. The eyes were dull and unseeing now. The pain inside Fen was almost too much to bear. It felt as if her own throat had been torn out. She could not breathe.

Something whispered behind her. The slightest of noises. Perhaps it was just the breeze. She turned. The moon peeped out from behind her cloud again and flooded the yard with silvery luminance.

The door!

I closed it!

But the door to the house stood ajar. The moonlight cast the entrance into relief—a thin rectangle of shadow set within white stone walls. And then the shadow grew as the door swung wider. For a moment Fen thought her father was about to step out, but then to her horror she saw that the stone walls were moving. No, something in front of the walls was moving— forms shifting. The moonlight and shadow slid off them like liquid. She blinked and rubbed her eyes. The forms gained definition and color. There was a tall, slender shape that at first she thought was a man, but then it turned its head, and she was no longer sure. The thing's eyes glimmered in the darkness like veiled stars. A long, thin blade curved from its hand. At its feet slunk two dogs, bigger than yearling calves, with massive shoulders and huge heads.

A word surfaced in her mind unbidden. A word she did not know. *Cwalu*. Death.

Again, the moon vanished back behind the safety of her cloud. Shadow reclaimed the yard. The shapes at the doorway blurred and vanished into the house. A scream clawed at Fen's throat, quivering on her tongue and springing tears from her eyes. But all she could manage was a whimper.

That was enough. The last shadow disappearing through the doorway across the yard halted at the sound. The hound's head swung from side to side, scenting the air. Two red eyes gleamed and fastened on her with dreadful certainty. Fen turned and ran.

Into the darkness of the barn she ran, heart pounding so fast it was a solid blur of agony, gasping, stumbling, arms windmilling. Tripping over a bale of hay to land sprawling. Palms stinging, blood in her mouth. The darkness was like water around her, holding her fast as if she were trying to run through the creek chest-deep, struggling, desperately reaching for the other side that was no longer there.

She heard the scrabble of claws somewhere behind her and a hoarse breathing that shuddered through her. Memory flooded her mind with a rush. Her thoughts drifted by. *I remember now. I've been here before. In my nightmare. I wish I was sleeping still.*

And she slammed straight into a wall. Wood. Stars burst across her sight. She felt splinters in her face, and her left hand burned with a heavy ache. She could not close her fingers. She nearly collapsed with the pain of it, but her other hand caught on the wooden rungs. She had run right into the ladder leading up to the hayloft. Frantically, she began to climb, clinging with her right hand and hooking her left elbow over the rungs.

Up.

Up. The ladder under Fen shook as the animal threw itself against the supports. The thing made no sound except for the harsh breath rasping in the darkness below. Her body cringed in anticipation of claws tearing at her, of teeth pulling her down flailing from the ladder to fall and fall and fall. She found herself over the top, sobbing and face down in the straw that littered the hayloft.

Fen turned and looked down. Below her, a pair of eyes stared up from the darkness. She could make out the shape of the hound—the lolling tongue and jaws of gleaming teeth, the head, the shoulders bunching and tensing. Tensing to jump! She threw herself backward, scrambling in the straw for anywhere, nowhere to hide. Fire shot up her arm as she fell on her injured hand. The hayloft trembled with the impact of the beast. Splinters and straw flew as claws raked the planks at the edge of the loft, scrabbling to gain a hold. Fen could smell the stench of the thing—a musk of decay mixed with a strange, sour damp. With a snarl, the hound fell away. She heard the thump of its body landing on the ground below.

And then only silence. A complete and awful silence. She strained her ears listening, but everything was quiet. That was even worse than hearing the hound, that dreadful breathing from her nightmare. Her thoughts raced through the silence.

Was there another way up onto the hayloft, a way she had forgotten? What was the hound doing? What if the other creature—that strange man with his sword in his hand—what if he was standing in the darkness below? Staring up, silently beginning to climb the ladder?

Fen crawled as quietly as she could to the edge of the hayloft and peeped over. Nothing. Only shadow. She peered out a little farther. And the hound surged up out of the darkness. Fangs snapped in her face. The thing's breath stank of death and blood and sour rot. Claws raked down the side of her arm. She screamed and flung herself back. The beast hung over the side, eyes staring and tongue lolling from gaping jaws. With a tremendous scrambling heave it kicked its way up onto the loft.

For a second there was silence. Fen was caught within the beat of her heart—a knell that paused in the midst of its toll, lingering in the act of being as if there was no need to beat any more. She stared at the beast, and it stared back at her. Saliva gleamed on its lips, illumined by a moonbeam.

The hound leapt.

It would only take a heartbeat. One more heartbeat.

She stumbled backward.

I hope it's quick, she thought.

So it won't hurt.

Please, no.

And then she was falling.

The trapdoor over the haymow. Someone left it open. *Papa will be furious. Magwin fell through here when she was small and broke her leg.* Fire lanced through Fen's thigh. She shrieked. Slammed down on her back. Musty hay. Alfalfa dust choking in her throat. Agony.

Fen looked up. Her vision was dizzy and muddled with white spots blooming in the darkness. Long, thin, curving spikes obscured most of what she saw. Red eyes glared down at her from high overhead. There was intelligence in them, assessing and weighing the situation.

She tried to get up, but the instant she moved her leg, she almost blacked out from the pain. One of the spikes sprouted from her thigh like the tendril of an obscene plant, transformed into steel and slick with blood. She had fallen between the spikes of the harrow. They rose up around her, protecting her, claiming her for their own, anointed with her blood like some strange, ancient altar of thorns.

Dimly, from far away, she heard a whistle. Darkness claimed her and she knew no more.

CHAPTER SEVEN
DARKNESS AND WATER

Jute woke to find himself alone in the room. A candle guttered on the table, melted down almost to its base. As there was no window, he was not sure how much time had passed. An hour? Another day? He tested his limbs. They ached, but no worse than a beating from the Juggler. He sat up and almost passed out. Dizzily, he forced himself to his feet.

Trust no one.

He glanced around, startled. But there was no one in the room, only the voice inside his head.

Trust no one.

"Even you?" he said. "Who are you?"

There was no answer. He tiptoed to the door, pressed his ear to the wood, and listened. Every house has its own sounds: the sigh of wood beams shifting slightly under the onslaught of wind and sunlight and time, the creak of a stone fireplace cooling around embers, the scrape of tree branches against a window, the stately tick of clocks. And then there are the human sounds: voices, footfalls on stairs and hall floorboards, the settle of a body's weight into beds or chairs, and the whisper of knives in the kitchen, punctuated by clattering pots and pans.

But there was nothing at all. Jute strained to listen, but there was only silence. He was afraid, for the silence held an anticipation, not unlike a ward—a coiled expectancy seeking its moment of violent release. He touched the door handle, expecting the tremble of a ward spell infused through the iron. There was nothing. However, the door was locked.

He turned out his pockets, but he did not even have a bit of fluff, let alone a piece of wire. Someone had emptied them. He frowned at that, for he had a habit of keeping his pockets stuffed full of interesting things that he collected: perhaps a polished mouse skull, some walnuts if he felt hungry, a ball of string, the remains of an expired ward that Lena had proudly given him, and always a piece of wire. But his pockets were empty now.

He examined the bed, but it had been made by a craftsman with no love of metal, for there was not a single nail in its frame. The chair Severan had sat in and the table by the door were no better. They looked to have been built by the same hands—notched and grooved with wooden joints.

The candle. It sat on a copper plate. Wax had run down and built up on the metal in draperies. The candle would not come unstuck from the plate when he tried twisting it, and he ended up splashing hot wax on his fingers. The flame went out, plunging the room into darkness.

He did not mind darkness. He never had, even when the Juggler had locked him in the basement for the first time. That had been years ago. He had been smart enough then, as a young child, to pretend terror and tears for the Juggler's satisfaction. Being locked in the dark had become the Juggler's favorite punishment for him. That and beating him. He'd choose the darkness over a beating any day.

Never mind that now. The candle.

He froze, unsure if the voice was sounding within the room or from within his head. The skin prickled on the back of his neck.

"Who are you?" he said.

I told you before, boy. There'll be time for that later.

The voice subsided into silence. Jute shivered, despite the stuffy air in the room. The candle came away from the plate in his hand in one wrench. His fingers found what he hoped for: a metal spike protruding from the center of the copper plate, ideal for impaling candles. Ideal for picking a lock. He bent the spike back and forth until it broke free from the plate.

It took him a while to pick the lock, for his hands were shaking so badly that he dropped the spike twice and had to fumble in the dark for it. But the tumblers of the lock were simple, and the door creaked open.

A glow flooded into the room. He peeked out into a gloomy hallway stretching into shadows on either side. High on the wall hung a lamp glimmering with pale light. The light flickered as if something moved behind the glass. A dark spot appeared on the lamp and then grew outward, no thicker than his finger, wavering toward Jute. He slammed the door shut.

An understandable response, but too late.

"What was that?"

A very nasty spell. Run!

Jute flung the door open and darted out into the hall. He had one glimpse of rippling, black tendrils wriggling toward him, with the lamplight streaming from their midst. But then he was running down the hall and into the shadows. A flight of stairs. His foot slipped on the first step and he caught at the banister to steady himself.

The stairway descended down into a high-ceilinged chamber shrouded in shadows. There was no way to tell whether someone or something lurked below, but Jute didn't care. He hurtled down the steps in panic. He turned at the bottom of the stairs and looked back up. A light shone at the top, and then a dark blotch spilled like fog over the highest stair. With a whimper, Jute plunged away into the darkness.

He tripped over a chair and fell. Bit his tongue and tasted blood in his mouth. He stumbled to his feet, disoriented. Felt the smooth wooden top of a table and skirted it. The shadows were thickening into almost discernable shapes. The moon bloomed through one water-streaked window. It was raining outside. Behind him, the sea of darkness flowed down from the last step and surged forward. Frantically, he looked around for a door.

"Dispel!" said a voice. The darkness vanished and ordinary shadow reclaimed the room. Two quick steps sounded and a hand grabbed Jute by the throat. He found himself staring up into Nio's face.

"How'd you get out?" said the man.

Jute could not answer. Nio's fingers tightened around his throat, choking him.

"I want answers," Nio said. "Now. Tonight. If I have to flay them from your flesh, one by one. I can't wait any longer on the qualms of my tiresome old friend."

Nio dragged him down a flight of stairs into a cellar. Water dripped from the stone walls onto a floor of mud and broken flagstones. The man flung him to the ground.

"The wind blows us where it wills," he said, his voice harsh. "There's no stopping it, no matter how we duck and hide."

He strode to the far end of the room, stooped over the ground, and levered up a grate set into the floor.

"Come here, boy," he said.

Trembling, Jute crept closer. The man grabbed him, once he was within reach, and pulled him to the edge of the hole. It was rimmed in stone and revealed a well of darkness. The noise of rushing water echoed up from far below.

"What do you see?" said the man.

"Nothing," said Jute, his voice shaking. "Darkness."

"Aye," Nio said. "Darkness. And there's water as well. Both restless and both in abundance. A quick lesson in wizardry, boy. Much of it is only the manipulation of what already is, of naming things and calling their essence, their *feorh,* to heel. In air, water, earth, and fire are the four ancient *feorh*—the stuff of creation itself—though there is a fifth of an even more ancient sort in darkness. When any of the four mix with darkness, there is unrest and pain."

The man spoke into the hole, three words of a strange language. The sound of rushing water stilled for a moment and then something rose up from the hole in the ground. It was the figure of a man, a grotesque parody with limbs that moved oddly, as if they had extra joints. It was formed out of water and darkness that swirled together. Gaps opened and closed in it with wet, sucking sounds. A chill exuded from its dark substance.

The man spoke again, a sentence in the same strange-sounding language, and the thing moved. It shambled straight at Jute. The boy stumbled away, scrabbling against the mud and flagstones for balance. The thing did not seem to move quickly, but wherever he turned it was there, sprouting extra fingers and limbs to hedge him in. Nio watched, his face expressionless.

The thing cornered Jute against the wall and descended on him in a dark, watery wave. He screamed, but immediately choked on water. Ice crept into him, soaking into his body. His bones ached with the cold. He could hardly move, even though he frantically strained to thrash his arms and legs. He could not breathe. He was weighed down, drowning. Darkness welled into his mind.

Nio snapped a word, and Jute felt air on his face, as if he had surfaced from being deep under water. He gagged.

"You'll talk, and talk freely," said the man. "This thing is hungry and wishes to feed."

"Yes, yes!" sobbed Jute. "Please take it away!"

"Not just yet." The thing tightened its grip on Jute. It was as if an icy hand held his entire body and was constricting its fingers. His limbs were numb.

"I would learn of you, boy."

Through a haze of pain, Jute heard himself begin to speak. Words tumbled out, one after another. Disjointed phrases gasped. Hissed through clenched teeth. Sobbed. His life was ripped from him, word by word.

Early faded memories of Hearne. The face of a woman who he himself had not even remembered. He clutched at the memory, frantic to examine her face for a second more, but the memory was gone, washed away by the pull of Nio's will. A summer sky with a hawk circling far overhead. The jumble of city streets and alleyways, mapped in his mind into impressions of angles, distance, time. This wall was climbable, this one was not. This door here never locked properly. Shops, taverns, and houses. The passing gilt carriages of the titled and wealthy. Faces of children. Lena and the twins. Dirty, tearful, laughing, cringing in fear. Hungry. Always hungry. Shadows.

Dimly, he was aware of Nio sorting through his memories, pausing on some but discarding most as quickly as they came up. An image of the Juggler floated to the surface—the first time he had met him, running down an alleyway from an irate shopkeeper. Nio seized on the memory. Questions came quickly, and Jute heard himself begin to speak of recent years.

The Juggler. Hunched over his kidney and onions every morning in the Goose and Gold. Stinking like a brewery. Malevolently eyeing his children— his imps if in a good mood, the shadowspawn if in a bad mood, blows and curses if drunk—as they slunk past him for another day of lifting purses in Highneck Rise. Another day in the markets and streets of the city.

The Thieves Guild. A grimace crossed Nio's face.

Careful.

Just as quickly as it had come, the voice was gone.

"The Juggler works for the Thieves Guild?"

Jute could not help himself. His voice continued, numb with hopelessness and the cold. The Thieves Guild. The little man named Smede who came every Sunday afternoon and drank a mug of ale with the Juggler and then took away a pouch of gold and silver. The fear on the Juggler's face. Whispers among the children. Memories of the older ones who left the Juggler's ranks to work for the smashers or the men who ran the docks. Or the few who went higher on the hill. Highneck Rise. Somewhere, it was rumored, somewhere higher on the hill of Hearne, there lived the Silentman, the head of the Thieves Guild. He ruled from a court hidden beneath the city streets. The Court of the Guild.

"Was this job for the Silentman?"

Yes.

Nio's eyes glittered in triumph.

"How do you know that?"

Ronan of Aum. The Knife. The hand of the Silentman. Walking through the door of the Goose and Gold. Silence falling over the room, followed by nervous chatter, glances flicking at the man dressed in black. The Knife. The Juggler's face slack with fear. Sitting at a table with morning sunlight slanting down. The Juggler's hand on his shoulder, forcing him forward. The Knife staring at him, leaning forward. A plate of bread and cheese going stale on the table between them. The details. Gone over again and again. The manor. Up a wall, down a chimney, into a sleeping house guarded by ward spells.

No matter, the Juggler had said. *Jute can handle wards. He's silent.*

"He knew the house," said Nio, grinding his teeth together. "How could that be?"

Once inside the hall, the door at the far end. Up the stairs and into a small room. That's where the box is. Somewhere in that room. It isn't a large place so it shouldn't be difficult to find the thing. Somewhere inside, a box the length of a forearm, made of black mahogany as hard as stone and fastened with catch and hinges of silver. A hawk's head carved on top, with the moon and the sun rising and setting behind. And if you open the thing, it'll be my knife in your gullet. Just stow it in your bag and back up the chimney with you.

Careful.

Nio hissed and spun away from the boy. "By the Dark!" he said. "Who has undone me?!" He turned back to Jute, his face twisted with anger. "Did you open the box?"

Careful.

No. He told me he would kill me if I did. Kill me. He did kill me.

"Did he tell you what was inside the box?"

No.

"What did you do after you found the box?"

Back down the stairs. Step by step by step. Back through the sleeping house. Tiptoeing silent as a mouse. Up the chimney toward the man waiting on the roof. But he wouldn't let me up. Darkness was creeping up the chimney after me. He made me hand the box up first. He took it away from me. And then the poisoned needle. And darkness. I fell.

"You've told me everything, boy?" Nio's face was inches away from his own.

Yes.

Yes.

The man snapped a word and the horrible, cold grip released him. Jute collapsed on the ground and sobbed with relief. Out of the corner of his eye, he saw the darkness of the thing subside beside him. Jute crawled forward. His body ached. The thing beside him kept pace. He could hear Nio stalking back and forth, muttering to himself and sometimes addressing the boy.

"What shall I do with you now?" said the man.

Jute heard his footsteps crunching this way and that on the broken flagstones.

"I realize you were just a tool, but you pose a problem for me. But how could they have known? No one else knew except for my fellow scholars, and it's unthinkable they would consort with the Thieves Guild. Unthinkable! What would the Guild want with it except for money? They must have been hired—but by whom? You know too much, boy, whether you realize that or not. We can't have that. Besides, I think our friend here is hungry, in his own peculiar way. Perhaps that will be best for all involved."

A wet tendril of darkness wavered out from the thing next to Jute and licked at him. He shied away from it, crawling forward mindlessly. His bones ached. A memory of sky faded through his mind. The summer sky of long ago, when he was a small child. His first memory. A hawk floated far overhead, black and remote against the expanse.

"The problem with the Guild," said Nio, "is they consider themselves free of any obligation to Tormay. To any of the lands of Tormay. Do you understand the repellence of that? Those who live in Tormay are obligated to Tormay, and this—this box that you stole—involves obligation of the highest sort. If the Guild was hired, they could've been hired by anyone.

31

Anyone with enough gold to satisfy the Silentman. The fool! The blind fool! Meddling in matters beyond him! But who could have known? A secret uncovered at the cost of many years! Who is my enemy? Is my shadow conspiring against me?"

Jute felt a different sort of stone underneath his fingertips. He inched forward. The darkness in the cellar seemed to be growing thicker. He could not see. The thing shambling next to him muttered damply.

"Our friend grows impatient." The footsteps turned and Nio's voice sharpened. "Boy!"

Jute's fingers reached into space. The hole in the floor. A stench of rotting sewage filled his nostrils. Nio called out a phrase—words that flung themselves through the air. The thing of water and darkness reached out a dripping hand toward Jute. And the boy threw himself forward, down into the hole. Behind him, he heard a wet gibbering and the furious shout of the man.

He splashed down into swiftly coursing water and was swept under. Tumbling around, he banged his head against stone. He bobbed up to the surface, choking and spitting. The roar of the torrent was in his ears. It was all he could do to keep his head above water. The rains, he thought dazedly. All the early rains. Summer has barely ended. Such strange weather.

He almost blacked out when the current slammed him into a stone bulwark that split the flow into two channels. His body spun off into the left-hand channel. The course angled down sharply, and he found himself careening along at a tremendous speed. Years of flow had worn the stonework of the sewers smooth and, even though he tried to slow himself, he could not gain any purchase on the sides of the channel. The current swept him under again.

I'm going to die, he thought.

No. For once, the voice sounded anxious.

Hold on.

Why?

Faster and faster now. There was no time for thought anymore. He fought his way to the surface for a gulp of air, and then the last of his strength was gone. Resigned, he curled himself into a ball, face tucked between his knees and hands laced around his ankles. Lights flared in his head—blots of scarlet and white pulsing with the beat of his heart. His lungs burned.

Hold on.

I can't.

You can.

It's always been like this.

What has?

Life.

Not anymore.

All at once, the sounds changed. Another sort of roar presented itself. The rhythmic surge of the surf. Growing louder. His mind groped to understand. The sea? And then he was tumbling through the air. Air. Rushing around him. His mouth flew open from sheer surprise and he sucked in cool air. He had one instant of a spinning view of the night sky, speckled with stars and ribboned with clouds. The moon stared down, her light gleaming on the sea and trailing off toward a horizon where dark sky and even darker sea met.

He hit the water hard, like a massive slap, and he was under but already fighting up toward the surface. He broke back into the air and treaded water, gasping. The cliffs of Hearne towered far overhead. Moonlight shone on a waterfall spouting from the mouth of the sewer high up on the cliff face. Wearily, the boy swam through the waves to the foot of the cliff and pulled himself up onto the rocks. He found a stretch of sand and, too tired to even feel the wet and the cold, fell fast asleep.

High overhead, a speck of black turned and wheeled against the night sky. The speck grew closer, gaining form as it neared—a hawk. He settled on top of a rock near the sleeping boy with a flutter of wings. Motionless, the hawk stared out at the sea.

CHAPTER EIGHT
NURSEMAID WORK

Ronan added the numbers up in his head. He frowned at his mug of ale. The numbers didn't add up. Not yet, at least. One or two more jobs might do the trick. Well-paid jobs, of course.

Supplies wouldn't come cheap. Warm clothing, furs, and skins, though he could certainly hunt and cure his own. That would take time and it had been years since he'd done such a thing. Line and hooks for fishing. Timbers for building a cottage. There weren't many trees growing on the Flessoray Islands, not as far as he knew. He'd never built a cottage before but he had a fair idea of how to do it. It couldn't be that hard, could it? Timbers for the frame, rocks for the walls—plenty enough of those on the islands—and turf over the top in layer after layer to keep out the wind and the weather. The timbers would have to be sailed over from Averlay. That would be expensive. Perhaps he could build a cottage entirely out of stone.

He sighed and took a drink of ale. A sailboat would be necessary as well. Maybe he could just sail the timbers out to the islands himself. He added the numbers up again in his head. It just wasn't enough. Even with the money coming to him for the chimney job. A dependable sailboat would cost a lot of gold. The sea wasn't his element. Not that he minded taking risks. You just didn't take risks with the sea.

"More ale?" said the innkeeper.

Ronan shook his head. The innkeeper swirled a dirty rag over the countertop and grunted something. It might have been about stingy thieves, or it might have not.

Perhaps if he did some freelancing on the side? The Guild was quiet these days. But the Silentman frowned on his men going off to earn a bit on the side. Thieves didn't obey the laws of Hearne, but they had to obey the laws of the Guild.

Maybe he could tutor a young noble in fencing. That wasn't thievery. Surely the Silentman wouldn't expect his piece of the pie from a swordsmanship lesson. There wasn't a better hand at the sword in the whole city. Except for Owain Gawinn. Perhaps. The Gawinns were known for their swordsmanship. Even his father had thought highly of the Gawinns.

Someone at the table in the far corner called for the innkeeper. The kitchen door behind the counter swung open and the scent of roasting meat wafted through the air. Beef and onions. Fresh bread. His stomach rumbled and he remembered he hadn't eaten yet that day.

"Lunch ready?"

The innkeeper nodded at him as he passed by with a pitcher of ale.

"Just on," the man said.

Stew. He inhaled appreciatively over the bowl when it came. There were still some good things left in life.

"That'll be a copper," said the innkeeper.

"Maybe with a loaf of bread it'll be."

The innkeeper grunted sourly but brought him the bread. It was fresh. Ronan tore off a hunk and dipped it into the stew.

Someone cleared their throat behind him.

Ronan sighed. "Can't it wait, Smede?"

"No, it can't. How did you know it was me?"

Ronan turned. Smede took a step back. He was a little man with a large nose and small hands that were always either rubbing together or investigating the surfaces of his nose, which was understandable as it was the only large thing Smede had in his possession.

"You smell of dust and ink and all the other nasty smells accountants smell of, molding away in your piles of parchments and gold. I'm eating lunch. Go away. The less I see your ghastly face, the better my life is. You disturb my digestion."

"Your words pain me," said Smede. "I've always had nothing but fondness for you, from the first day the Thieves Guild took you in—a wayward lad with an eagerness for fighting and all the sordid activity that carries on in our back alleys."

"Activity that makes you and your betters quite rich," said the Knife. "Blood on my blade is gold in the Guild's coffer."

"Gold offers more serene constancy than anything else in this world, be it noble titles, the love of a beautiful woman, honor at arms. To see it mount up in gleaming piles, to lock it up tight in strongboxes, to let it clink through your fingers, to tot the numbers up in fresh ink—purest joy! I fail to see why songs are not penned in its praise. Love, honor, valor—bah! Show me a bard and I'll show you a babbling fool."

"Why are you here, Smede? My stew is getting cold."

"Ah yes. The Knife is known for getting to the point." Smede wheezed once in honor of his own humor. "Economy of words. Being the Guild accountant, I should appreciate that."

The little man lowered his voice.

"Plainly put," he said, "the Guild has a job for you that must be done immediately. It'll pay well, of course."

"How much?" Ronan spooned up some stew and scowled at the accountant.

"Enough."

"I said, how much?"

"The amount remains to be seen, but it'll be generous. Rest assured. We have found ourselves yet another rich customer." Smede appropriated the stool next to Ronan. "Perhaps I should have a mug of ale? I don't drink the stuff often, but it might help me experience your degraded culture." He signaled to the innkeeper for ale. "Ahh, not bad, not bad at all," said the accountant. He licked foam off his lip with a pale tongue. "Poor man's wine, isn't it? Perhaps I should get away from my desk more, see the sights, take in the culture of our fair city Hearne? I'm sure you, my violent friend, know all the best spots and all the—"

"What's the job?" said Ronan.

"The job? Yes, the job. Let me tell you about this job."

Smede leaned close, whispering between sips of ale. Ronan listened and mopped up the last of his stew with chunks of bread. When he was finished speaking, Smede leaned back a bit unsteadily and gulped down the rest of his ale.

"That's it?" said Ronan.

"That," said Smede, "is it. An' I seem to have run out of ale as well. Mebbe another mug? Innkeeper! S'more ale!"

"Why me? If there's good gold in it, I don't mind taking the job, but surely this is something more suited for—for—"

"For a n-nursemaid?" hiccupped Smede. The accountant buried his nose in his fresh mug of ale.

"Yes. A bleeding nursemaid."

"Because you're the Knife," said Smede. He rubbed his nose and peered furtively around the room. "Because you're the best, the absolute best an' our customer wanted the best the Guild has to offer. Silent an' swift! Most importantly on this job—silence! Discretion! Not a word to anyone! The best!" He banged his fist on the table. "The best, I tell you!"

"Right," said Ronan. He shrugged.

"Innkeeper!" bawled Smede. "S'more ale!"

"My friend will be paying for my lunch," said Ronan to the innkeeper.

"Lunch!" echoed Smede.

"Thank you, my friend." Ronan clapped the little accountant on his shoulder. "Have some more ale."

"S'more ale!" hollered Smede.

Ronan turned and left the inn.

He had not realized how far gone the day was. The sun was already past its zenith. There was a chill in the air. He flipped his collar up and strode along, not bothering to mind where he was going.

It was a strange job, to say the least. Definitely not the sort to boast about afterward. However, he could see the wisdom in having the likes of himself doing the job. He, more than anyone in the Guild, understood the need for discretion. Loose lips shed blood. He shook his head. Who'd have thought the regent of Hearne himself would be hiring the Thieves Guild to do his dirty work?

He found himself down on the docks. Waves crashed against the seawall. Gulls circled through the sky. A fishing boat was rounding the breakwater. He could hear its lines creaking in the wind. The sea was alive with light. Something shivered and tightened inside him.

The regent.

Who'd have thought it?

CHAPTER NINE
FEN AWAKE

Fen desperately wanted to stay asleep. It was so much more comfortable in the darkness. The darkness was soft, and she had the notion that waking up might prove to be painful.

It'll be bright, she thought. *The sun in my eyes will be bright and I'll blink and squint like one of those little barn owls caught outside in the daylight. They must hate that.*

The barn.

Something about the barn. Something dreadful had happened in the barn. And then she was no longer able to hold onto sleep. She drifted up through the depths, growing lighter and unbearably lighter with each exhalation. Her body shivered alive with agony. Her leg was burning. She opened her eyes and remembered. A shriek burst from her lips, but she bit down hard the instant it escaped her mouth. She lay trembling and listening. There was only silence. Morning sunlight slanted down through cracks in the wall. Dust gleamed, hanging in the light.

Fen was able to inch her way up by getting her left foot onto the axle of the harrow. She stood up as slowly as she possibly could. The spike slid greasily through the hole in her thigh. Tears ran from her eyes and her teeth chattered. Her body quivered in agony. She could not see for her tears.

She must have blacked out again, for the next thing she knew she was lying face down in the hay. From the slant of the sunbeams she could see it was late afternoon. She looked up. For a moment she thought Hafall was alive, stirring from his nap just inside the barn door. The shape of his body, shadowed by the light outside, moved and seemed almost to rise. Fen limped forward, and the crows stooping over the corpse rose in a flutter of wings. They hopped away, croaking in irritation at her. Sobbing, she stumbled after them, scooping up dust, straw, anything to throw at them. But her left arm was numb and would not obey her. She tripped and fell flat on her face. Behind her, the crows settled back to their meal.

Movement caught her attention across the yard. A pair of rats rocked back on their haunches and stared at her with beady-eyed malevolence. They were crouched over a body lying across the threshold of the miller's house: a tall man with a head of hair nearly white blond in the sunlight. The same color as her hair, but stained and spiked with blood.

38

She could not breathe. Her heart was bursting, too big to be held within her small chest, and she screamed and screamed and screamed until the world dulled down into gray around her, until there was nothing except the sound of her voice dying away into a whimper of nothing that no one heard, that meant nothing within the darkness falling on what could have been a perfect sunlit day.

CHAPTER TEN
THE EDUCATION OF NIO

Nio stomped up the tower stairs. He slammed the door shut and stalked to a window. From there he could look from his house out over most of Hearne. And beyond. East. Something there had drawn his attention for the past few months. First in a dream and then, whenever he was within the tower, in unconscious habit.

Tonight, though, he glared out over the city. He saw nothing. The stone walls, the brick houses faded by so many summers' suns, the heights of Highneck Rise mounting toward the higher cliffs crowned with the regent's castle, the broken hulk of the university standing in a jumble of spires and towers and turrets huddled in ruins over the secrets they still held. Everything was washed pale in the light of the moon. It was all a blur, for rage does not sharpen sight, as some are wont to say; it merely blinds.

The work of half his life lost in one night. Stolen from this room by a boy. Years of study, of tracking down forgotten tomes to find a single line of text, a casual reference in a book of history moldering in a dusty library. It had taken him three years alone to get into the royal tombs of Harth—forbidden to all but the ruling line and the deaf and dumb servitors that guarded those tombs—just for the sake of one fresco fading into incomprehensibility on the wall of Oruso Oran II's mausoleum.

All lost.

Stolen by a boy.

Stolen by the Thieves Guild.

How had they known?

The boy stared back at him in his memory. Skin white with fear, eyes hollowed with shadow, the gaunt face and even gaunter body. A skeleton. Nio ground his teeth together. His hands curled into fists. The boy would be a skeleton when he was finished with him. He would flay the flesh from him. He would break his bones with his bare hands. He would—

No.

With an effort, he stilled the tumult in his mind. Such thoughts would not serve him now. He needed to think. It had all been so close, just within his grasp. If only he had been able to figure out how to open the box.

He would find them. He would find them all. This so-called Knife, the enforcer of the Guild. The fat man. What had the boy called him? Oh yes—

the Juggler. They would tell him everything, once he had found them. They would beg his permission to speak. They would give him more threads to follow, until he had made his way to the center of their web and discovered what was there to be found.

It had begun forty years ago. When he had been a student under Eald Gelaeran in the Stone Tower, far to the north of Hearne, on the Thule coast. There, the last true library of magic existed, preserved since the destruction of the university in Hearne. For the tower was a school of wizards, a secret place not known to many. Those who did know had no cause to share such knowledge with others. The tower could be found only if one already knew it was there. The place was woven about with spells. Travelers who came along the moors tended to find themselves on twisting paths and heading east or south or straight over the cliffs into the sea when they meant to go north.

He had been a quiet boy, even for the Stone Tower. The other students spent their free time playing on the moor or climbing the rocky cliffs there that fell down to the sea. He never joined them, and they, in the unthinking manner of boys, were cruel with their words and actions. But he taught them otherwise with his fists and later with the aptitude he demonstrated in learning magic. It is unwise to bully someone who can enspell spiders and send them swarming over your sleeping body at night.

He learned quickly, much more quickly than he let on to those who taught in the Stone Tower, for there was an innate cunning in him that cautioned against revelations of any kind. When he saw the old wizards were soon reaching the limits of what they were willing to teach, he determined to find his own manner of study. This he did by stealing into the private library of Eald Gelaeran and reading the books there page by page, stolen minute by stolen minute.

One day, Eald Gelaeran set out on a journey to Harth. Nio surmised the wizard would be gone for at least a month, traveling as he did by ship to Hearne and then further south to Harth by horse. On the day the old curmudgeon set sail, Nio crept into his library and stole a book. The book of Willan Run.

He did not know why he chose the book out of all the others.

For thirty days and thirty nights, the book of Willan Run lay open before him. Strange spells worked their way into his memory. Incantations muttered beneath his fingertips. Shreds of forgotten history wrote themselves across the pages: old wars and rumors of wars in far-off lands, countries he had never heard of before that seemed to have no part in Tormay and its eight duchies. Much of what he read he did not understand. He did not concern himself over this, however, for his mind was hungry and he stored the words in his memory.

On the tenth day, he turned a page and heard the sea, smelled the green earth, felt the wind on his brow, and was warmed by the heat of the fire. He read of the four ancient anbeorun—the stillpoints—those beings of power who walk the boundaries of the world of man and beast and keep watch against the Dark. Four words spoken in the first language, in the tongue that is called *gelicnes*.

The four words spoken became the four beings who ruled and held sway over all the *feorh*—all of the essences of what is. Everything was theirs to command, from the creatures of the sky, earth, and sea, to the foundations of stone, wood, water, and flame.

Nio's imagination was caught. He devoured the rest of the book by candlelight at night, or in the afternoons, lying on his stomach and hidden in the tall grasses on the moor. The book went back onto the desk in Eald Gelaeran's library even before the white sail was seen beating its way up the Thulish coast.

He dreamed of the anbeorun. He dreamed of what he did not know. The dreams filled him with a longing for wide open spaces, higher fields, and places from which one may stand and see things more clearly. And he dreamed of power. Thrones and dominions. The heights that ascend above and beyond all else.

But dreams are dangerous things. They are not to be indulged lightly or deemed just the perfume of sleep's flower. In dreams, the sleeping self reaches for things beyond normal life. It ventures through unknown lands and, without realizing, disturbs the thoughts of others who make their home in dreams just as man makes his home in the world. With certain of such creatures it is perilous to draw their attention.

All souls are like dwellings shuttered and locked against the night. If one dreams too much, then a light grows and shines from behind those shutters. That, by itself, can be enough to draw notice from whatever stands outside in the darkness. If one continues to dream, day after day, then perhaps the door of the dwelling creaks open, and the sleeping soul wanders forth into the night, shimmering with the light that is the mark of life. The darkness is wide and the night is complete. Even a little light may draw attention.

So it was that the Dark woke to the existence of young Nio. It considered, watched, and waited.

A month later Nio left the Stone Tower and wandered across the duchies of Tormay. He arrived at the city of Hearne, where most people end up who have nothing better to do with their lives. Even then, perhaps nothing would have happened had he not signed on to a caravan that was heading toward Harth. Who knows? It is foolish to speculate on what might have been if another path had been taken. At the beginning of a life, there are many paths to choose from. At the end of a life, one looks back and realizes there was only one path all along.

The caravan master was pleased with his new hire. Travel and trade were always dangerous. He needed someone conversant with magic, even a fledgling wizard. Goods could be maliciously enspelled and there was always the inconvenience of unfamiliar wards in foreign cities.

Crossing the desert, they stopped on the outskirts of the ruined city of Lascol. Sheepherders kept their winter camp there, and the caravan-master always made a good trade bartering for their wool and fleeces. Bored, Nio wandered into the city ruins and spent several hours wandering about. Stone and fire-blackened timber formed a jagged mosaic around him.

It had happened then.

He found himself standing in a courtyard overgrown with weeds. A crow perched upon the sheared-off top of a pillar. It regarded him with one beady eye. The bird bobbed its head from side to side and fluttered off the pillar and onto the cracked flagstones below. It seemed almost as if the bird knew him. It hopped away and then stopped to look back at him.

The message was unmistakable. Nio followed the crow, not bothering to think why a bird would behave in such a fashion. It led him deeper into the ruins, through hallways choked with rubble, past collapsed walls, and around fissures that gave him glimpses of darkness below. The crow stopped from time to time, teetering on its claws and waiting until he came near. The sun gazed down through the gaps in the broken timbers. The stones shimmered with its heat. Sweat trickled down his back.

The bird halted at the foot of a marble stairway. The steps spiraled up until they ended in midair. The crow hopped up five steps and then pecked under the lip of the sixth step. One eye swiveled back to look at him. It pecked at the marble again.

Nio had known what to do, almost as if someone had spoken the words aloud. Kneeling, he felt under the lip of the step. A catch clicked under his fingertips and the face of the step swung open to reveal a recess. A book lay within the hollow. He heard a rustling flap behind him and turned, but the crow was gone.

Nio gazed out over the city of Hearne. The book. The writings of Willan Run had opened the door—true—but the book from Lascol had opened his eyes to what lay beyond the door. Strange. After all these years, he still did not know who had written the thing. The books of the wizards always had some hint as to which of them had been the writer, some mark or feel of the person reaching forward from the past. But the book from Lascol was different. It was a mystery that had intrigued him for years but was unimportant in the light of other questions. Such as who had hired the Guild, and where was the box? How had they known?

And what was in the box?

Had the thieves managed to open it?

The thought made him grind his teeth together. All the learning of forty years at his command and he had not been able to open the cursed thing. He wasn't even certain what was inside. The enchantment woven about the box had been so beyond him that he had not been able to find the end of the weave, the knot, the last syllable muttered into being that provided the final knit of the spell. What he was certain of, though, was that whatever was inside the box had been instrumental in the death of one of the four anbeorun. He was sure of it.

Hunger rose up in him at the thought.

The book from Lascol was explicit in what it wrote of such an occurrence. *If the life of an anbeorun be taken, and here I speak of the four great wanderers—Aeled, Eorde, Brim, and Windan—then that which hath taken life shall possess it until the blood of another is spilt by that same instrument. E'en death to life be returned by such a blow and with it the essence of the wanderer springs anew. But this be a perplexing matter, for the anbeorun cannot be known in form or custom, for they are not bound to the ways of men. And e'en if thou hath the fortune to encounter one such as these, with what will thou fill thy hand and strike?*

Nio shivered at the thought. Shivered in anticipation of the life and power flooding through him. Which would it be? The strength of the sea? The solidity of the earth? The fury of the wind shrieking through the heights, or the hunger of the fire?

But the box was gone.

Severan and the other three old fools scrabbling in the university ruins had never understood the promise of the box. They had thought it only a curio, an oddity. He had been careful to not dissuade them of this. He had never told them all he had learned. They knew it perhaps contained knowledge of the anbeorun—that was all—another tool to combat the Dark. Knowledge of the anbeorun could be found in other places.

No. They could not be trusted with the whole truth. They were content enough to hunt in the ruins, looking for scraps of the past. Looking for the so-called *Gerecednes*. The Book of Memories. The fabled writings of the wizard Staer Gemyndes. Looking for a book that did not exist.

The box.

Glass shattered as he drove his fist through a windowpane. Far below, he heard shards breaking on the street. The pain of it cleared his head. Blood trickled down his hand. Blood. There was always a use for blood. An idea bloomed in his mind. He turned and went down the stairs.

The house was quiet these days. Originally, the entire party searching within the ruins of the university had stayed in the house. As the exploration progressed, they had determined there were safe areas within the university, and they had moved there to be closer. To be closer to what they might find. And now the house was his, alone.

Well, not quite alone anymore.

Nio lit a candle in the kitchen and went down into the cellar. The candle guttered and shadows danced along the walls. The room was empty at first glance. The stone walls gleamed with moisture and shrouded with the tattered leavings of a thousand generations of spiders. Water murmured from the hole in the center of the floor. The same hole that the boy . . . With a grimace, he focused his thoughts. The room waited. Then, with an effort, he spoke.

"*Wesan.*"

Something stirred in the gloom. Shadow coalesced into a blob that wavered and stretched until it had achieved the semblance of a figure. The wihht. Water beaded on the floor around it, rolled toward the two feet and then vanished, as if blotted up by a dry bit of cloth. The addition of water lent the form definition, but it was hazy and Nio could see through its edges. The creature had lost much of its essence since the night he had spelled it into being. Pity that the wretched boy had escaped. His life would have given the wihht vitality.

"*Neosian.*"

The thing shambled toward him and stopped, several feet away. He could feel the chill rising off of it. A smell of decay filled the air. There was not much strength left in the wihht.

It took a tremendous amount of power to shape the feorh of anything, whether it be remaking wood into stone or a blade of grass into the petal of a flower. Simple things, but they required careful concentration. The crux of such fashionings was in the renaming. The true name of a thing had to be reshaped into a different name. Difficult enough with a blade of grass, but to fashion a wihht was a different thing. Who could mix darkness and matter and bend it to a human will? He doubted even old Eald Gelaeran would have been able to do such a thing.

A voice whispered inside his head that Eald Gelaeran would never have chosen to do such a thing.

Nio bit his lip. The voice died into silence. He had the will to succeed. The book he had found in Lascol had certainly taught him a thing or two. It was dangerous to fashion darkness, but darkness offered certain benefits— yes, *benefits* was the right term to use—that other materials would not give. The water woven into the wihht lent placidity and made the fashioning easier to control.

But it needed a third element to add strength. He held out his bleeding hand. The wihht before him did not move. Portions of its form faded in and out of visibility. Gaps opened up in its torso, so he could see the wall beyond, and then drifted closed again. A drop of blood fell from Nio's hand and plashed to the floor. It beaded into a ball and rolled toward the wihht's foot. The blood vanished.

The thing whispered wetly in satisfaction and then extended its own hand. The two hands—shadow and flesh—melded and became one indistinct mass. Nio felt warmth creeping up his arm and then back down, like a tide moving sluggishly through his flesh. The sensation made him feel sleepy, but he knew better than to close his eyes.

"Enough!" he said, and he took a step back, pulling his hand free.

He was exhausted, but he held himself still. The wihht snarled but did not move. For a moment, there was no change in its appearance, but then it gained form and substance. The limbs took on definition; fingers appeared and divided; the torso thickened, broadening across the shoulders. A head rose up—a thing of clay as if made with clumsy hands—it had only a daub of a nose, a gash for a mouth. There were two holes for the eyes, as if the potter had merely plunged his thumbs into the clay to fashion sockets. These two holes lay under a slab of a brow and, though they were filled with shadow, Nio could detect a point of light in each, fixed upon him. He read intelligence there and nodded in satisfaction. It was good enough for his designs now, despite the startling appearance of its face. Besides, he did not fancy giving it any more blood. It would not do for the thing to develop a taste for him.

"I have a job for you," he said. "In the city. Listening and watching. But first, we'll have to find you some clothes."

CHAPTER ELEVEN
THE HORSES'LL MISS YOU

They left early the next morning, with the sun just up over the Mountains of Morn. Yora refused to leave the kitchen; she sat in a corner with her apron bunched against her face. She only hunched her shoulders when Levoreth kissed the top of her head. Outside, the stable hands stood in a row in front of the barn, caps clutched in their hands. They stared at Levoreth, barely acknowledging the duke's admonitions to look after the horses and to be sure to mind Yora. The youngest, the boy Mirek, stumbled forward after being kicked by those nearest him. He touched Levoreth's stirrup and then snatched his hand away, his face coloring.

"You'll be coming back soon, M'lady?" he said.

She smiled down at him, not trusting herself to speak.

His face brightened. "The horses'll miss you, M'lady." He ducked his head, backing away.

She turned one last time at the river ford. Sunlight shone on the manor's stone walls. The cornfields around it were soft and thick with the gold silk of their tassels. The hills rose beyond in green slopes. The air was still, as if time had stopped at this place, finding nothing to age and content to leave things as it had found them. The dust of their passing hung in the air and gleamed with light. But as the roan clattered down onto the riverbed and splashed across, Levoreth felt the touch of a breeze on her face.

It grew warm as the party rode along. Dolan tended to have long summers. This year was no exception despite the unseasonal rains of the past months. The men-at-arms loosened the collars of their leather jerkins and tipped their helmets back. At the head of the column, the duke rode alongside Willen, the old sergeant. They chatted back and forth, trading thoughts on horses and tactics and whether or not there was any truth to the rumors of wizards returning to Tormay. The duchess rode behind them, sidesaddle on a placid mare. She eyed Levoreth, who had opted for a split skirt and was riding astride.

"My dear," she said, "I'd think you one of those unsavory Farrows if I didn't know better."

"They're the best horsemen in all of Tormay," said Levoreth.

"And the best thieves and killers," returned her aunt. "So it's said."

"So it's said."

"Hmmph."

It was true. In addition to being the best horsemen in the four kingdoms, the Farrows also were acknowledged as being extremely handy at theft and killing. To be fair, the Farrows tended to steal only under great mental duress—such as when confronted with a beautiful horse or a beautiful woman. However, the Farrow men were polite enough to never steal a beautiful woman without stealing her heart first. As for killing, that only happened if the clan itself was threatened, or if someone came along who was stupid enough to steal a Farrow horse or a Farrow woman.

Certain members of the clan had been known to kill for hire, but they were shunned by other Farrows. The most famous of these had been Janek Farrow the Blackhand, who had climbed the tower of Tatterbeg on the northern coast and fought the wizard Yone. Their struggle broke the tower into ruin. Dying, Yone had cursed Janek, that everyone Janek loved would be brought to heartbreak, ruin, and death. Janek fled to the east, determined to forget his family so that the wizard's curse would not come to settle on them. He disappeared and was never heard of again. The other famous Farrow, of course, was Declan Farrow, son of Cullan Farrow, who had stolen his father's sword.

The roan danced under Levoreth, drunk on sunlight and fresh air and the prospect of a lengthy and leisurely outing. Levoreth patted its neck and brooded on Declan Farrow and Farrows in general. Odds were, Declan Farrow was still alive, for the incident that had resulted in his disappearance had happened only fourteen years ago. He would still be a young man. At least, young by her standards, and Levoreth smiled to herself.

The road turned to the west. A few oaks grew in the rolling grasslands. They stood like sentinels of the Lome Forest, which lay miles further to the southeast. Crickets hidden in the grass rasped their music, buzzing cheerfully of the last days of summer. Occasionally, the hooves of the horses stirred them up into sight and then the little creatures would hop lazily away to safety.

Levoreth hummed under her breath, picking up the note of the crickets. Blackbirds swooped by with their wings flashing blue in the sunlight. She borrowed the melody of their song and wove it into her own. She pursed her lips and turned the tune into a whistle.

"Lovely," said her aunt, riding near. "What is that, my dear? A folk song?"

"Just an old tune about the earth. I think they're all based on the same handful of melodies."

"It puts me in mind of green things. Rather like one of those songs the girls sing while out in the harvest."

Levoreth smiled.

CHAPTER TWELVE
THE MOSAIC IN THE CEILING

With a sigh, Nio shut the book of Lascol and rose from his chair by the library fireplace. He put the book back on the shelf. The firelight flickered on his face as he stood a while in thought. A musty odor of parchment and leather filled the air—the scent of books, of time stopped and caught by words.

The book of Lascol contained an index of anything relevant to the subject of the anbeorun. *Aeled, Eorde, Brim,* and *Windan*. The guardians of fire, earth, sea, and wind. The four wanderers who had walked the world since the beginning of time, bulwarks against the Dark so that man and beast could live their lives in peace. It had taken years to track down everything referenced in the book, all the other books, the inscriptions in tombs and castles, even a tapestry in the manor of Duke Lannaslech in Harlech. Shadows, that had been a close one. If he had been discovered there, his life would have been forfeit. The lords of Harlech did not suffer strangers gladly, least of all a thief prowling their halls at night.

Forty years searching, and the final answers still eluded him. The information contained within the book had not proven to be enough. It was silent in several areas. Such as what could kill an anbeorun. Or what the origin of the anbeorun was. But at the end of the day, there was only one question that mattered: *What was in the box?*

A noise drifted up from below in the house. Nio went to the door, opened it, and listened. The wihht had returned. He heard the front door close, and then there was silence.

The wihht was waiting for him in the hall at the foot of the stairs, motionless in the shadows. Only its eyes moved as Nio walked down the steps. The candles in their sconces on the walls flamed to life when Nio muttered a word.

Lig.

Light.

It seemed there was more detail in the creature's face, more pronounced cheekbones and a fuller nose. Odd. He put the matter from his mind. He was honest enough to realize he did not know everything about fashioning something as complex as a wihht. Little was written on the subject, for not many wizards had ever dared to fashion the darkness.

"What did you learn?" he asked.

The thing answered him with a hoarse voice that was strangely soft, as if it had no lungs to breathe with and so make normal speech.

"Many things were learned, master. What would you wish to hear?"

"Tell me about the fat man called the Juggler."

"He cares for a band of children who live and work together. Without father or mother. Orphans. He works for—this group of thieves, this—" It paused, stumbling for the word.

"Guild."

"Guild," repeated the wihht.

"Go on."

"The Juggler controls their lives."

"Ah," said the man. "He would've certainly known more than the boy. Describe the Juggler to me so I'll know him when I see him."

"This one is a short, fat man with a round face. A round face like the smaller sun that lights the night."

"The moon. It's called the moon."

"A round face like the moon."

"Does he have a real name, other than this Juggler nonsense?" asked Nio.

"This was not learned," said the wihht.

"And what of the man called the Knife?"

"Less can be learned of this one."

"Why?"

"He is feared, master."

"Well," said Nio, "there must be something you can tell me of him."

"His name is Ronan and he comes from a town called Aum, in the duchy of Vo. No one believes that. But no one knows better."

"Aum's a ruin, a haunt of jackals and hoot owls. No one's lived there for over three hundred years. He has a past that's not to be found out and everyone be damned if he cares if they try. Arrogant of him. What else did you learn about him? This is of no use to me."

"He is a tall man," continued the wihht. "He is a man with dark features as if he has seen much sun. No one in this city is reckoned his equal with the sword or knife."

"Weapons don't concern me. What else?"

"That is all," said the wihht.

"What? Not even where he lives?"

"No, master. That was not learned."

"Friends, a lover, a favorite inn?"

"No, master. That was not learned."

"Is that all you have to say?" said Nio. "We'll have to start with the fat man. Curse the Guild! They're a stealthy, sneaking bunch, and curse that paltry excuse of a regent for letting them flourish in his city! Speak of the rest of what you saw today. Maybe some trifle will come to light that might be of purpose."

The wihht's hoarse voice mumbled on. A picture emerged of children flitting through the marketplace, of sunlight painful in the wihht's eyes, of small hands filching from barrows and the pockets of unsuspecting passersby. Men in taverns, gossiping over tankards of ale, of hidden things and the long arm of the regent, the Guard of the city and their captain Owain Gawinn. Locks, wards, streets, and doors. Roofs, back alleys, walls, and grappling hooks. The Silentman, rumored to be hidden in his labyrinth of tunnels under the city. Travelers from distant lands. Merchants, traders, noblemen. The Autumn Fair approaching. An inn called the Goose and Gold. After a while, the wihht ran out of words and stood silent before Nio. The moon glanced in through the window over the front door.

"Tell me more about the inn you mentioned," said Nio.

At that same moment, there came a knock on the door. For a second, Nio froze and then he jumped to his feet. His mind feathered forward and he felt a familiar presence at the door—impatience, age, someone tapping their foot and grumbling. Severan and another. One of the other so-called scholars from the digging party in the university ruins.

"Quick," he said to the wihht. "Into the closet there. Don't make a sound until I release you!" The creature obeyed and Nio locked the closet door behind it. At the front door again came the knock.

"Coming!" he called.

Severan stood on the threshold. Water dripped from his nose. It was raining and dark outside. A fat little man bobbed up and down behind him.

"Catch our deaths of cold, Nio, waiting for you," said Severan. "It's bad enough breathing dust and mold in that confounded ruin day after day."

"Come in," said Nio, forcing himself to be agreeable. "Ablendan, I haven't seen you for some days. I'm surprised you tore yourself away from your beloved rubble."

"Well worth choking on mold," said the little man, "seeing the find we made today. Amazing! Haven't seen anything like it before. With what we've found, I tell you, we're one step closer to finding the *Gerecednes*! Why do you stay cooped up in this dreary house, poring over your books? You don't know what you're missing."

They clumped into the front hall and hung their cloaks over some pegs on the wall. Severan stopped and turned, his nose twitching.

"What's that smell in here?" he asked. "Almost like mice dying in the walls, but worse."

"It's worse in the cellar," returned Nio. "There's an open drain into the city sewers and I'm afraid the rains have stirred some muck up. You'll get used to it after a while."

"No sign of the boy?"

"He vanished. I can't fathom how he managed it. Clever wretches, these thieves."

Severan shook his head. "At any rate, no one will be able to open that blasted box. Probably just rubbish inside once the thing's open. It's not like it was a book. Now that would've been a loss."

The two arrivals suggested some bread and cheese and maybe a mug of hot ale to take the chill off. Nio agreed with as much goodwill as he could muster. In the kitchen, Severan stuck his nose around the door leading down into the cellar. He sneezed and frowned, but said nothing.

"What brings you out from your beloved ruin?" asked Nio. "And what's this find you speak of?" He sipped from his mug and watched Severan over the rim.

"A mosaic," said Ablendan. "We were digging in the west wing, just past that hallway with all those wretched dog wards—can hardly take a step through the place without some cursed hound appearing and chasing you from here to the moon. We were puttering about there and the floor gave way, revealing a blocked-up stairwell. So down we went, shone the lantern around, and there it was! Covers the whole ceiling."

"There are many mosaics in the university," said Nio.

"Ah," returned Severan. "But this one moves."

"Some kind of warding spell?"

"No," said the other. "The mosaic doesn't pose any detectable danger. Rather, its stones rearrange themselves according to what's said aloud in the room. At first we thought it was just a beautiful but pointless decoration. The stones shifted and flowed around each other as we stood below gazing up and gabbing back and forth all the while in a confusion of talk. It was only after we fell silent that the mosaic ceased its movement. Then, when one of us spoke singly, the stones moved with his speech."

"So stones move to the sound of a voice, like pigeons fluttering around Mioja Square at a child's yell." Nio shrugged. "Interesting, yes. Unique, yes, but hardly worth rushing all the way through the city in the rain to tell me. More cheese?"

"No, no," said Ablendan. "Yes, more cheese. The mosaic's much more than that. It shows you what you speak of, as if a mirror of your words."

"Is this true?" asked Nio, turning to Severan.

Severan nodded. "As far as we can tell, the older the tongue, the more precise the picture. I spoke about my cottage, naming the earth beneath it, the moor, and the sea beyond, giving such names as I know are bound into the land, and the stones of the mosaic rearranged themselves so as to show me my old place far up the coast of Lannaslech in Harlech, with moon flowers growing up its walls and onto the roof as I know they must be at this late summer's time."

"Amazing!" said Nio, startled despite himself.

"It shows the exact present," said Ablendan, "for old Adlig, on a whim, described us and soon there we were, gazing up at ourselves, blinking and gaping just as we were doing at the moment. A lot of fools we looked."

"This mosaic could be a powerful tool!"

"It could be," acknowledged Severan. "But the picture it shows is warped, as if seen through a crooked glass. Happily, though, we think you might have the key to this problem. Part of the key, at least."

"My possession of such a key is unwitting. What is this thing you think I have?"

"It's a guess on my part," said Severan. "Only a guess, but one I'm convinced will prove sound. Upon each of the four walls of the room are smaller mosaics inlaid, high up on the wall, just out of arm's reach—one for each of the walls. They are fashioned of the same stones but lifeless and unmoving in their pieces, while the large mosaic shifts at the sound of our voices. Naturally, this drew our attention and we noticed that a border framed each of the four smaller mosaics—"

"That's why!" broke in Ablendan. "That's why we thought you might have the answer! And then, we'll ask it to show us the *Gerecednes*!"

"I'm still confused," said their host. He forced a smile. "Why do you need me for answers?"

He thought of the closet door and wondered if wihhts ever grew restless or out of sorts. He would have some disagreeable explaining to do if the thing decided to emerge.

"You?" returned Severan. "Well, the first of these borders is carved with all kinds of fish, seabirds, and waves. The second has a pattern like flames of fire. The third is covered with trees, plants, and animals. The fourth is carved over with a single, unbroken line that flows—no—rushes about like—"

"—the wind!" said Nio, his eyes widening. "The four anbeorun!"

Severan nodded. "Eorde, Brim, Windan, and Aeled. We think their four separate mosaics awakened might prove the proper unlocking of the larger mosaic. And we were right, for between us we could speak a handful of ancient names related to the earth, to Eorde. The little we knew proved enough, and the mosaic bounded by trees and plants and animals came to grudging life and portrayed a wolf. A great head of black fur with staring, silver eyes. At that moment, the stones in the portion of the huge ceiling mosaic nearest to that wall instantly shifted in subtle ways so that that part of the larger mosaic became sharp and clear."

"A wolf?" said Nio. "Why would it be a wolf and not a horse? How odd."

"Eh?" said Ablendan. "What's that?"

"It's peculiar that Eorde should be represented by a wolf rather than a horse. Many of the legends written about her mention a horse. The men of Harlech claim their own equine bloodlines are descended from this companion of Eorde, the great horse Min the Morn. But maybe the historians have it wrong. Might her companion have been a wolf instead of a horse?"

Severan shrugged. "Who knows the mind of the anbeorun, even Eorde, despite the stories depicting her as friendly to the race of men? At any rate, Nio, we all know you're an expert in such lore. Your knowledge might unlock the three other small mosaics."

"Perhaps," said Nio. An idea bloomed in his mind. "Perhaps."

The three men set out into the rain and darkness. Nio did not worry about the wihht waiting in the closet, and he was right in doing so, though he did not realize why. The Dark is patient, and the wihht was fashioned mostly of shadow by now, as a great deal of the water had trickled out of it in its day of creeping around the city. It had left many damp footprints behind.

Nio's heart quickened as they made their way through the city. The thought of what the mosaic could do was intoxicating. Could the present be revealed, spied upon as it advanced with every clock tick? The box! Perhaps he could discover where it was with the mosaic. And the boy as well. I will be able to see him and so find him. Nio was glad of the rain and the dark and the hood about his head, for his face was so twisted with malice at these thoughts that his companions would have been startled to see him.

They hurried across the cobblestones of Mioja Square. It was deserted at that time of night. Light shone from the windows of the buildings around the square, but the university ruins loomed dark and lifeless. In a trice, they were up the steps and ducking through the little door that opened up like magic—it *was* magic—tucked away to one side of the real doors, massive things that looked more like the tombstones of giants than anything else.

Severan produced a lantern from his cloak. He muttered a word and it flamed to life. Light flickered on stone walls. Everything was grimed with dust. The floor was strewn with rubble. Their shadows ran along the walls beside them, waxing and waning with the wavering of Severan's lantern. Darkness crowded up on their heels. Anyone else would have been lost after ten minutes in such a place, but the three knew the university ruins well.

"I don't think I've ever been in this part of the west wing before," said Nio. "There's a powerful warding spell here. I can feel it."

They paused within an arch opening into a hall lined with slender clerestory windows. Moonlight and shadow alternated in slices of luminance and gloom.

"As I said before. An impressive spell." Ablendan's voice sounded suspiciously cheery.

"Don't tread on the blue tiles," said Severan. "Though, if you do, the dogs can't pass the far threshold. They're quick brutes, but they need a second or two to materialize and that's enough for a running start."

Near the halfway point it happened. The light was poor, and the pattern of blue, black, and white tiles was bewildering to the eyes. The blue and black tiles were so near in color that they could only be safely distinguished apart in daylight. At any rate, Ablendan trod on a blue tile, and all three heard the feathery whisper of a ward activating.

"Oops," said Ablendan. He took off for the far door, bounding like a child's rubber ball. The others ran after him, though Nio saved a breath or two to curse him as they went. Many other blue tiles came to life in their wake. Paws scrabbled and teeth snapped behind them.

"Safe," called the little man, flinging himself over the far threshold. The other two almost tripped over him, so close behind were they.

"That is not a child's game of tag!" gasped Severan, mopping sweat from his brow. "I'm too old to be playing such a thing, and the beasts want blood if they win!"

"You did that on purpose!" said Nio. He scowled at Ablendan.

"My eyesight is quite poor at night."

They all turned toward the hall. The pack stood just on the other side of the door. They were magnificent brutes, all with fur tinged blue and eyes an even brighter blue that glowed with light. Their teeth gleamed white. Some paced back and forth in agitation, but most stood stock-still, eyeing the three men. They did not bark or growl, but their rasping breath was audible.

"Astounding, aren't they," said Ablendan. "Brilliant spellcraft. Lana Heopbremel of Thule. Apparently, she had a thing for wolfhounds. They'll fade in a few minutes."

They clattered down the stairs. The room below was well-lit with torches. A tall man with a nose as big as a vulture's beak pounced on them as they reached the bottom.

"Where have you been? Half the night gone and I had to give old Adlig a tincture of sluma leaf, so worked up was he. Look at the mosaic. It's moving as we speak. There's Adlig snoring away in bed. At least what you can make out. Confound the thing! If only it were clear. Just imagine if we can coax a glimpse of the *Gerecednes* out of it. Nio, what've you been doing all these days hiding away in that gloomy house? Do you know any of the ancient names for the wind?"

"Peace, Gerade," said Severan. "Give him a moment and we'll see what he can add. The wolves were just chasing us."

Ablendan laughed at that, but Nio stepped forward, ignoring them. The place smelled musty and the air felt heavy, as if it had lain within the stone confines of the room for hundreds of years. He gazed up at the ceiling. Overhead, the mosaic rippled with movement, surging in silent mimicry of the sound of the men's voices. Thousands of tiny stones gleamed in the torchlight—white, black, brown, scarlet, shimmering yellow and glossy green, vermilion, dull gold, and a blue gleaming like the summer sky. His eyes flicked to the smaller mosaics, high up on each of the four walls of the room. Four smaller stars ringing the larger fifth. A strange constellation. The wolf stared down at him with silver eyes from the wall on his right. The other three were blank. Their stones were a uniform, dull brown. Behind him, he heard several impatient coughs. He ignored them.

The wolf in the small mosaic was a puzzle. Four small mosaics. Each one framed with the traditional signs of one of the four anbeorun. It would make sense that each, when revealed, would represent the four corresponding companions of the anbeorun. Unless, of course, they would show things such as actual earth or sky or water or flame. But the earth mosaic containing the wolf disproved that. Perhaps the four little mosaics were intended to reveal enemies? But that was illogical. The wolves were the subjects of Eorde.

According to the legends of the anbeorun, each of the four wanderers had a companion of sorts—an entity that was an extension of themselves, a shadow of their being, an echo of their voice. Only Eorde's companion was identified in the legends with any certainty. A horse named Min the Morn, whose hooves had shattered the earth in the north and formed the hill country of the Mearh Dun. However, the wolf's face staring at him from the little mosaic cast doubt on that.

There was hardly anything known about the companions of sea and sky and fire: a hint in a treatise, a suggestion in an obscure codex, an idea woven into the strictures of an ancient weather-working spell. And then there were the guesses inspired by an excess of learning. For example, some maintained that the companion of fire was a dragon, as no other known creature was better suited to the inherent power of flame. Logical, but logic is only one lens of many through which to examine existence.

"Come on," said Gerade behind him. "Have at it! We've been waiting long enough on this blasted mosaic."

"Well, then, you can wait a bit longer," said Nio.

The mosaic was magnificent. He could sense a weaving of power so delicately designed it was as if he could hear it as music. It was a melody played on the edge of his thoughts. He stood in awe, for the fashioning was beyond his understanding. The blue stones shimmered above him, standing out from the rest. Blue like the sky washed with sunlight.

Sunlight.

"Sunlight," he said. The stones shifted slightly, as if encouraged.

"*Sunne*," he continued. "*Brunscir, beorht.*" And the mosaic over them flared into a near white yellow. The room flooded with light. It was so blinding that everyone had to shut their eyes.

"*Sweart*," said Nio, and the radiance vanished as the mosaic went dark.

"Light and darkness," said Severan from somewhere behind him. "You picked the only two things in existence that require no clarity. Blurred or focused, both are the same to our eyes and, I wager, to this mosaic."

"I was only curious to see the stones transform," said the other.

"But what about fire, wind, and sea? Do you know any of the ancient languages that might describe the three?"

"Of fire I know a fair amount," Nio said reluctantly. "And of wind, three words gained at great cost. I am loath to share them. But of the sea? Nothing, for the sea has never been interested in man's affairs. All the books I've read are silent on the subject. The sea remains a stranger and, I think, always shall. The sea is unknowable and unstoppable. She's an alien land of unfathomable depth and distance and darkness. Even the fishermen who venture upon her waters, day after day, even they do not know her. They take their livelihoods from her, yet they know she'll demand their lives one day. Brim, the eldest of the anbeorun, is a mystery to me. And my study has been considerable."

"Yes, yes," broke in Gerade. "Your study is considerable, but my patience is not. So what about fire and wind? Speak, man, and bring some clarity to this confounded mosaic."

"Very well," said Nio.

But he would not speak a word until the other men retreated to the far corner of the room. They grumbled at this, but he was unmoved. His knowledge had come at a price and he was not inclined to share it. He first approached the small mosaic bordered with carved flame on the left-hand wall.

"*Brond, byrnan, sweodol, ond lig,*" he said quietly. "*Fyr.*" The stones of the fire mosaic shifted slowly and then the dull color of them darkened. The music on the edge of his thoughts changed. The new melody sounded uncertain and ominous.

Would it reveal a dragon? Nio's pulse quickened. "*Bael!*"

The stones adjusted themselves into darkness etched with darkness. Within the absence of color there was the suggestion of a face. A human face. No. Nearly human. There was something wrong with the eyes. Something slightly off. Unbidden, the memory of a sketch in an old book came to him. He gaped at the little mosaic in astonishment. But only for an instant.

"*Undon*," he said, and the image blurred somewhat until the face was no longer recognizable. The others hurried forward. From where they had been standing they had only been able to discern the stones' movement rather than detail. They gawked at the little mosaic.

"What is it?"

"Were your words enough? You brought color to it. That's more than we could do."

"I suppose those are eyes and something of a face, but it's impossible to tell where it begins and leaves off. Perhaps there, right where that deeper shadow—"

"You needn't be so secretive about a few old words, Nio. Why, I'll tell you the thirty-three curses of Magdis Gann in exchange, if you want."

"Much better than our efforts, but is that all you can do with fire?"

"Yes," said Nio.

"Rather like a fire salamander, I'd say."

"What? Are you crazy? Who ever heard of a fire salamander with black scales?"

"Perhaps a black dragon," said Ablendan. "I read somewhere—I can't remember where—that if the gefera of fire is a dragon then it must be a black dragon."

That gave them pause, and they all studied the image uneasily.

"Why black? That doesn't necessarily follow. Might as well be a red dragon. If there actually is such a kind."

"The worst of the lot, supposedly. A black dragon?"

"I certainly hope not," said Gerade. "Surely they've all died out or have fallen asleep. No one's seen a dragon for five hundred years."

"Rubbish, Ablendan. Don't believe everything you read."

"I can't remember where I read it. Anyway, has anyone gone looking for dragons recently? I thought not, so it's illogical to assume there aren't any."

"Who'd be dumb enough to go looking? There might be some left, beyond the northern wastes, but the cold will keep them asleep."

"Theoretically."

"The seventh stricture of dragons states that the heart-flame of a dragon can be dimmed by nothing except death. Therefore, the cold would have no effect on them."

"Nonsense!"

They might have continued arguing had Nio not shooed them back to their corner. He wanted to try some words on the wind mosaic. They complained, but they had no choice. Wizards and scholars were not fond of sharing hard-won knowledge. Basic knowledge, such as what was taught in the Stone Tower on the Thule coast, was shared freely. Anything beyond that was jealously guarded, kept to trade with others for a word here or a newly discovered thread of history there. All of the men in that room possessed knowledge unknown to the others. Though they grumbled at Nio, they understood and would have done the same had they been in his position.

He gazed up at the lifeless mosaic of the wind. He was uneasy now, thinking of what stared down from the fire mosaic. So what lay behind this one? Something else just as disturbing? He knew only three words of the wind, surely not enough to bring much definition to the mosaic stones.

"*Fnaest, rodor, ond styrman,*" he said.

The tiny stones sprang into life, flowing around each other and lightening in hue. The little mosaic became a patch of blue sky from which a hawk's head stared down. Black eyes and black feathers tinged with silver. Blurred, but clear enough to recognize. He was surprised that only three words could bring clarity to the wind mosaic, when six had barely done the same to the fire mosaic.

Still, how could you measure the power of one word against another? Some scholars argued that the purer the form of the word in relation to the first language spoken, the more power it contained. Others said words gained power according to how they were used. Some maintained that certain words were influenced over the years by the Dark. Words that had been twisted into a mockery of their original intent. Power flooded through these words easily, but it was power that could only be used for evil. Such words were few and far between, and anyone who discovered one was bound by honor to destroy whatever clues, whatever writings or artifacts led them to the word.

"A hawk," said someone behind him. They had silently advanced while he had stood lost in thought.

"Were you expecting a rooster?"

"It makes perfect sense," said Severan. "A hawk as the companion of the wind. You can see the storm's cruelty in his eyes and the softness of the breeze in his feathers."

"Excellent," said Gerade. "We've made some progress, despite the sea. This hawk, the wolf in the earth mosaic, and our mystery creature of fire. I'm puzzled about the wolf. The anbeorun of the earth, Eorde, has always been friendliest to the race of man. She's always popping up in our history.

There's a decent amount known about her. Everything I've read, from Staer Gemyndes on down, suggests that her companion is the legendary horse Min the Morn."

"Perhaps the little mosaics don't represent the four companions?"

"What, are you saying a hawk would be the enemy of the wind? You, my friend, are stupider than you look."

"Enemy or companion. Those seem to be the only logical options."

"Staer Gemyndes must have got it wrong. Unbelievable!"

Severan shook his head. "Even the wisest must be allowed the luxury of failure. Let's see how the mosaic will work now, despite the lack of the sea."

Nio left them then, arguing about what pictures they should call forth, while the huge mosaic overhead swirled with the sound of their voices. He wanted to use the mosaic, but for that he would need the room to himself. He didn't want the others to see what he was interested in. Particularly Severan. He wondered what their reaction would be if they found out he could bring the fire mosaic closer to clarity, and that he knew one word of the sea. One word.

He trudged up the stairs and wove a wisp of fire from some moonlight. The flame lit him through the long hall as he picked his way around the blue tiles. The mosaic would find the boy and the box for him. He would return later—after all was quiet and the old fools were snoring in their beds. Let them dream of finding the lost book of Staer Gemyndes.

When Nio reached his house, he stood a while in the entrance hall, dreading what waited him within the closet there. His mind was tired. He opened the door. The wihht stood within.

"Go down to the cellar," he said. "Wait there until I have further need of you."

Silently, the wihht obeyed him. As it shuffled past, the thing looked at him furtively with one sidelong glance. Nio went up to his room and cast himself onto his bed. He immediately fell asleep.

CHAPTER THIRTEEN
THE HAWK

Jute woke in the gray light of morning. For a moment, he did not know where he was, but then memory flooded back in with the surge of the nearby surf. His clothes were cold and damp against his skin. Pebbles and sand grated beneath him. He sat up and then wished he hadn't. The sky tilted overhead. His head ached.

Careful.

Something moved at the edge of his sight. He turned to see and then scrambled backward, staring, until he was painfully stopped short by a boulder.

Careful. The voice sounded amused. *You have been through enough to kill most people.* The hawk watched Jute with unblinking black eyes. His feathers were a glossy black. Around the eyes and the edge of the cruel ivory-colored beak, the feathers softened to silver.

"You—you're a hawk!" said Jute.

A hawk. That will do well enough.

"But birds don't talk!" said the boy.

To most people, no. We could not be bothered. You are different.

"What do you mean?" The boy leaned forward without knowing it.

Something akin to a sigh escaped the hawk's beak.

There are those fated to fly faster and higher. Those who have always held the sky in their hearts. Some who fly higher than others. And then there is you. You cut yourself on the knife, did you not?

"I never meant to touch it," protested Jute.

At that, the hawk's wings unfurled with a whisper of feathers. A breeze fanned the boy's face. Further down the beach, the surf rolled up the sand toward them.

Do not speak so! Thank the wind, the sky, every star in the heavens. Blessed be the house of dreams that you touched the knife. Knowing what one was meant to do, or not meant to do—this knowledge is beyond the understanding of man, beyond the wizards, beyond you. Even you.

"Who am I?" said the boy.

The hawk sprang into the air with a beat of his wings.

That will be learned one day at a time. Suffice it for now to stay alive. Walk softly, for things wake that should not have been disturbed. You would do well to avoid their attention. Above all else, listen.

"Listen? To you?"

To me, yes. Amusement, once more in the voice. *Listen to the sky. Listen to the wind.*

The hawk mounted into the sky. Morning light gleamed on his feathers.

For now, be content with staying alive, youngling.

"Wait!" he called, but the hawk wheeled away into the blue and was lost in the sunlight.

CHAPTER FOURTEEN
STOLEN APPLES

Arodilac Bridd was the orphaned nephew of the regent and his heir apparent, as Botrell had no offspring in evidence, or any other living relatives. Arodilac was sixteen, a gawky boy, teetering on the brink of manhood. His head was thatched with hair as yellow as straw, and guileless blue eyes blinked from his face. He had the thick wrists of a natural swordsman, but his hands were still awkward, and, at the moment, they were knocking over a mug of ale.

"Oh, sorry," said Arodilac.

Across the table, Ronan hurriedly pushed his chair back. He mopped at his pants and thought about the Flessoray Islands. He had been there, once, when he had been young. His mother's family came from the coast east of the islands. Older cousins of his had taken him out in a boat. The day had been cold and clear, with the light on the white sail and the wave tops so bright they had brought tears to his eyes. On the horizon, the islands rose remote, too far for a day's outing. He had stared at their silhouettes with all the dreaming intent of boyhood. Even now, he still felt the longing. The pale sunlight of the north, serene and gleaming on the lonely sea. Solitude and peace. He sighed.

"Tell me how it happened," he said. "From the beginning. Don't leave any details out, even if it means your honor at stake."

Arodilac fidgeted with a spoon, his face reddening.

"Well, you see—it's Ronan, isn't it?—you see," he said, "it's not just my—"

"Or if it's her honor at stake," interrupted Ronan. "I don't care. I'm a thief and we don't care about things like honor. All I care about is getting the job done and getting paid."

Arodilac glared at him for a moment from across the table and then turned to stare glumly out the window.

They were seated in an anteroom in the servants' quarters of the regent's castle, the door locked and two Guardsmen standing outside to discourage any interest. It wasn't proper for thieves and nobility to be seen together, though many nobles were adept at robbing their people and the odd thief or two managed to be noble on occasion.

Ronan had never been inside the castle before. Normally, he would have been fascinated by the chance, attentive to every detail of how the remote and near-legendary ruler of Hearne lived. As far back as the history of the Thieves Guild reached, there had always been an unofficial truce between the Guild and the regents of Hearne. In return for not stealing from the castle and the families of the regents, the regents refrained from executing thieves except for the most grievous offenses.

This day, however, Ronan would have rather been anywhere else. Anywhere else than sitting across from this slack-jawed idiot who probably didn't even clothe himself and whose wit was evidently in reverse proportion to his family's wealth. True, he would earn a lot of money for the job, but it was all he could do to sit there politely. Well, somewhat politely.

Arodilac leaned forward, one elbow on a filled scone. Blackberry jam oozed out.

"She's like one of those, whatchamacallits," he said.

"That's helpful information," said Ronan.

"Yes," said the regent's nephew. "One of those—what are they?—the tallish flowers with the single white bloom unfurling up, just like her graceful neck—what are they called? My mother used to grow them in her garden."

"Mustard grass? Deadly nightshade?"

"Lilies. That's what they are. White spring lilies. She's like a slender, white spring lily. Lovely as the first day of spring—"

"It usually rains on the first day of spring. A downpour."

"—and as graceful as the best filly the Farrows ever raised."

Ronan, whose eyes had been glazing over, jerked upright. He snorted.

"So what you're saying is she's a flowerlike horse on a spring day."

"That's it!" said Arodilac. "That's her. Why, you said in half as many words what I couldn't say in twice the amount. How did—"

Ronan's fist crashed down on the table.

"Blast it all to the seven walls of Daghoron!" He cursed with all the fluency of a Thulian sailor waking up the morning after the first night home in port. His head was beginning to throb, which lent his words vigor. He had not joined the Guild for this.

"What was that last bit?" asked the regent's nephew. "The part about the jackass and the thingummy? Fascinating stuff—I must confess I've never—"

Mugs and plates jumped as Ronan's fist crashed down again on the table.

"Never mind that," he said. "What's her name?!"

"What?"

"Her name!" said Ronan.

Her name was Liss Galnes, and she was the daughter of Cypmann Galnes, a widower and merchant who, by virtue of his wit and his wealth, was the regent's advisor on matters of trade. The Galnes family lived in a mansion in one of the more secluded streets of Highneck Rise, a stone house surrounded by a walled garden. Liss was an only child, and her father had kept her from the social circles of the court, judging that such a place was no fit environment for a child. This was a view he held privately, of course, for, although he entertained doubts regarding Nimman Botrell's mental capabilities, he did not doubt the regent's capacity for sudden and malicious judgment.

Liss was raised mostly alone, except for her father, a few servants, and a succession of tutors. She learned needlepoint and the history of Hearne, although facts on this subject became sparse, of course, once one reached the Midsummer War and the reign of Dol Cynehad, the last king of Hearne. She learned to play the spinet and how to figure compound interest, though her father grumbled that compound interest was no suitable pastime for women. She read Harthian poetry in its original form—slowly and with much frowning, of course—and she learned how to run a household. She also became an accomplished gardener and grew the best apples in all of Hearne. This was how Arodilac Bridd met her.

"The best apples you've ever tasted," said Arodilac.

"Get on with your story," said Ronan, gritting his teeth.

Cypmann Galnes was in the habit of carrying fresh fruit with him wherever he went, said Arodilac. Even to the castle. The regent, who was given to three vices—horses, women, and food—availed himself of some fruit Galnes brought one day, and, after his appetite was piqued with an apple, inquired where the merchant found such delicacies.

"In his garden, of course," said Ronan, eyeing a pewter pitcher and wondering if beating Arodilac over the head with it would, in any way, speed up the storytelling.

"In his garden," echoed the youth. "And then, do you know what happened?"

"No, but you're going to tell me."

"Uncle pulled me aside after dinner, and said there was something he wanted me to get for him. He wanted apple pie for dessert, the next day, and the best apples were to be had from the garden of Cypmann Galnes. And if he didn't have his apple pie, he'd be cross."

"So what'd you say?" asked Ronan, intrigued despite himself by this private side of the regent.

"I told him that, once when I was small, Cypmann Galnes thrashed me for chucking pebbles at his horse."

"Rightly so. I would've done the same."

"He only laughed and told me to get some of those apples."

"Which are in that garden."

"In the garden, yes," agreed Arodilac. "I pointed that out to him, and he told me to steal them."

"What?"

"He told me to steal them."

"So the regent's muscling in on the Thieves Guild? Let the fruit vendors look to their knives, or they'll be paying double in protection."

Arodilac fell into a reverie, gazing out the window. Twilight was falling, and the oak trees that stood alongside the castle wall were dappled with shadow and blurred light.

"The house is at the end of the Street of Willows, and it was one of those trees that I climbed to make my way over the wall. Cypmann Galnes was working at his warehouse down at the docks. I swung over the top and Liss was there, sitting under a tree and doing needlepoint. She didn't say anything. She just watched me. I figured it'd be best to leave with whatever dignity I had left. Of course, it's easier to get into that garden than get out. After watching me slip and fall several times in trying to jump for the top of the wall, she brought me a cup of water. It was a hot day."

"Over such little things have kingdoms fallen," said Ronan.

Arodilac reddened. "She's unlike anyone I've met before. Not like all the girls at court fawning around me, cooing like pigeons, all beady-eyed over my title and not ever seeing me."

"You didn't tell her who you are."

Arodilac looked away. "Not until her father caught us together. He was angry. He went and told Uncle."

"And you intend to marry her?"

He looked up. "Yes! We love each other."

"You're the heir to the regency of Hearne," said Ronan. "Who you marry won't be left up to you. Horses and the nobility. Both bred with an eye for bloodlines. No doubt there's a duke's daughter being groomed somewhere. You'll be foisted on each other, whether you like it or not, for alliance, for blood, and for money."

"I don't care about such things," said Arodilac.

"What you care about doesn't matter," said Ronan. "What I care about doesn't matter. All that matters is that your uncle has hired the Guild to tidy up. So tell me, and with few words, why the regent hired thieves to clean up after his nephew."

Arodilac's eyes slid away from him. "Just some letters I wrote to her. That's all."

"Letters?"

"I promised we would be wed. My uncle would be embarrassed if—"

"Do you take me for a fool, boy? A letter, no matter how idiotic, is not going to matter a whit to the regent of Hearne. With all the beds and mistresses he's worn out, he won't be bothered by his nephew's indiscretions, even if you ran about the city, naked as the day you were born. Tell me the truth."

The boy hung his head.

"I gave her my family ring," he said.

"You did what?"

"I gave her my family ring. I don't know why I did it! Something came over me, but she doesn't know what it actually is. She just thinks it an old ring, only dear because it comes from me."

Wordless for once, Ronan stared at him. The boy winced.

"I know, I know. And it isn't just my old family estate bound into it. Uncle's been teaching me the wards of this castle."

It was customary within the noble families to pass a ring down, from father to eldest son, or whichever heir was to assume the title. All the ward spells guarding the estate were bound into the family ring, so that whoever wore it, anywhere at any time, would always be aware of any dangers threatening the estate. What's more, whoever bore the family ring could safely pass through the wards.

Possession of the family ring of one of the noble houses of Tormay was every thief's dream. With such a ring, one could pass unchallenged into the richest estates of the land. But even though the house of Bridd was reputed for its wealth, this ring was much more valuable. It disarmed the ward spells guarding the regent's castle. Ronan shook his head. He could hardly believe it.

"Are you telling me your uncle's been teaching you his castle wards and then weaving the spells into your ring as he goes?"

Arodilac nodded.

"And she's hidden it? Refuses to give it back?"

The boy nodded again.

"She says she wants something in exchange," he said. "But she won't tell me what."

The words hung in the room, like dust glinting in the sunlight. There was irony in the fact the regent had called in the Guild to solve his problem. A missing ring containing his castle wards was bound to turn up. Such things always did.

A ward-bound object attracted certain kinds of people who came near it. The problem was that most people attuned to such things tended to use their knowledge in illegal activities. Many of them worked for the Guild. Others worked alone. The regent's decision to hire the Guild to find the ring—some of the people who would be most tempted to use it against him—was a clever move. Bound by their own honor code, the Guild would not be able to use that which they had been hired to recover.

"What does it look like?"

"A gold band carved in the shape of a hawk, with rubies for eyes."

"The mark of the wind," said Ronan.

"My family has always honored the wind lord and the sky." His head came up, proud once more.

"Tales for old women."

"Don't hurt her," said Arodilac.

"What do you take me for? The Guild doesn't turn its hand against children."

An image of the boy sprang unbidden to his mind, falling down the chimney into darkness. Ronan got up and pushed through the door, past the two Guardsmen, wooden at their post, and then down a hallway and out into the gloomy evening. The air smelled like wood smoke and coming rain.

CHAPTER FIFTEEN
WHAT THE TRADERS FOUND

Murnan Col hailed from Averlay in Thule. He was a trader who worked the coastal route of villages down to the duchy of Vomaro and all places of interest in between, including, of course, Hearne. Once in Vomaro, he always turned inland to Lura to acquire more expensive items for the return north. That spring, however, a bag of pearls bought off a fisherman convinced him to venture south, down through the desert to the city of Damarkan in Harth.

Harth made him nervous. He wasn't sure why. Perhaps the desert stretching on forever and ever into heat-shimmered distances. Perhaps the odd beauty of the Harthians themselves with their dark skin and their bone-white hair bleached by relentless generations of sunlight. Or maybe it was their courtly grace, their politeness, and the liquid cadence of their speech—all so different from the rougher customs of the north.

He grimaced, shifting in the saddle. Shadows, but it was a long road up from Damarkan. He'd be glad to get back to Averlay and his own bed. Cwen. How long had it been since he'd seen her? Four months? Much too long to leave a good woman idle. No telling what she had gotten up to in his absence. He smiled to himself.

Damarkan had been profitable. The pearls had brought the court chamberlain of Oruso Oran IX stalking through the marketplace, attendants scurrying along at his side. A cold man serving an even colder master, if the stories were true, but he had been fair in his dealings with the trader and he knew good pearls when he saw them.

Murnan turned in his saddle. The pack train straggled out behind him. Four heavily laden mules and the giant Gavran twins bringing up the rear, smiling as ever and singing one of their endless ballads. The sea and death and the melancholy of unrequited love, no doubt. They were young and didn't seem to think about much else.

An hour would see them down into the valley of the Little Rennet River. They had stopped there on the way south. The villagers had been friendly, eager for news and a chance to trade for his iron, wool, and the small kegs of salt so dear to inland folks. He'd promised to buy some cheap silk in Damarkan for the miller's wife. She'd be pleased with the bolt of ivory-colored cloth he'd found—smooth to the touch and full of light. There was to be a wedding in the family. A daughter. He frowned. Perhaps it was high time he married his Cwen.

They smelled the village before they saw it. Faintly at first but then stronger and stronger—the sickly sweet odor of rotting flesh warmed by the sun. The trader's horse shivered under him.

Murnan loosened his old sword in the saddle sheath. "Gann, tie up the mules and stay with them. Loy, come with me." His hand flexed on the sword handle. Not that he was any good with the thing, but you had to try. That was what life seemed to be about.

The stench grew as they rode down the trail into the valley. With each step, the horses grew more restive, trying to sidle off the path and head back up the incline. They came around a bend and a stand of pine. The village lay before them. Murnan reined in.

"The birds," he said.

Below them, among the houses standing together beside the stream, crows rose and settled in flurries of wings. Dark blots clumped into bigger masses as if huddling together for intimate meetings. Here and there, buzzards were visible, waddling about the ground or stooped over the awkward, broken-looking shapes littering the earth.

"Shadows!" cursed Loy.

They galloped down the slope. The birds rose at their approach, sluggish and slow as if so heavy with their meals that they could only struggle up into the uncertain support of the air. Murnan could see Loy turning green beneath his sunburnt skin. Bile burned up inside his own throat. The dead were everywhere: lying in the clay and stone of the pathways between the cottages, sprawled across doorways, crumpled against walls.

They had been dead for perhaps a day, he reckoned. He swallowed, trying to calm his stomach. Even though the bodies were torn by bird beaks, there was enough definition left to suggest recent death. Perhaps even less than a day. *And if we had not tarried another day in Damarkan?* He shuddered.

His horse twisted and he caught a glimpse of a panicked white eye. He soothed the beast with soft words and touch. The horse shuddered and subsided under him.

Loy exclaimed. Murnan turned to look. Further down a path between two cottages stood a girl. She was a skinny little thing, no bigger than a shadow and with white hair tangled around her head. For a moment she stared at them, and then whirled to run. Loy jumped off his horse. It took only several steps of his huge strides to catch her, for the girl ran awkwardly. She screamed once when he scooped her up and then her body went limp.

"What shall we do?" asked Loy. His jaw was clenched in anger. The girl was tiny in his arms. She dangled there like a child's broken doll.

"She's unconscious?"

"Aye. Skin's burning. She's got fever."

"We're four days' ride from Hearne. If we push the mules. Back with her to your brother, and I'll do a quick scout through the rest of the village. Perhaps there are others still alive."

But there weren't any other survivors.

Murnan stood for a while over the body of the miller. The man's eyes were gone, pecked away by the birds, no doubt, and his sockets stared up at the sky. There would be no wedding for his daughter. He turned away.

CHAPTER SIXTEEN
SPYING ON JUTE

Nio returned to the university ruins in the morning.

Mioja Square already bustled with people. Vendors called back and forth, vying for the attention of customers. Nio was so wrapped up in his thoughts as he walked along that he failed to notice Severan hurrying toward him, hand raised in greeting. At the last moment, though, the old man must have somehow thought better of it, for he ducked behind an apple cart. Nio swept past, head down and brow furrowed. Severan stood and looked after him, but then he made his own way in the opposite direction, away from the university and into the city.

As Nio expected, the university was silent within. He double-checked anyway and stood motionless for several minutes, eyes closed and listening to the silence looming around him. He let his awareness drift through the expanse of the ruins. Countless halls, chambers, courtyards choked with rubble, mold, dust, and silence. Towers crumbled in magnificent disarray or still standing proud over the city. Stairways climbing into the sky. Secrets and shadows and old memories soaked into stone, still stained with blood and tears centuries after the living had been brought down into dust. And the slumber of his fellow searchers, floating across his consciousness like dandelion seeds drifting in the air. No one was awake.

Nio frowned. Only three sleepers. The fourth was not in the university ruins.

He came to himself and opened his eyes. It was as he expected. Though the absence of one so early in the morning was a bit surprising. They all tended to stay up late, arguing over discrepancies in this history or that, or quarreling over inflections in long-dead words that had not been uttered out loud in hundreds of years. With such a habit, they all slept until noon every day.

Scholars. His lip curled. All of them hid behind the title scholar, rather than the dubious distinction of being a wizard. Both studied the same kinds of things. A wizard, however, sought to apply his learning to life. A scholar did not, being content to learn, observe, and record. It was a distinction that had arisen after the Midsummer War and the ill repute that conflict had given wizards. These days in Tormay, hardly a wizard could be found in any of the duchies, unless you counted the tame court wizards of Hearne and

Harth, who existed only to ply their parlor tricks at parties to amuse the nobility. In truth, it wasn't safe to be a wizard.

Ridiculous.

Things would be different. Someday. He would see to that.

The morning sunlight poured in through the thin clerestory windows of the west wing hall. The blue tiles shimmered benignly, as lovely a blue as a summer sky. He picked his way around them, though he deliberately stepped on a blue tile just before the threshold. Safely on the other side, he turned and watched the dog rise up from the floor. A blue vapor, like steam rising from a kettle spout, thickened until it grew opaque and took on solid form. The creature snapped at him once, but then settled on its haunches not two feet away. They regarded each other silently, the man and the beast, and there was interest on both sides.

It has intelligence woven into it, thought Nio. It isn't just a mindless ward created to strike out blindly. Those eyes are assessing me. Thinking. Planning.

He marveled at the craft, wanting to understand and possess the knowledge that had gone into the making. The dog stared back at him. After several minutes, the thing grew transparent, and then it was only a blue mist that drifted down and vanished into the floor.

He stood in silence beneath the ceiling mosaic for a while. It waited in a meaningless jumble of colors. He wondered what the others had sought from it the night before. The three smaller mosaics were still in the same state as when he had last seen them: the hawk, the wolf, and the red eyes of the fire staring down from within darkness. Only the mosaic of the sea was featureless, secure within its border of carved fish, seabirds, and waves.

First, there was the fire mosaic to restore.

"*Brond, byrnan, sweodol, ond lig,*" he said. The stones shifted, the colors sharpening. "*Fyr ond bael!*"

And then the image was clear. Not as clear as it might have been, had he possessed more knowledge of fire, but clearer than what the others had seen last night. It stared down at him. It was similar to a man, yet not. The face was formed of shadow. The eyes were coals, banked and smoldering behind the lids.

A sceadu.

His heart quickened and his mouth went dry. A sceadu. A being woven out of the true darkness at the beginning of time. According to lore, only three of them had ever existed. No one had ever seen one since the days of Staer Gemyndes, and even he had written guardedly of them in his books. But there had been a sketch of a sceadu in one of his histories. Nio shivered and tried to doubt his own eyes. There was something oddly familiar about the sceadu's face. What was it? The wihht. That's what it was. A hint of similarity between the two.

The wihht, he thought guiltily. But seldom do I exercise such a spell. It is always on behalf of a greater need, when there are no other choices available. I will unmake the wihht once I have no more need for it. Besides, I would never have dealings with such a thing as a sceadu.

What could it mean? The fire wanderer, Aeled, served by a sceadu? But perhaps we had it all wrong. Perhaps these four smaller mosaics signify something different and do not represent the four companions of the wanderers. After all, the three visible are all black in color to some degree. Surely that might represent some sort of tie to the Dark, like the sceadu. Might they all represent enemies of the wanderers? The purpose of the anbeorun is to guard against the Dark, all the histories agree on that, so how could one be served by a creature of the Dark? Also, the earth mosaic should portray a horse, not a wolf. The horse Min the Morn. Were all the old writings wrong?

He pondered on this a while, but he could not come to any conclusion and so turned his attention to the lifeless mosaic of the sea. Sometimes it was better not to think about certain things.

Only one word of the sea. That was all he knew. The memory of its cost was still painful. Even after all these years, he wasn't sure if he had been cheated. Was there value in the word? Or was it merely a lifeless sound? He had never been able to devise a test. He wet his lips with his tongue and then spoke.

"*Seolhbaeo.*"

The word whispered in the air. It sounded like the ocean surf sighing on the shore. Nio held his breath. What sort of creature would be revealed? He was not sure he had pronounced the word correctly. The old man who sold the word to him had refused to say the thing out loud, but had written it out on parchment, which he then burned after Nio memorized it. *Not a safe word, lad,* he had said. *No telling who might hear. Things listen, they do.*

For a moment, Nio was sure he had been cheated. The old man had swindled him. But then the little mosaic came alive. Its stones did not move like the other mosaics. Rather, all of its stones turned blue. A deep, greenish blue the color of the sea. There was nothing else. Just the color. The blue seemed to heave and sway as soon as he looked away, but whenever he stared straight at the little mosaic, it was still.

Elated, he turned his attention to the huge mosaic overhead. He described the box in detail. Black mahogany. Old silver hinges and catch. The lid carved with a hawk's head, the moon and the sun floating behind. Whorls curving in and out of each other on all four sides.

The mosaic sprang into life. The definition of color and shadow was more precise than what he had seen the previous night. The tiny stones shifted around each other. Colors blurred into other colors. Then the mosaic went still. The picture it presented of the box was indistinct. Not because of a lack of focus, but because the box was obviously in a dark place.

Nio cursed out loud. The mosaic was thrown into confusion by his words. The picture of the box vanished into a jumble of color and nonsensical shapes as the mosaic sought to portray what his cursing looked like. He had to laugh at that, and then he restored the original view of the box. When it was once again visible, he studied the picture.

The box was on a shelf in something like a closet or a cupboard. A faint bit of light shone from somewhere, perhaps a crack in the door. The space was lined with shelves crowded with boxes of all shapes and sizes, stacks of books, bulging velvet bags, and a heap of necklaces crammed into one corner and spilling over the shelf's edge like a waterfall of gold. Obviously, the hideaway belonged to someone wealthy. The Guild.

Nio cursed again, but was prudent enough to do it under his breath. There was no self-evident way to shift the angle of view the mosaic presented. If he could see the outer door of the hideaway, then he might gain a clue as to where the thing was. Perhaps if he waited? Did the mosaic maintain its views in the changing immediacy of the present? If true, then he might see someone open the hideaway to take or leave an object. His eyes gleamed at the thought. But what if one of the old men came down the stairs and caught him here? He couldn't risk that.

But what if finding the box was no longer important? What if whatever had been inside was no longer there?

The thought sickened him.

The boy had known where to look in the house. Someone had instructed him how to beat the guardian ward. That indicated magic at work. Ridiculous, to think the boy knew such arts. Someone powerful had set up the theft. That same someone might have known how to open the box. If he could find the boy, then he would unravel him like a thread and find his way, inch by inch, back to whoever had hired him.

The boy.

The frightened face appeared in his mind.

"A boy named Jute. Within the city of Hearne, most likely. Slight for his age. About thirteen years old. Ragged, probably. Dirty, I'm sure. Thin-faced. Straight black hair." He wracked his memory, trying to recall details.

"Dark brown eyes. Old bruises on his face, I think. Slender hands. The hands of a thief. A thief. *Oeof*." He held his breath and watched the mosaic.

The stones shifted. Colors rippled. Lines blurred into being and then rearranged themselves into shapes. A stone warehouse, long sweeps of wharves, the blue stretch of sea and sky behind. Figures bending over crates spilling over with silver. Silver. Fish. The docks. And there in the foreground, a boy clambering up from the beach. It could have been any one of the hundreds of street urchins afflicting the city of Hearne. But then, the boy turned toward him, almost as if aware of his gaze, and the dark eyes and face sprang into clarity.

Nio whirled and leapt up the stairs. He stopped, cursed, and ran back down.

"*Undon,*" he said to the little mosaic of the sea. The blue grayed into dull stone. He muttered a word at the mosaic of fire, and the image of the sceadu lost clarity, devolving into the indistinct mass of darkness and two red eyes that had been there before. He snapped a few words at the mosaic overhead until it swirled into a confusion of color and shape.

He ran for the stairs. There was no time to lose.

CHAPTER SEVENTEEN
THE PERFECT PLACE TO HIDE

Jute made his way along the foot of the cliffs until he came to the sweep of beach curving along the city walls toward the harbor. He hunkered down behind a boulder and thought for a while. At least he tried to think, but this proved to be difficult, as he was shivering with cold and growing hungrier by the minute.

It was some help, though, to think about the hawk. The whole affair was so strange that it diverted his thoughts from his miserable state. He had a memory of someone saying there were certain animals that could talk— beasts that had been enspelled. Perhaps it had been one of the older boys. Some of the Juggler's children had come from privileged backgrounds, children who had run away from families wealthy enough to have afforded schooling.

What had the hawk meant?

Things wake that should not have been disturbed. You would do well to avoid their attention.

Did the hawk mean things like the horrible creature in the cellar? Even though he was already shivering, this thought made him shiver even more. *For now, be content with staying alive, youngling.* He might be able to manage that, if he could somehow get warmed up. Some food would help too.

Several fishing boats were drawn up on the beach. Fishermen were stretching out their nets to dry on the sand. Others carried wicker baskets of fish from the night's catch to the wharves further along the beach. Bigger boats were tied up along the wharves, prows in and crowded for space. Costermongers sold the fresh catch from their stalls. Housewives, cooks from the city's inns, stewards, even the blue-liveried servants from the regent's household prodded and poked and sniffed their way through piles of bass, snapper, and flounder, along with buckets of oysters and baskets of eels twisting about themselves like tangled black velvet ropes. Someone had caught a pair of sharks, and the brutes hung by their tails at the side of a stall, seawater and blood trickling from their jaws.

Past the wharves, an immense pier on stone pilings extended out into the harbor almost to the breakwater that sheltered Hearne's port from the sea. Larger oceangoing vessels were moored along the pier. Slim, doublemasted ketches, sturdy schooners from the northern duchies of Tormay, and huge galleons from Harth flying the golden flag of the house of Oran. Even now, a brigantine with square white sails running up was coming about, turning toward the gap in the breakwater and the sea beyond.

Jute stood and discovered his legs were trembling so badly he could hardly walk. Hunger drove him forward, however. He slunk down the beach toward the wooden arch named Joarsway, or the Fishgate, as it was called by the locals. One of the fishers, an old man mending a torn net, called out to him, but Jute flinched away at the sound of his voice.

The Fishgate neighborhood of the city was a warren of inns, shops, and dwellings, built in a hodgepodge fashion of stones and thatch and timbers and plaster. In places, the narrow streets were cobbled, but this was rare. Most streets were merely dirt packed to the hardness of stone by years of traffic and weather. Due to the night's rainfall, the alleys and shadows were slick with mud. Jute made his way through the crowded streets. His stomach hurt.

He did not know the Fishgate neighborhood well. It was one of the poorer parts of the city and the Thieves Guild did not waste time robbing poor people. The Juggler's children never worked the Fishgate streets. It was not that the Guild had sympathy for the poor; rather, they preferred to go where the money was.

Within the shadow of an alley, Jute paused and looked around. The back of his neck prickled as if someone was watching him. But there was no one there. The alley was heaped with rubbish. Other than that, it was empty. Three children ran past the mouth of the alley, threading through the crowd and shrieking with laughter. A stout woman trundled past in pursuit. With a grunt, she lunged and caught the smallest boy by the ear and hauled him off.

"But Mama, I don't want to go!" Jute heard him squeal before the two vanished out of earshot. He felt nauseated and tired. His stomach spasmed. Sunlight angling over the wall fell on his face and he looked up toward the sky. It was empty and blue.

Jute let himself drift out into the crowd. The street opened up into a small market square bustling with life. An open-air butchery stood on one corner, with haunches of beef, pork, and mutton hanging red and fly-speckled from a crossbeam. Links of sausage glistened in looped piles alongside folds of rubbery tripe and stacks of muttonchops. The *thwack-thwack-thwack* of the butcher's cleaver on the chopping block could be heard. At another stall, cabbages and wilted lettuces lay heaped on canvas. Shriveled potatoes sat mounded in baskets. The stink of fish filled the air, and a board slung across two barrels gleamed with piles of their slick silvers and blues and blacks. A small boy sloshed water onto the fish from a bucket and scratched himself, yawning. Flies buzzed around his bare feet.

A spicer stood guard in front of his wares and eyed the crowd. Jute could smell the pepper and cinnamon from where he stood, and he drifted toward the man, his nose twitching. The smell was pungent, even amidst the stench of fish and the butcher's goods. Strings of dried chilies in green and yellow and red dangled from the awning next to braids of garlic. Behind the man were bowls of spice: chunks of rock salt, peppercorns, tiny green cardamom seeds, golden ginger, paprika in dusty shades of scarlet and orange, and brown cinnamon. Jute sniffed, his mouth watering.

The spicer scowled at him. "Are you going to buy my spice or just stand there, smelling it up? Run along, you wretch."

Reluctantly, Jute moved away. At the far corner of the square, a baker did business. His oven exhaled the fragrance of yeast and salt. Jute edged closer and stared. What happened next would have been normally unthinkable for a boy of his abilities. Filching a loaf would have been child's play for any of the Juggler's children, but the past few days had taken their toll. His hand trembled on a loaf of bread and the baker glanced up.

"Thief!" yelled the baker, lunging for him. Flour billowed in the air around him. He missed, but the woman standing next to Jute did not.

The baker beat him soundly with the wooden paddle he used for shifting loaves in the oven. A crowd of people gathered and called out advice. Business picked up, and the baker's assistant scurried about with armfuls of bread. Concerned the paddle would not hold up, the baker dropped Jute onto the cobbles and kicked him. The boy tried to crawl away, but the baker danced around him like a fighting rooster.

"This is what we do to your sort in the Fishgate!"

"Tsk—you'd think Hearne was run by thieves these days. How much are the large ryes?"

"Two for a copper! The baker's assistant waved a loaf in the air. "Fresh an' hot from the oven!"

"That'll teach him!" said a crone.

"Aye, Mistress Gamall," said the baker, his boot connecting with the boy's ribs. "We should be concerned with the schooling of our youngsters." He stepped on Jute's hand and smiled in satisfaction as he heard the bones crack. The boy blacked out and then came to, gasping, as the baker kicked his stomach. He caught a glimpse of sky spinning overhead, empty and blue.

"Hold, baker!"

Dimly, Jute remembered the voice, but he could not place it. He heard a brief, angry exclamation from the baker. And then the sky was blotted out by a face peering down into his own. Brown eyes, faded, dusty clothing, a ragged cloak. The old man. Severan. The crowd drifted around them, the man kneeling next to the crumpled boy. The baker stomped back to his stall.

"Can you get up, Jute?" asked Severan. The boy shivered from his touch.

"I'm sorry for that," said the old man.

"Sorry!" spat Jute. His voice cracked. Tears tracked down his muddy cheeks.

"I can't fault you for judging me on the company I keep," said the old man. "I fault myself! But trust me for now. You must be away from here immediately."

"Back to the house and that basement?" said the boy.

"Darkness take me, boy, if I lie. I didn't intend you any harm and you won't be going back there. Not if I can help it. We've both learned a thing or two these last days."

Jute tried to pull away from him once he was on his feet, but he was too weak and Severan held onto his arm. The old man seemed to know the neighborhood of the Fishgate well and led Jute through a maze of alleys and twisting streets. He moved fast for an old man. The boy was soon stumbling on his feet, barely able to keep up, but the man would not release his hold on him.

"Leave go," gasped the boy. "Let me go. You'd take me back to him and—and that thing!"

Severan hustled him down an alleyway and did not stop until they had rounded a corner. He glanced around before he spoke, but there was no one in sight.

"Hear me out, boy. I mean you well. I never dreamed he would do such a thing. Such sorceries are forbidden!"

"Then you saw it?! That, that—"

The old man shivered. "You can know someone—think you know them—and then in one instant what you hold true is discovered to be false. The mask is peeled away and a strange visage is revealed. A chance trick of the light and suddenly a stranger is looking back at you. Last night, I happened to be at Nio's house. Questions had arisen in my work that only Nio could answer. When I walked in the door, I sensed something strange. A scent in the air made me uneasy. The place quivered with the vibration of unseen magic. Somewhat similar to what you hear, boy, when you are about your thievery and listen for ward spells, but this was a tremble in all material at hand, as if something of the Dark had been recently near. Echoes, if you will. A kind of footprint peculiar to the Dark.

"I had uneasy dreams last night," continued Severan. "When I awoke, I determined to go and confront Nio with my fears. Perhaps the thing, whatever it was, had crept into his house without his knowledge? I would not damn an innocent man with assumptions. But I saw him in Mioja Square this morning. He was oblivious to my presence. Something in his demeanor changed my mind and I did not approach him. What if the evil was in the house by his design?"

"He did it," said the boy, shuddering. "He spoke and something came up out of the sewer in the basement! Darkness and water all mixed together. It felt like ice when it touched me!"

"You should have died there. Luck was on your side. The thing you speak of is called a wihht. The essence of darkness married with some item of our world. Such creatures cannot be created except through an evil will, for they can only be used for evil. This sort of magic is forbidden. It is accursed. When you use the Dark for your purposes, it uses you as well." The old man sighed. "Whatever possessed you to rob that house of all others?"

The image of the Knife stooped over the chimney sprang to Jute's mind and again he heard the whisper floating down through the darkness. *Come up, boy. Come up.* And the long arm reaching down for him. The Guild had a long arm indeed, and it could still reach him in this city. He stared at the old man and did not answer.

"I decided to investigate for myself while the house was empty," said Severan, "for Nio was heading in the opposite direction when I saw him. The place was silent and filled with shadow. All the windows were shuttered. The air smelled of decay. It grew stronger as I entered the kitchen. The door to the cellar was ajar, and I eased it open to look down the stairs."

Jute clutched his hand.

"And you saw it?" he said, his voice shaking. "Did you see it?"

"Not at first. It was dark inside. I crept down a few steps and thought to call forth a flame to aid my sight. I'm not a wizard, but one needn't be a wizard to attempt certain modest things. But at that moment, below me in the darkness, I saw two dim points of light. Perplexed, I thought them a pair of candles. But then, to my horror, they slowly moved my way. I heard a wet, whispering noise as of sodden flesh pressing against stone. A form gathered shape out of the darkness. I turned and ran up the stairs with my heart pounding so painfully in this old chest of mine I could hardly breathe. I did not stop until I was out of the house and halfway down the street. I had to see the thing, to prove to myself—but for you to have been in that house . . ."

"It was a job." A spark of defiance flared in Jute's eyes. "The Guild needed the Juggler's best for that chimney, and I'm the best of his lot."

"But why that house?" Severan shook his head. "I don't know much about wihhts. However, creatures of the Dark all share certain similarities.

One is that they do not easily forget a scent. The wihht will remember your smell and it'll sniff its way through this city in search of you."

Jute sat down on a wooden crate. His face was white.

"I'm as good as dead," he groaned.

"Not if we act fast. We have some time, I think. I'm no tracker, but I think any scent would get confused in the Fishgate. The stink of fish is nauseating. Even a wihht, let alone a bloodhound, will have trouble here finding your scent. You'd be a sight safer if you hadn't tried your luck with the baker. People remember that sort of thing. It gives them something to talk about over their ale. Wihhts do have ears."

"But where can I hide?" said the boy. He looked up at the sky. "Where can I hide?" Severan got the odd impression that the boy wasn't speaking to him.

"I have the perfect place," said Severan briskly, "but we must be quick. The more time you spend in the streets, the more chance the wihht will pick up your tracks."

He urged Jute to his feet and they hurried off. They made their way through the back alleys of the Fishgate, avoiding the busy streets. After a while, they came to a narrow passage that emptied out into a crowded square.

"Mioja Square," gasped Jute.

Severan grabbed his arm. "But, look you beyond the square."

"There are so many people! I might escape the wihht, but what if someone from the Guild sees me? They think I'm dead. I'll really be dead then!"

"We'll have to risk it," said Severan. "This is our best chance. You see, just beyond the square? That's where we're going."

Mioja Square teemed with life before them. Market stalls, barrow vendors, jugglers, musicians, a throng of humanity. Looming above it on the other side of the square was a massive edifice of black stone spires, squat towers, arches, and crazily angled roof planes that gleamed ancient green copper in the sunlight, rimmed with balustrades and festooned with every manner of gargoyle, glaring and grinning down at the city.

"That's the old university," said Jute. "No one goes there. It's full of magic and death and all sorts of ghosts."

"True to a point," said the old man, smiling. "However, the place is so steeped in magic that the wihht would have immense trouble finding your scent there. Besides, the Guild would never set foot in the ruins, so we're killing two birds with one stone. We don't need them and the wihht both hunting you. You should be safe within the walls. Reasonably safe. Oh, you needn't look like a frightened sheep, Jute. Most of the stories you've heard about the university ruins aren't true, and the ones that are true—well, you step carefully once inside those walls and you're safe enough."

Here, Severan paused, as if unsure as to how he should proceed. "I'm a scholar of sorts. Some years ago, several of my colleagues and I were granted permission by the regent of Hearne, Nimman Botrell, to conduct a search of the university grounds. It's been unoccupied and locked up since the end of the Midsummer War, more than three hundred years ago."

"Yes," said the boy, remembering stories told late at night by the older boys. "And for good reason!"

"Oh, piffle. Worn-out reasons from long ago. Perhaps in the years following the war—the first hundred or two hundred years—there was wisdom in that. I'll be the first to admit that, er, not just anyone should wander about the university. There are some interesting wards within the grounds that have survived the years intact. Some of the most deadly wards ever spelled. But don't worry, boy," he said hastily, for Jute's eyes were widening. "My colleagues and I are well suited for what we do. If we weren't, the regent would have never given us permission. Besides, he's gambling he'll have his cut out of whatever we find—a greedier man I've yet to meet."

"If I take one step out into the square," said Jute, "the Silentman will know instantly. Half the barrow vendors are in the Guild's pay. Pickpockets and cutpurses everywhere. Worse still, we, the Juggler's children, always considered the square as our play field. They know my face. I'm sure to be seen!"

"Wait here," said Severan.

The old man hurried off across the square and disappeared among the vendors and the crowds eddying about the carts and stalls. The boy hunkered down behind some garbage and stared out at the square. The thought of his old playmates worried him. Would they turn him in for a copper coin and a kind word from the Juggler? He wasn't sure, and the uncertainty was worse than the hunger in his belly. Lena wouldn't squeal on him, but she was only one among dozens. The twins. They probably wouldn't say anything either.

Mioja Square was the proving ground of the Juggler's children. It was where the children honed their skills at picking pockets in hopes of graduating to the richer pickings of the Highneck Rise district. His first lift had been a wallet filched from a fat man inspecting bolts of silk at a draper's stall. But he had been too eager, and the man had whirled around. Jute had sprinted away, the wallet clutched to his chest. The fat man could not keep up for long and stopped, gasping and hurling curses after the boy. Jute had collapsed in a fit of nervous giggles, once safe, and the Juggler had been pleased later. Three gold pieces as shiny bright as butter.

The Juggler.

Shadows.

It felt like a hundred years ago.

The Juggler. The Knife. The man's face swam into his mind and he saw his lips move, forming the words: *Remember, boy. Don't open the box, whatever happens. If you do, I'll cut your throat open so wide the wind'll whistle through it.* He shivered, remembering too well the man's hand drifting down, the needle prick on his shoulder, and the night sky receding away as he fell down the chimney. Something tight and hot congealed within his chest, a point of almost physical obstruction that made him swallow convulsively. And for the first time in his life, Jute hated.

A breeze rustled down the alley and blew across his face, waking him from his reverie. Footsteps sounded and he looked up to see Severan.

"Here," said the old man, handing him a folded up cloak. "Put this on. Pull the hood down over your face."

There was one bad moment when they crossed the square. Right next to Vilanuo's barrow—he sold fried bread—Jute looked up from within the shadow of his cowl to meet Lena's glance. Lena, of all people. She was turning away from the barrow, gnawing on a slab of greasy bread dripping honey. Her eyes flicked up, blue against the ravaged, ward-scarred skin. An uncertain frown drifted across her face, followed by blank eyes and dismissal. But Jute had already turned away, steeling himself from breaking into a run. Sweat trickled down his back. Lena was his closest friend among all of the Juggler's children. *Had been*, said part of his mind. *Trust no one.*

He hurried to catch up with Severan stalking through the crowd. Some beggars sat lazing in the sun on the steps of the old university. They scattered like a flock of ragged starlings as Severan and the boy came toward them, shambling to the outer edges of the steps and down to the square.

"Your precious ruins are safe, scholar," jeered one old man as they passed. "We've been hard at guard."

"Aye," said Severan. "I warrant your smell's enough to do the job."

This elicited a chorus of cackles from the other beggars, and they drifted back to their spots in the sunlight pooled on the steps. The front doors were massive, ironbound affairs, with chains wound through the double handles. They were secured by a rusty lock. As Jute stepped closer, he felt his skin prickle and go cold.

"This is warded," he said. "Heavily warded." He could feel the curious stares of the beggars behind them.

"Yes, yes," said the old man, not paying attention to him. "Ah, there it is."

Jute blinked in astonishment. Where there had only been a stone wall before, a small, dark opening yawned.

"Hurry," said Severan. "It'll only stay open for a moment. We can't have one of these old fellows sneaking in after us. One of them did that several months ago. Never saw him slip inside. Didn't find him until later. What was left of him. He didn't survive much more than an hour."

Jute snorted. "I can be a lot quieter than a beggar."

"I'm sure you can," said Severan. "But an alarming number of the ward spells here aren't attuned to noise. The university isn't a safe place."

"I thought you said it was safe," said Jute, but they were already through and there was only stone behind them where the opening once had been.

"Safe?" echoed the old man. "Did I say that? Well, yes, of course it's safe. In a relative sort of way, perhaps. Safer than the streets of Hearne! The wihht won't find you in here. Er, at least, that's my hope."

It was dark inside after the morning sunlight, and at first Jute was aware only of an echoing space before and above him. As his eyes grew accustomed to the darkness, he saw stone pavement stretching out in front of him for a great distance. Rubble lay scattered across it. Pillars rose up in rows running along either side of the floor. Some of them were shattered and broken off at different heights. Shafts of scarlet, gold, and azure light slanted down through clerestory windows of stained glass. It was a place of shadows, despite the light falling through the stained glass.

"Come," said the old man. "Food and a bed for you, and then later we'll talk of what must be done. For now, however, walk behind me and don't speak unless I speak to you. There are certain wards within this place that are disturbed by the sound of human voices."

The boy wondered why Severan had bothered to say *human voices* instead of just *voices*. At the end of the row of pillars, there was a series of doors. These led into a maze of corridors and stairways so full of twists and turns that Jute was soon hopelessly bewildered as to their direction. Dust lay over everything and stirred in their wake.

From time to time, the old man stopped and mumbled a sentence or two. He spoke so quietly, however, that Jute could never make out what he was saying. But he knew the old man was disarming wards, for he always stopped in places where the air quivered with expectancy, and whenever the old man finished, the quivering sensation was stilled. The expectancy was everywhere—that listening quality every ward has, regardless of its function. The air rustled with it. Jute prided himself on never having yet encountered a ward he could not lull into complacency through his own silence. Here, however, the coiled, listening expectancy of the ward spells was different than anything he had ever known. The back of his neck prickled. He imagined eyes watching from every dark doorway and from behind every pile of rubble they passed. Once, he whirled, sure he had heard footsteps, but there was nothing except the empty corridor behind them.

It seemed as if they walked for hours, through shadows and archways, down long malls and past stairways twisting away in every direction. They picked their way through gaping holes in crumbled walls. They crossed a hall filled with light so bright it made his eyes ache. The roof, high above them, was shattered and open to the sky. The wind moaned through the broken ribs of stone overhead and Jute looked up, thinking of the hawk. They came to a warren of corridors relatively untouched by ruin. Severan opened the door to a room furnished with a bed, a wooden chest, and a table and chair.

"Wait here," said the old man.

When he returned with a plate of bread and cheese and a withered summer apple, he found Jute snoring on the bed. The boy had fallen asleep on top of the blankets. It was chilly in the room, and the old man rummaged in the chest for a woolen blanket. He laid it over Jute and then left, closing the door quietly behind him.

Jute lay on his back under a night sky. He had the strange sensation that he could feel the entire earth pressing up underneath him. Mountain ranges, plains, long ribbons of river shining silver in the moonlight. Distant lands. Deserts chilled and shrouded in darkness. Forests lost in shadows of green midnight. The whole of the earth pushed up against his back, as if he were on the prow of a gigantic ship rushing through the night, propelling him through a vast darkness in which only a few stars gleamed. The wind touched his face. He heard in it the echo of a mighty tempest blowing toward him from an impossible distance away, blowing and howling among the far-off stars and spinning dusts of space.

He wanted to reach the sky, to hurl himself up into it. To unravel into the night until there was nothing left of himself. To be freed from the hold of the heavy earth. The breeze whispered to him of the older winds roaming free, far above the plodding earth. A tremor shook him as he strained upward, but he could not lift a hand from the ground. The blades of grass growing from the earth under and around him held his body fast in their gentle embrace. Stone shifted beneath him like bone scraping on bone. The earth held him close, whispering to him with the sounds of rustling leaves and the mutter of worms as they pushed their patient way through the loam.

No. It cannot have you, said a worm.

No, agreed another.

It has nothing to give you, rustled a leaf. *Nothing except the emptiness of sky.*

Nothing.

You must not forsake the earth.

You will wither like this leaf, said a worm in satisfaction.

Aye, said a leaf. *The best and truest of fates.*

He will wither like you.

Aye, agreed the leaf.

The worms murmured together in lines that moved so slowly and smoothly he thought he could feel the damp earth eaten and left in the wake of their tiny passage.

He will fade into worn hues.

Muted from last year's bold spring.

He will tatter in the wind.

Teeter on a shivering branch.

And lose his breezing balance.

He will fall to drift on down.

And so lay with the whole of earth.

Pressed against his crinkled back.

Aye, rustled the leaf.

"But the sky," he said. "It's so perfect and clear. I wish. . ." He could not say what he wished. The worms had nothing more to say either. The leaf, however, rustled one more time.

Aye. I have seen the sky before. Before I fell.

He cried out in longing and awoke. The dream faded from his mind, as dreams do, and he was conscious only of regret and the memory of sky.

CHAPTER EIGHTEEN
ANDOLAN

The town of Andolan nestled in a valley within the Mearh Dun, or the Horse Hills as they had been known hundreds of years ago, before Dolan Callas had first ridden north during the settling of the lands of Tormay. It was written that Dolan Callas fell in love with the region for three things.

First, for the hills themselves and the prairies stretching from the cliffs in the west on the sea's edge to the Mountains of Morn in the east. Each season was more beautiful than the preceding: lush green in the spring spotted with the scarlet poppies like drops of blood, all of which burned into gold under the summer sun, followed by the rust of autumn and the stark snows of winter.

Second, he was drawn by the wild horses that claimed the hills and prairie of the Mearh Dun as their own. The love of horses runs strong in the blood of every Callas, and Dolan Callas was the first of that line.

Third, and most important, Dolan was caught by the gray-green eyes of a peasant girl whom he saw as he rode along the banks of the river Ciele in the heart of the Mearh Dun. Legend has it the girl was washing laundry at the river's edge. Dolan reined in his horse on the other side. The girl's black hair, bright and dark together as a raven's wing, fell across her face as she bent over her work. She did not look up, even though she must have heard him approaching, for the Ciele is a narrow river. At the nicker of his horse, she finally glanced up. Her name was Levoreth, as so many women of the Callas family down through the years have been named. He built Andolan for her and she bore him three sons. So began the lineage of the dukes of Callas.

The duke's party clattered over the bridge crossing the Ciele and came up the road winding toward the two old towers that guarded the southern gate. Lights gleamed in the town of Andolan, for the sun was lowering in the west. The men-at-arms laughed and talked among themselves. They were glad to be back—good ale and good friends at the castle, the warmth of their homes and wives. The guards at the gate were already standing at attention, for the tall form of the duke was distinctive at a distance.

Children skipped alongside the horses and chased after pennies the duke tossed for them as the party rode through the streets. Men and women called cheerfully from porch stoops and windows and from market stalls shuttering for the night. They tugged their forelocks in respect to the three members of the Callas family. The duke and duchess were loved in Dolan, but especially in the town of Andolan. The dukes of Callas had never forgotten the peasant girl who had become the mother of their line. It was in honor of her that the castle doors were always open to the townsfolk. Equally so, it was just as normal to find the duke sitting outside the local tavern with the old men who had nothing better to do than warm their bones in the sun and swap tall tales.

Grooms ran out to hold the horses' reins as they clattered to a halt in the castle courtyard. Two hounds lollopped up and sniffed dutifully at every horse before making for Levoreth to slobber happily all over her hands. The old steward Radean emerged from the front door and tottered down the steps. Servants peered smiling from lamp-lit windows. The Callases were home.

The days whisked by in a whirl of activity. There was much to do before setting out for Hearne and the Autumn Fair. Melanor decided none of her dresses would do and, catching Hennen at an opportune time when he was sneaking a pork pie in the larder before supper, convinced the duke to part with the necessary gold.

"I think Levoreth could use a few new things, too," said the duchess.

"You women are going to beggar the duchy," said her husband, edging around so that he was standing between the duchess and the remains of the pork pie sitting on the shelf.

"Nonsense," said his wife. "We're the only reason the land hasn't gone to ruin, with you buying up every horse in sight and paying a king's ransom for whatever four-legged creature the Farrows trot through here."

"What?" said the duke, foolishly rising to the bait. "Madame, you speak of things you know nothing of. Horses are the treasure of Dolan. That last colt—she'll be faster than Min the Morn, or I'll eat my best cloak—was worth every penny I paid."

"And how much was that?"

"Er . . ."

"I don't suppose you'll grudge Levoreth and me a few pieces of gold."

"A few pieces? Why, I know that just one of your dresses—"

"Hennen, you have crumbs on your chin," she interrupted. "And we'll need to get some shoes too. Several pairs each."

"Oh, all right," he said.

Levoreth would have smiled if she could have heard them, but she was walking down by the river Ciele. She did not care about new dresses and shoes. The few she had she was comfortable with, for they were faded and known, like old friends. Green and growing things fascinated her: the change of seasons, how the earth accepted the coming of the rain. And the homey parts of everyday life never ceased to tire her: the scent of bread baking, the cooing of a baby, the flicker of a hearth fire at the end of the day. And then there were horses. She was a Callas, through and through, in every best sense of the name. Every Callas loved horses.

One of the hounds had followed her from the castle and now was snuffling among the rocks by the river's edge. Every once in a while, he would stop and raise his head to stare at her, as if to reassure himself of her presence. She sat down on a slab of rock. Light glittered on the water. The sun rode up the arch of a perfect sky. She leaned back, rested her head on her shawl, and slept.

She dreamt of a young girl standing on a savannah of grasses waving in the wind. The girl's face was remote and still. Sadness pooled in the shadows under her gray eyes. Her hair streamed away from her in black tresses. She gazed away into the distance. The girl turned, slowly, to look at Levoreth.

Levoreth awoke with a start. The hound was nosing at her hand. It woofed happily when she scratched its head, and then it flopped down at her feet. She lay back and slept again.

This time, she dreamt of a winter sky. High overhead, a hawk floated on the wind, wings stretched wide. Its cry thrilled through the air, fierce and cruel. Far off across a snowy plain, a figure walked toward her. She could not tell if it were man or woman, as the distance was great. A roaring rose in her ears. Wind howled through the sky and whipped across the snow. A flurry of ice stung her skin. Indistinguishable at first, but then clearer and clearer, a voice called to her from far away.

Levoreth.

I am Levoreth Callas. He stopped for me, and I looked up. I chose to look up. I took his name.

Levoreth.

It is mine. I never wanted much.

This time, she awoke with a hand touching her shoulder. One of the maids from the castle was kneeling next to her. The hound sat up and yawned.

"Miss Levoreth," said the maid. "Milady would like you to come for your fitting."

"All right, girl," she said. "Run back and tell her I'll be along shortly."

"Yes, miss." And the maid scampered across the meadow toward the town walls.

Levoreth sat for a moment, staring down at the river. Its liquid voice sang of the valley, of the heather on the hills graying into autumn, of the mists that rose in the mornings on the plain and melted away under the noonday sun. Through it all was the murmuring memory of rain, of the storms in the Mountains of Morn that brought life to the Mearh Dun.

"And the hope of rain, yet again," said Levoreth out loud. The hound looked at her quizzically. "So it ever goes, and the years are preserved. May it ever be so and may the Dark never wake in Daghoron." She scratched the dog's ears, and it growled with pleasure. "Come, or Melanor will grow impatient and take it out on the poor tailor."

The tailor proved accommodating to Melanor's wishes, even though he sighed at her demand that all the clothes be finished in two days. He was a melancholy man with sad eyes and the air of an undertaker.

"Honestly," whispered the duchess, "you'd think we were being fitted for our shrouds. But he's positively the best tailor north of Hearne. Something terribly sad must've happened to him."

"Or perhaps," said Levoreth, "he has corns and his shoes are too tight."

"You think so?" And the duchess spent the rest of the afternoon scrutinizing the poor man's shoes until he grew so flustered that he jabbed Levoreth with a safety pin as he was measuring her for an evening gown.

CHAPTER NINETEEN
STARTING THE JOB

Ronan spent some time watching the comings and goings of the merchant Cypmann Galnes. He had heard of Galnes even before Arodilac Bridd had told him his story. The man was well-known among the merchants and traders of the city. He was wealthy, powerful, and equally comfortable among the nobility of Highneck Rise and the roughnecks of the docks. It wouldn't do to anger a man who had the ear of the regent. Even if the regent was paying for the job.

Obviously, the man was aware of his daughter's circumstance. And angry. The best thing would be to find out his habits and then rob his house when he wasn't home. There was no need to anger him any further. Strange, though, that his daughter wanted the Bridd family ring for something. What was it Arodilac had said?

She wants something in exchange. But she won't tell me what.

Strange.

It was raining—a chilly downpour, unseasonal but welcome enough to the gardens and greenery parched brown by summer—and this dreariness plunged him into a brooding study. The rain reduced the city to a blur of stone, punctuated by the glow of lights in windows—taverns, shops, homes—all promising warmth and respite from the damp and dark.

Water ran on the cobbled streets; it streamed from cornices and peaks and spouts. It flowed along through the gutters and gurgled down storm drains. In Mioja Square, in the heart of the city, the fountain began to overflow, sheeting water across the square. The vendors had already packed up their handbarrows and stalls and scurried away. Nobody shopped in weather like this.

Cypmann Galnes stalked across the square, oblivious to the rain and oblivious to the shadowy form of Ronan trailing behind him. As far as the thief could tell, they were the only two souls out in the city that morning. He flipped his collar up and shivered. Rain ran down his neck. A curse escaped his lips as he splashed through a puddle.

Normally, such a job would be given to one of the runners, one of the children fresh from the Juggler's pack. Someone with enough brains to follow and keep their mouth shut, stay invisible, and hang about in doorways, waiting for someone else to move, someone else to think, someone else to act. But the instructions Smede passed on from the Silentman had been explicit. The regent wanted no one else from the Guild working on the job, no one else from the Guild even knowing about the job. The potential of embarrassment for the regency was too great.

Ronan smiled sourly to himself. He appreciated the trust that the Silentman obviously thought him worthy of. Still, he'd much rather be sitting in an inn somewhere, a mug of ale in hand.

We all have our jobs to do.

Almost, he stopped to turn around, to see who had whispered the words, but it was only his memory stirring. Darkness filled his eyes and he saw the chimney yawning open underneath him, filled with shadow. He felt dizzy, as if he were teetering on a height. As if he was the one falling. He strode on in the rain, shoulders hunched against the wet and the cold, and against the past.

Nothing personal, boy.

We all have our jobs to do.

Cypmann Galnes owned a warehouse near the harbor. Here, the city continued its hustle and bustle in spite of the rain. Water was a customary part of life, whether in the sea or raining from the sky. Even now, the docks swarmed with fishermen unloading the morning catch. Rain hissed on the swells rising and falling against the pilings. A schooner nosed up against the dock, its mainsail dropping with a clatter. Ronan could hear the calls of the sailors as ropes were flung and made fast. He huddled in an archway and watched as the merchant disappeared through a door down the street. A moment later, lamplight flickered from behind a window. The merchant would be there until late in the day. His routine was predictable. Ronan trudged away.

CHAPTER TWENTY
THE GAWINNS TAKE IN AN ORPHAN

They drove the mules hard. The twins no longer smiled and sang, even though Loy took to crooning wordlessly over the girl. She did not wake from her sleep. Her body grew thinner with each passing hour until it seemed she was only a collection of bones wrapped with skin. From time to time, Loy managed to trickle drops of honey and water between her lips.

"Her skin feels like fire," he said. "And the wounds on her leg stink of rot."

"Tomorrow morning we'll be there," said Murnan.

"Might be too late."

"Aye," said the other twin. "If these lazy mules of yours weren't weighted so heavily, we'd make better time. Be there by nightfall."

The twins both glared at the trader. He tried to stare them down but could not.

"All right!" he said. "Have it your way. It'll mean less for all of us at journey's end."

After a hasty discussion they decided on the copper ingots, as well as a pair of silver cats that had caught Murnan's eye in Damarkan.

"For a wedding," he said to himself. "They'd have been a perfect wedding gift. Cwen loves cats." But then he subsided into silence, for his thoughts turned to another wedding and the miller's face staring up blindly at the sky.

They buried the copper and the cats at the foot of an oak in a dell near the river Rennet. It was beginning to rain. The mules stepped out eagerly, now that their burdens had been lightened.

"Ten hours," said the trader.

It was closer to nine hours and just into night when they reached the gates of Hearne. The horses steamed with sweat in the light of the flaring lamps and the mules refused to move once they clattered under the stone arch. A young officer emerged from the guard tower.

"Sir—"

"I need a physician. Quickly, and the best you know!"

The officer raised his eyebrows.

"Physicians don't just come for anyone, sir. Even in Hearne, only a few practice and they cost a—"

"What's this?" said a voice behind the officer. A man sauntered down the steps of the guard tower. The young officer stepped to one side and saluted him.

"Murnan Col, is it not?" said the man.

"My lord?" said the trader.

The lamplight drew the man's face out of shadow, revealing a bony visage with startling blue eyes and dark hair falling over his forehead.

"You sold me a pair of emeralds a year ago," said the man. "Perfectly matched. Had them made into earrings for my wife."

"Ah!" Murnan's face lightened. "Owain Gawinn! My lord, surely fate has brought you here. I'm sorely in need of your assistance. I know a good physician's hard to find, but not for the regent's Lord Captain of Hearne."

"For yourself, no doubt," said Owain, though he didn't mean it. His eyes had already noted the form cradled in Loy's arms.

"Several days ago, my lord, as we came up from Damarkan, we arrived at a village on a tributary of the Rennet. A little place I've traded at before, pleasant and friendly folk. This time, however, when we entered the village we found a charnel house out of the worst nightmare! Every person slain except for this one poor girl we brought away, and she is gravely wounded. Perhaps it would be a kindness to let her die, seeing her people are gone, but who knows why one is left to live?"

The captain's face had stilled at the trader's words.

"How were the villagers killed?" he asked. His voice was quiet. "Did you take time to notice?"

Murnan's face twisted in disgust. "Their bodies were disfigured by the birds and rats feeding, but it seemed they died in one of two ways. Some had deep wounds, thin and precise as if stabbed by knife or sword. Others had their throats torn out as if by a wild beast."

Owain Gawinn said nothing more after that, except to snap an order to the young officer at the gate. Soldiers dashed out with fresh horses, and in a matter of seconds the trader and the twins found themselves hurried along through the streets of Hearne. The rain and the darkness and the looming walls around them passed by in a blur of clattering hoofs and the muttered talk of the soldiers. Owain rode at their head, but he seemed a shadow flitting through the night, only just in sight and always out of reach.

The street climbed up a steep rise. The houses were larger there, mansions, for the most part, set back behind walls and gardens. The rain rustled overhead in the branches of trees sheltering the street. They came to a gate in a high wall. Owain called out, and the gate swung open. They entered into a courtyard. Light spilled from doorways and windows. Servants came forward.

"Welcome to my house," said Owain Gawinn.

The regent's own physician came and tended to the little girl. He was an old man with a stern face, but his hands were gentle and the girl's labored breathing eased under his touch.

"Her blood's tainted with a strange poison," he said. He bled her with a knife into a stone vial, though Loy scowled and grumbled in the corner so much that he had to be ushered from the room. Owain's four children peeped in through the doorway, all with his blue eyes. Sibb, his wife, swept in and out with hot water and a cool hand that seemed to do just as much good, if not more, than the physician.

Murnan Col left that same night, relieved and heading north to Thule and home. One twin, Gann, went with him, but Loy stayed behind in the house of Owain Gawinn, for, as he said to his brother, he had felt the little girl's life ebb away in his arms over the course of those past days and he wished to see her whole again before he left.

Her fever broke after three days, and the wounds on her arm and leg began to heal. But even though she opened her eyes, she would only stare at her visitors. Not a sound escaped her lips, despite Owain's repeated attempts to question her. Finally, his wife banned him from the room.

"She'll speak when she's ready," she said. "Until then, you'll have to wait. Now go, before I lose my patience."

"Know your place, Sibb!" said her husband. But then he laughed and kissed her. He was a wise man and knew that his wife was wiser still in most matters.

The days passed, and still the girl remained silent. All of them grew used to her grave eyes—Owain, his wife Sibb, their children, the servants, and Loy—though Owain wondered what it was that she had seen. This was not the first tale he had heard of such killings, but it was the first time he had encountered a survivor.

After some time, the girl plucked up enough courage to venture out of her room, but only if Loy was in view. Besides Owain's wife, he was the only one she would suffer to pick her up. But even for him she remained silent and solemn, despite the many ridiculous faces he would make for her benefit. Not a night went by without a nightmare coming to her, and it was only then she made noise—screaming as if she were looking into the darkness of Daghoron itself. The household waited patiently for her improvement and speech. She remained mute, however, and so the family grew to expect nothing more of her, though Sibb wept over her sometimes at night.

CHAPTER TWENTY-ONE
VANISHING STAIRS

There was food on the table when Jute woke up. After he ate, he investigated the room. There was nothing worth stealing. Wool blankets and old books would not bring much from the barrow sellers who bought from the Juggler's children. The room adjoined another room with nothing in it except for a window opening out onto a stone casement. He crawled outside and sat in the morning sunlight. The stone was already warming with the sun. He was at a great height, well above the rooftops of the city. Above him, the university spires towered even higher, up into the clear sky. Far below, the hubbub of Mioja Square drifted up to him. People bustled like ants among the brightly colored awnings of the stalls.

The city sprawled around his vantage point. The sea was a brilliant line of blue to the west. To the east, huddled near the university walls, was the ugly mass of the Earmra slum, where the poorest of Hearne's poor lived and worked. To the north, of course, the rooftops sloped sharply up toward Highneck Rise, at whose highest point rose the gleaming white stone towers of the regent's castle. He had never been inside, or even close, for the castle was so heavily warded it set his ears buzzing if he got within a hundred yards of the place. According to the Juggler, the castle of Nimman Botrell was filled with the most fabulous treasures imaginable.

The Juggler.

His jaw tightened. A breeze blew by his face, prompting him to look to the sky, but there was nothing there—no hawk riding the winds—only the empty blue.

The view from the window only held him so long. By noon, his boredom outweighed his fear of the university and the terrors Severan had hinted at. He opened the door to the hall and peered out. No one was there. The hall was silent. Even better, he could not hear any ward spells whispering in his mind. What was it Severan had said?

An alarming number of the ward spells here aren't attuned to noise.

Then what do they listen to if not noise?

He rubbed his nose and thought hard about this for a moment. He hadn't met a ward yet he couldn't beat. The trick was to be as silent as the sky. Silent and empty, and the spell would reach right through you and find nothing.

Jute crept down the hall.

He tripped his first ward twenty minutes later.

After some time prowling about the warren of hallways, he came upon a marble door carved with whorls that seemed to creep in and out of each other. He pressed his ear against it and listened. There was only silence. More importantly, there was no ward whispering in his mind. He opened the door and found himself standing on a platform jutting out over a huge, gloomy space of darkness. He edged over to the side to look down. He could see nothing below. But surely something was down there. He had to find out.

Happily enough, a staircase curved down from one side of the platform. The steps were visible some distance down in the darkness, reflecting a hidden light source he could not make out. Jute tiptoed down the stairs in silence. However, after some time, he became aware of a noise. He froze. It was the quietest of noises—similar to a finger tapping on stone. Just a simple, peaceful tapping.

Or so Jute thought.

He took another step down the stairs, listening hard. After a few more steps, he realized the tapping increased in rapidity the further he descended. He retreated back up the stairs a way and paused. Sure enough, the tapping slowed back down.

If Jute had understood the history and nature of the university, he would have promptly ran back up the stairs and hurried to the room where Severan had left him. And there he would have waited until the old man returned. But Jute didn't. He was a stubborn boy and he was also a curious thief. It was a combination that didn't always prove healthy.

He tiptoed down the stairs, listening with all his might to the tapping as it increased in tempo with every step he took. He still could not tell where the stairs ended, as no floor was visible below. By this time, the tapping was so fast that surely the next step down he took would result in the tapping becoming a single, unbroken blur of sound. He took one more step and found this to be true.

It was at that moment the stairway began to vanish. The steps below him disappeared, one by one, climbing up toward him. He turned and ran. There was one horrible spot at the end where he felt the step under his foot soften and he looked down to see the thing vanish. He lunged for the platform at the top of the stairs and hauled himself, sobbing for air, up over the edge.

Jute lay on his back, his heart hammering against his ribs. After a while, he noticed with horrified fascination that, far below the platform, the stairway was reappearing. The stairs shimmered into view, one by one, mounting higher and higher. The last stair materialized under his fingertips, and he snatched his hand away as if the cold stone would burn him.

Severan was waiting in his room, perched on the wooden chest.

"Have an apple," he said, waving at a pile of withered specimens on the table. He took one for himself and bit into it. Jute picked up an apple and promptly dropped it on the floor. His hands were shaking.

"Ah," said Severan. "You found Bevan's stairway. I felt it vanish. My colleagues also did. We figured it must have been a large and unlucky rat, though I had my suspicions. No one's ever reached the bottom of those stairs. Alive, that is."

"I can't just stay cooped up in here!" said Jute.

"It's either stay cooped up or have the wihht find you," said the old man. "Or have your neck broken in any number of ways. The wards in this place are deadly. Can you get that through your thick skull?"

"The stairs vanished right underneath me!"

"You shouldn't have been wandering around. I don't doubt you're bored, but, trust me, you were lucky. Those stairs killed a lot of people during the Midsummer War. Bevan was an unusually creative wizard. He was the one who figured out how to mask the warning buzz that wards give off. Once he'd discovered that, it wasn't long before all the best wards in this place were woven for silence. Though—did you hear a tapping noise when you were on the staircase?"

"Of course," said Jute. He bit into an apple. "What do you expect me to do? Sit in here until I grow old and die?"

"Most people would never have heard any tapping, which is how Bevan designed it. However, if you heard it that means you'd probably be able to recognize many of the wards in these ruins, one way or another. So I suppose it would be safe for you to see a bit of the place. Though," he warned, as Jute's face brightened, "you must use your wits, which you obviously didn't do on the staircase."

"I'm alive, aren't I?" said the boy.

"Next time, if you hear noise, no matter how quiet, get away from that place as fast as possible. Furthermore, don't go below the ground level and do not go outside, whatever you do. Some of the entrance wards are strong enough to reduce a house to rubble. The wards in this place are much more sophisticated than the variety people buy in the marketplace for their homes and whatnot. Any noise, any movement, changes in color or temperature, even a change in odor—treat them as signs of a ward listening to you."

"What if it's just a mouse scurrying by?" said Jute.

The old man sighed and reached for another apple.

"A mouse," he said. "How I wish the world was that simple. You obviously know nothing about the Midsummer War. If you did, even the mice in this place would give you cause for concern." He settled back on the wooden chest and began to speak.

CHAPTER TWENTY-TWO
SCUADIMNES AND THE MIDSUMMER WAR

"Long ago," said Severan, "all Tormay was united under a monarchy that ruled from the city of Hearne. The duchies of Dolan, Hull, and Thule in the north and those of Vo and Vomaro in the south all gave their allegiance to the king. Harlech, of course, far to the north, minded its own business, as it has always done and always will. The deserts of Harth, beyond Vomaro, gave their loyalty to no one, though the tribe of Oran was beginning to establish itself in those years by seizing control of the oasis trade routes. The duchy of Mizra did not exist in those days."

"What?" said Jute, blinking. "Mizra, where all the gold comes from?"

"Mizra, where all the gold comes from. There're more important things to know about Mizra than that. The Guild is obviously selective in what it teaches its budding criminals. Mizra, at the time, was a wilderness, east of the mountains of Morn. No one ever went to Mizra and no one ever came from Mizra. Anyway, at the time, the university in Hearne was a center for the study of history and certain other topics. It was a place of wonder, a repository of knowledge so vast that men have never known its like. Students came from every walk of life."

"To learn how to be wizards?" said Jute.

"Not just wizards," said Severan. "It was a place for scholars as well. Besides, no one learns how to become a wizard. You either are or you aren't. Wizardry is just a trait like any other trait. Some people are born with the knack of understanding animals or throwing the perfect clay pot or knowing just when to whisk a cake out of the oven. The university taught how to control and refine the trait of wizardry. The trait itself can't be taught."

"But what about ward-weavers?" asked the boy. "Fat old Arcus in Mioja Square offered to take on Wrin as his apprentice, and Wrin's stupid as a rock. I once gave him a piece of tin and he thought it silver."

Severan waved his hand in the air. "You can teach a dog to do tricks if you're patient and have plenty of bones to keep the rascal happy. Anyone can learn a few bits of wizardry, but it doesn't mean you're a wizard. Most modern ward-weaving is tomfoolery and only fit for keeping out rats and mice. As I was saying, er, what was I saying? Oh, yes. The university! The university was a vibrant place, a marvelous mix of the best minds of Tormay.

All dedicated—well, mostly all—to preserving knowledge of Tormay's past and the study of the Dark. For if one does not know the past, one cannot guard against the future."

The day was darkening outside. Severan rummaged in the chest and found a candle. He lit it and set on the table. The light flickered on their faces. Shadows trembled on the wall. The old man settled back on his seat and continued.

"But then an unfortunate thing happened. The old king died. His son, Dol Cynehad, ascended the throne, and the wizard Scuadimnes was appointed advisor to his new majesty. Scuadimnes was the senior archivist at the university, a quiet man of no distinction other than his remarkable memory. It was said that every word in every manuscript of the archive was held within his mind. One need only go to him and ask where might one find a treatise on cloud formations, or hedgetoads, or sicknesses caused by the touch of a lich, and he would select the pertinent work. Plucked, mind you, from thousands of scrolls and scripts and books. No one was sure where Scuadimnes came from originally. Some said Vomaro. Others said that he was a farmer's son from Hull. Still others said that he came from Harlech, though that's unlikely, as few wizards have ever come from that land.

"Scuadimnes set about poisoning the young king's mind against the university and the wizards. Any power not in the hands of those who rule is found suspect by them. This is a dangerous inclination to exploit. Slowly, Scuadimnes twisted the king's thinking until he regarded the wizards with suspicion. And then enmity. And then fear. Edicts were proclaimed, limiting new students to only those approved by the king's council. Taxes were levied on wizards and the practice of the arts on behalf of others. The council of the university did not suspect the involvement of Scuadimnes at the time, for he came to them in those days with honeyed words, protesting his lack of influence over the king and his dismay at the cruelty of the throne."

The old man stared at the candle flame.

"They believed him," he said. "Even though they must have known. They must have! But it's easier to pretend all's well than to awake and confront the Dark."

"What happened then?" said the boy.

"What happened then?" echoed the old man. He sighed. "The Midsummer War is what happened then. It began with murder. The body of Volora Cynehad, the king's grandmother, was found in her rooms. A harmless old woman who was only important by virtue of who her grandson was. Murdered in a hideous manner that pointed to wizardry of a dark and learned sort. The dean of the university was arrested and died in the royal dungeons under mysterious circumstances. Students were beaten in the streets of Hearne. Mobs tried to break into the university grounds. The wizards avoided confrontation at first, but the violence spiraled out of hand. It was only a matter of time before the royal army attacked. And attack they did.

"The deceit of Scuadimnes was then revealed, for many of the younger wizards, students mostly, turned on their peers and masters. Bought long ago by promises of power, they aided the king's soldiers and transformed the university into a raging battleground of sword and spear and the magic arts. The nights of Hearne were lit up by the eldritch glow of the struggle. Three times, the battered remnant within the university threw their attackers from the school. And in the evening after that last time, an awful sight was seen."

"What? What was it?" said the boy. He stared at Severan with wide eyes.

"The gates of the royal castle were thrown open, and out marched the dead, in row upon row. Warriors and wizards alike, woven back to a strange half-life by the arts of Scuadimnes. Fathers and husbands, sons and brothers, brought back from the grave to fight again. Their wounds gaped, and they bled darkness instead of blood. They called to each other in strange, whistling voices as if the wind spoke through them instead of their own breath. Terror fell on the city. The inhabitants fled. They carried word of the horror through all of Tormay. The duchies mobilized in confusion, readying themselves to march on Hearne, but to what end? To save it from wizards, or to save it from the hand of the king?"

"And the wizards here in the university?"

"They died almost to a man," said the old man sadly. "They died not understanding why. To be faced with the greatest puzzle of their lives and to not be allowed even a hint of the answer was a terrible thing. The genuine wizard is not as interested in the exercise of power as he is in discovering answers. Who was Scuadimnes? How was he able to command the dead? What was his intent?"

"His intent?" Jute stirred. "Didn't he gain control of the king?"

"He did, but it didn't seem to be his goal. Scuadimnes disappeared after the university was destroyed. The army of the dead wandered the city streets for days, witless and stumbling on limbs that slowed until they no longer moved. And when the armies of the duchies of Tormay arrived at the city gates, they found only the dead—the truly dead—within. Hearne was as a tomb, the silence broken only the harsh cries of the carrion fowl feeding in the streets. Thus it was that the monarchy of Tormay ended. The king's body was found in the castle. None wasted grief on him, because the land bore a larger grief. A regency was installed in Hearne, and the duchies went their own ways, each seeing to their lands and no longer giving fealty to

Hearne. And so the years have come to our times and our own regent, Nimman Botrell."

"But what does this mean for Mizra?" said the boy. "You said the duchy there had something to do with the Midsummer War."

"Excellent. Listening is the first step on a long road."

"The first step on a long road to what?" asked Jute.

"Wherever it is you're going, of course. Ah, Mizra! What a strange land it is! They say a traveler can, in a single day, traverse from icy crags to deep canyons where smoke rises from crevices in the ground and the earth is warmed by the fires smoldering far below the surface. As I said, no one lived there before the Midsummer War. It was considered a dangerous, inhospitable land. After the war, however, some of the king's court found refuge there, and the duchy of Mizra was born. There was a sort of humor to the matter, for it was the king's treasurer, Maom Gifernes, who found gold there in the spot where the city of Ancalon now stands. His family has held sway there ever since. Brond Gifernes rules today in Ancalon. He's an able lord, despite his youth—so they say—but I've never been to his land."

"When I was in the basement," said the boy, "that thing—was it something like the dead warriors of, of —"

"Scuadimnes?" The old man paused, as if reluctant to answer.

"Was it the same? He told me what he did as he fashioned it, calling down into the sewers. He told me it was darkness and water woven together and that anything fashioned with darkness would cause pain. Four things, he said. Any of four things with darkness. Fire and water, earth and air."

Severan nodded. "I don't think Nio capable of the dark arts of Scuadimnes, but the shadow behind such men remains the same. It's always the same. Forcing fire, earth, water, or air to join with darkness can only result in evil. Those four things are the materials of the four ancient anbeorun, the four stillpoints around which all life revolves. They were created to stand against the Dark, so how then can they be forced into union with their enemy? They are a bulwark against evil and have always been beyond the understanding of man. Even the wizards know little of the anbeorun, though certain small things have been discovered. It's said there exists a book called the *Gerecednes*, that it contains knowledge of the anbeorun, but this is only what some believe. Legend says that the *Gerecednes* is a wonder, a book so fascinating that anyone would be content to sit and read it forever." He sighed. "Finding that book is the main reason my fellow scholars and I came to these ruins."

"What about Nio? Does he search here as well?"

Severan nodded reluctantly. "He's a man of letters, a scholar of history and things lost. I can't bar him from this place, for he was one of our original company when we struck our deal with Nimman Botrell, the regent of your city, five years ago. He has the right to enter here. But the university grounds are huge. None of my peers know of this room here and this area of halls. I really wouldn't worry about Nio. The air here is jumbled with the memories and currents of magic. It would be impossible to find the one faint thread that is you in this vast place."

CHAPTER TWENTY-THREE
THE GOOSE AND GOLD

Nio, of course, did not find Jute down by the docks. It had been a foolish idea. In his haste, he had not considered the fact that it took a good half hour to hurry from the university to the docks. By the time he reached the wharf, there was no sign of Jute. This sent him into a rage, and he spent the rest of the day cursing and stamping about his house. It was only later that he recalled what the wihht had told him. There were other avenues to investigate. What had the wihht said? Something about an inn the Thieves Guild patronized. The Goose and Gold. He hurried downstairs, shrugged on his cloak, and slammed out the door.

It took Nio a vexing amount of time to find the inn, for as with Fishgate it also was in an area of the city where he rarely went. He should have had the wihht explain the location with more detail. The inn was situated on a street called Stalu, which was ironic, as the word referred to the business of robbery. Not in one of the ancient languages, of course, but in an old trade language fallen into disuse about two hundred years ago. A wooden sign hung above the inn's door. It showed a golden goose on a black field. The paint was faded and peeling.

How interesting. He could sense the usual confusion of ward spells around him. Weak and badly woven—fitting quality for such a neighborhood. Spelled into doors, windows, gates, and walls. About as sturdy as spider webs and just as easy to brush away. The curious thing was that there was a very powerful ward in one place, hidden behind shabbier wards. Intrigued, Nio let his mind drift out, feathering past the layer of cheaper wards. He ran a mental finger over the closest loop of the ward. Impressive. Old, subtle, and so cunningly woven that he could not find any loose ends in the weaving. It wasn't work he recognized. Not many wizards would be capable of such a thing. He withdrew his mind as soon as the ward woke to his presence—woke—wards weren't sentient the way a man is, but the better wards did seem alive.

He looked about to see where the ward was situated. It was a shabby house, a three-story affair several doors down from the Goose and Gold and on the opposite side of the street. Broken shutters, stone walls grayed and pitted by the years gone by, and a slate roof pocked with missing tiles. Not the sort of place one would think necessary to guard. But someone obviously did and had the money to do so. Nio had been many times to the Highneck Rise district—dinners or soirees put on by bored nobility who thought to amuse themselves with the scholars grubbing about in the university ruins. But even there, in the richest neighborhood of the city, one would not find a ward like the one guarding the old house.

He would return to investigate on another day. He was always hungry to learn. He wondered what demanded such protection. But not today. There was a box and a boy to hunt, a fat man and a master thief to find, and the trail of the Guild to sniff along until it led him to whoever—or a whatever—had commissioned the theft.

A whatever.

Where had that thought come from? The histories mentioned other beings who once lived in these lands—Tormay, and the older countries lost in the east centuries ago. Beings other than the ogres and giants and dragons and such that existed uneasily on the fringes of man's civilization. For some reason, the image of the sceadu staring from the mosaic sprang into his mind.

Nio muttered a few words under his breath, and then opened the door of the Goose and Gold. He had an impression of shadow and odors of food and ale and tobacco, but then his eyes adjusted to the gloom. Men sat around tables, busy at their lunch and busier at their ale. A fire crackled on the hearth. Stairs rose up on one side to a second floor. Lodging available for travelers, no doubt. Grime blackened the timbers in the ceiling. The rumble of conversation lulled when he entered, but it picked up again. He nodded to himself, satisfied. The obscuring worked. It was a minor weaving, but one he had never tested before.

He sat down at a small table in one corner and looked around. From the looks of the clientele, the inn was favored by the rank and file of the Thieves Guild, and not their masters. To Nio's eye, everyone seemed on the oafish side. Pig-eyed, thick-necked dolts with fat hands and small heads. He had trouble imagining anyone in the room burgling a house successfully, let alone stealing their grandmother's eggs.

"What'll it be, love?"

A serving girl materialized at his elbow. She was young enough to be his daughter, but her eyes were much older. Faded brown and looking right through him.

"Ale and—what do you have for food?"

"Beef stew and bread," she said.

"All right, then."

She returned with a platter and a tankard. The ale was decent and the bread was only half stale. He eyed the crowded room while he ate and considered what to do.

An old man lurched up to his table.

"Spare a copper, mister?"

"Perhaps," said Nio. "If you can answer a question."

The old man swayed closer and tried to look knowledgeable. He breathed wine fumes in Nio's face.

"Do you know a man called the Juggler?"

"Aye, I do," said the old fellow. "He's like a son to me. A dear son."

"Bring him to me and you'll have your coin."

"Bring him to you?" repeated the other.

"Yes."

"Maybe a drop of ale first. Just to ease the dryness, you know. It's terribly dry in here."

"Go on."

Nio turned back to his lunch. The old man shuffled away, mumbling to himself. A few minutes later, someone slid in across the table from Nio.

"Here he is, and I'll have my coin."

He looked up. The old sop was standing by and, across the table, sat a fat man. Nio fished a silver piece from his pocket.

"As promised."

He tossed it through the air. But before the old man could grab it, a hand darted out and snatched it.

"Hey there," protested the old man.

"You don't rouse me from my drink for nothing, Gally," said the fat man. "Here's a copper. That's enough for some ale. Get on with you."

Grumbling, the old man took the coin and shuffled off toward the counter.

"You shouldn't throw away silver on garbage like that," said the fat man. "No telling what those around here'll do if they catch wind of money."

"I'm touched by your concern," said Nio.

"Right you are," said the other. "I don't like to see folks taken while I'm around. Gives the place a bad name, and we don't want that. Now then, old Gally told me you wanted a word."

"You're the Juggler?"

"Fifteen years and counting. Took over for my father before me, as he'd done for his. It's a family thing. One Juggler after another. Fathers and sons. Tradition ain't a thing to be taken lightly. What can I do for you? You seem a gentleman of distinction—not the sort to frequent the Goose, if you don't mind me saying so. Is it a spot of trouble you're reluctant to bother the city guard with? Need a word spoken in someone's ear? Bits and bobs you want scooped up? Something found, something lost?"

"Something lost," said Nio. His mind feathered out to touch the Juggler's thoughts. But then he stopped and withdrew, for a ward shielded the fat man's mind. It was a cheap one, probably just a bauble carried in the pocket. He could have broken it easily, but such dispelling always generates attention, and he did not want that.

"Well, now," said the Juggler. He turned and signaled to the serving girl. "Lost things don't always want finding. It can take effort and skill. But you've come to the right man, assuming you're a man of generosity, that you're a man of liberality, that your purse is ready to aid me in my search. Why, I've got the cleverest little hands in the city. Just right for finding things."

He waggled his stubby fingers in the air. Nio knew, though, the man was not talking of his own hands.

"The item I've lost," said Nio, "might be difficult to find."

"And why's that?"

"I think other people might be looking for the same thing."

The serving girl materialized at the table and plunked down a tankard of ale. The Juggler took a swig and shook his head happily.

"Other people mean problems, headaches for me, say, if I were to find this missing thing you speak of. Headaches can be expensive. Especially if they're mine. But I know you wouldn't want me to suffer needlessly."

"Of course not."

"Gold has a medicinal quality."

"Naturally."

The Juggler smiled. "I think we're in agreement. Now, what is it you need to find? A chestful of coin wandered into someone else's coffers? Deeds, diamonds, a mortgage paper in need of disappearing?"

"No," returned the other. "Nothing like that. I first need to find a person."

"You refer, sir, to a series of jobs. If there's a first, then there must be a second. Series of jobs are more costly to accomplish. It's the focus that must be maintained, you see. The follow-through. Often I see the young lads setting up shop, thinking to do me out of my business, but I never worry. And d'you know why? The follow-through. They have no follow-through."

"I need to find a man known as the Knife."

The Juggler flinched, but recovered so quickly that Nio was uncertain of the reaction. It had been only his eyes flicking open wide, and a glimpse of something behind them. Fear, thought Nio.

The Juggler leaned forward, his voice quiet. "Why would you want to look for such a man? There are a lot of men in Hearne, but only one Knife. Might be easier to find someone else."

"As you said, there's only one Knife. I've heard he's a unique sort of person."

The Juggler glanced around the room and then back at Nio.

109

"A city crammed with people and you're bent on finding this one man? Being picky can be hard on your health. Why, I remember when I was a young lad, examining a merchant's storeroom. It was filled with all kinds of wonderful things. Being young and lacking wisdom, I took my time to find only the best, as opposed to grabbing what I could and making a hasty exit. Imagine my surprise, as I knelt there attempting to determine whether a cube of Harthian jade was more valuable than a bolt of gold-threaded silk, when the master of the house barged in. The ensuing unpleasantness would have been avoided had I been content with lesser things. What a valuable lesson!"

"I can always go elsewhere for help."

"No, no," said the Juggler. "I'm sure the man can be found. It's just that . . ." Here, his voice trailed off and he gazed pensively down at the table.

"Money is not an object."

"Ah," said the fat man. "That always helps."

They came to an agreement, though Nio found the fat man as stubborn as a Vomaronish moneylender. But he did not care. The box was priceless in his eyes. He would have been willing to give a fortune for it. Still, it was somewhat irritating to be cheated.

"It just so happens," said the Juggler, "I might know a thing or two about the Knife's habits."

"I expected nothing less of you." Nio slid several gold coins across the table.

"Now I remember," said the Juggler. "There's a house on a street called Forraedan. Heading west, it's the seventh house, past the south market square. The Knife visits there most Thursday nights—a certain young lady. I'll have a word with him beforehand. He'll be pleased to meet a gentleman of your distinction." The Juggler paused and then added, "And the rest of the gold?"

"You'll have it once I've met him," said Nio.

CHAPTER TWENTY-FOUR
OLD RESEMBLANCES

That evening, the autumn feast was held at the castle in Andolan. It was early in the season to celebrate the autumn harvest, but with the duke and duchess soon leaving for Hearne, this could not be avoided. Besides, no one cared. A feast was a feast, and the people of Dolan seized any chance to get together and eat and argue and drink large amounts of wine. All that day, the lords of the holdings scattered throughout the reaches of the Mearh Dun had been arriving with their retinues. The whole town was invited, though it was tacitly understood that children were not welcome.

"It's not that I don't like children," said the duke. He fiddled with his cravat and frowned at himself in the mirror. "They grow up, mostly, which seems to work out. It's just, as children, they do better far from me and, er, vice versa." The duchess smiled and said nothing. She had been doing this frequently in the last two weeks. It made her husband uneasy.

The duke and the duchess went down together to greet their guests in the great hall. Three tables ran the entire length of the hall. At the far end, raised on a dais, was the high table. Candelabras filled the hall with light. A throng of townsfolk and crofters eddied about the hall, threaded through by servants offering mulled ale. The duke and the duchess stopped to chat with villager and holder alike. Here was Weorn the miller, talking oats with Gan Ierling and his three silent sons who farmed on the high plain. Several traders in town from the southern duchies were arguing amiably in one corner about the spring market in Hearne. And there was Slivan Hyrde, the largest sheepholder of the hills, flirting with the young widow of Foren Mallet.

"Already set her cap," said the duke in his wife's ear, "and her man not in the ground thirty days."

"She's merely looking after herself," said the duchess. "I would do no less."

"Oh, you would, would you?" said the duke loudly, outraged.

"Shush, Hennen. I'm teasing you."

A serving boy appeared in a doorway and blew a strangled-sounding note on a horn that startled the hall into silence. He scampered away, and Radean the steward, looking pleased with himself, tottered onto the dais.

"Lords and ladies, gentlefolk," he called, his old voice cracking, "My Lord and Lady Callas bid you welcome to the autumn feast. Please take your places."

The assembly moved toward the tables. Radean steered select guests to the high table. The duke got to his feet, cup in hand, and a hush fell over the hall.

"Friends," he said, "Thank you for attending my lady wife and me this evening. The Callas family lives to serve this land, and you are this land, every one of you. Long ago, when Dolan Callas first rode north into the Mearh Dun, he saw a wild countryside. He saw promise. He saw—"

"He saw a woman!" cackled old Vela Hyrde from the far side of the room. The hall erupted into laughter and the duke grinned.

"That he did. The first Levoreth Callas, your own sturdy Dunnish stock, whose blood runs strong in all our veins and who our family has honored every hundred years by naming so another girl-child." Here, the duke broke off at the sight of Levoreth attempting to unobtrusively edge her way toward the dais and the empty chair next to the duchess.

"And here's my niece, our own Levoreth!" called the duke, raising his cup of wine. "Back with us after these two years!" Heads swiveled, necks craned, eyes stared. Levoreth turned bright red and dropped into her chair.

"To Levoreth!" roared the duke, upending his cup.

"To Levoreth!" roared the hall back at him, raising their cups.

"Is he already drunk and the meat not served yet?" said Levoreth, frowning at her aunt.

"We'll live, my dear," said Melanor. "Besides, you should have been on time."

"Dolan!" bawled the duke, downing another cup of wine.

"Dolan!" echoed the hall.

"More wine!"

"Aye, more wine!"

"Let the feast begin!"

A procession of servants filed in and out, bearing the choicest of summer's end and the beginning of the fall. Grouse and quail, roast boar, trout from the Ciele, and haunches of venison. Baked squash, pickled onions, snap beans as sweet as honey, leeks smothered in dill sauce. Fragrant loaves of crusty bread. White rounds of goat cheese redolent with thyme. Pies, cakes, pastries stuffed with the last peaches of summer, pear and strawberry tarts. And through it all came more and more pitchers of wine: the smooth reds of Harth, the darker flavors of Mizra, and the unpredictable vintages of the north.

Levoreth toyed with some trout on her plate and then set her fork down. She did not have much of an appetite. Some bread and cheese would do. Glancing up, she caught the eye of the eldest son of Gan Ierling staring at her. He had a vacant look on his face. Particularly with his mouth hanging open. Like a sheep, she thought, and she scowled at him. Flushing, he turned away.

"Really, Levoreth," said the duchess. "You shouldn't do that. It's bad manners, and people think you're peculiar enough as it is. Besides, those Ierlings can be muddle-headed. If you glare at him too much, he'll probably fall in love with you."

"Nonsense," said Levoreth.

"How odd," said the duke.

"What's that, dear?" said his wife.

"Have you known Ginan Bly to ever miss a chance at a good meal?"

"No, I haven't. Though I recall he seems fonder of his wine than meat." And here the duchess looked at her husband, for he was in the act of refilling his own cup.

"I'd never noticed." Hennen took a sip. "At any rate, he isn't here."

He would have said more on the subject, but the sight of a roast boar's head teetering by diverted him. Resplendent with apples and plums and a stuffed grouse perched inexplicably in between the beast's ears, it was borne on the shoulders of two servants who seemed just as old as Radean the steward. They maneuvered up to the dais and plonked their burden down in front of Levoreth. She forced a smile but then ruined the effect by scowling and waving the platter away.

"I have it!" said the duke conspiratorially, in what he obviously thought was a whisper directed at his wife. He set his empty wine cup on the table and eyed it suspiciously for a moment before leaning over.

"I have it!" he repeated again. Heads turned in interest from along the high table. "Do you know why, my dear, I always feel like a little boy around our niece?"

"Later, Hennen. Have you tried this peach pastry yet? I must confess that Ada works absolute magic with the—"

"It's because she's the spitting image of my great-aunt! You know, my grandfather Toma's sister, or, er—I can't remember whose sister she was—somebody's sister, I'm sure. I lived in terror of the woman, ever since she caught me smoking cornsilk behind the barn with the stable boys. She came after me with a horsewhip. Wasn't able to sit down for a week! Horrible woman! I think she drowned in the spring thaw when I was twelve. She has the same sort of glare—like she's doing now."

"Within families," said Levoreth, "resemblances have been known to happen. Perhaps it did not occur to you, but that's why you look, sound, and behave like your father—a more pigheaded man I do not recall."

"My dear," said her aunt.

"It came to me," said the duke stubbornly, "quite clearly. While I was drinking my wine."

"Precisely," said Levoreth.

The advent of an enormous trifle, borne by several staggering servants, prevented the conversation from going any further. A collective, drawn-out sigh was heard from the other members of the high table who had been attending the exchange the duke and his niece. Old biddy Clummian, who was standing on her seat down at the second table, snorted in disappointment.

Levoreth looked out across the hall. Ierlings, Hydres smelling of sheep, flaxen-haired Meyrtts and their Wendish cousins. Mallets, Feorlins, Farlins, Ealu Fremman and his six sons. Munucs—pious to a fault, every one of them—solemn Murnans, old biddy Clummian who knew every bit of gossip there was to be had in Andolan and was never loath to pass it along. Sceohs, fat Wynn the cobbler, merry Elpendbans, and the dour Hyrian family. They were all crowded elbow to elbow, eating, drinking, talking, laughing, arguing, red-faced and cheery in the candlelight.

Dolan.

Her people—if something like that could be said. Her heart turned over in her chest. They were a stubborn lot, set in their ways and determined not to see beyond the ends of their noses. But that same quality was also what kept Dolan strong and rooted in the Mearh Dun, right on the edge of the cold north and bounded by the dangerous beauty of the Mountains of Morn.

Levoreth sat on the windowsill of her room later that night and brushed out her hair. Lights shone in the village clustered around the castle. She could smell wood smoke in the air. Two years away. Perhaps she was losing her touch. Falling asleep all the time and dreaming about the past. Dozing off during the day. Getting into ridiculous arguments with the duke in front of half the town. How mortifying! She smiled.

Dreaming about the future, said the voice within her mind. She frowned at that, but then sat for a long time, staring out into the night. Her daydream down by the Ciele. The young girl standing on a windswept plain. Black hair flowing. Gray eyes emptied of everything except sorrow. She looks like me, Levoreth thought, startled.

Precisely.

Like I looked six hundred years ago, when Dolan came riding up the Ciele and I ignored him until he could only sit on his horse, foolish and red-faced, staring like a boy at his first midwinter feast. Maybe I was foolish as well, lingering for thirty years and watching him age before my eyes. But I bound him to this land, another bulwark against the Dark. That was no violation of who he was, for he had already grown to love this place before I strengthened his resolve. I gave him three sons to carry on and sink their roots deep into the Mearh Dun. A fair trade by anyone's lights. It cannot be said I did wrong there. I loved him.

But the girl—I was never that sad when I was her age. How long ago was that? I can't remember. Perhaps I never was young. I thought it was all a lark, a wonderful adventure unfolding. I never realized. Perhaps that's what went wrong. Not badly wrong—but enough. Not realizing. I put down roots of my own without knowing it. The better part of six hundred years spent returning to these hills and inventing yet another Levoreth to weave through the descending generations of the Callas family. That was a mistake, she thought tiredly. Tormay is bigger than just the duchy of Dolan. I have been remiss and must set about fixing that. There is still time. But Min loved these hills. And I never thought I'd fall in love. I never thought I'd love this family so—my children and their children's children continuing on and on. At any rate, there's been no hint of the Dark for so long, besides the news the wolves brought me of the sceadu in the mountains. And even that creature proved to be long gone. It might not even have been a sceadu.

Yes, but have you been hunting these past years?

She lay back on her bed and promptly fell asleep, without even blowing out the candle. The wind wandered in through her window and, after investigating the hanging drapes of her bed, snuffed the candle out. It blew back outside into the night sky and headed south, winging its way toward Hearne, further to the Vornish lands and the deserts of Harth beyond.

For the first time in a long while, Levoreth did not dream.

CHAPTER TWENTY-FIVE
AN ENJOYABLE CRISIS

"You've got that look on your face again."

"I do? What look?"

Owain Gawinn tried to rearrange his features into a pleasant smile but could not. He was not fond of smiling. His wife, Sibb, was sitting by him, knitting a scarf from red wool. The needles clacked in her hands.

"There," said his wife. "You're doing it again."

"Doing what?"

"I know that face, Owain," she said. "That's the same look you got the day you told me you were leading a troop to Vomaro to hunt for Devnes Elloran. Intent, inscrutable, as solemn as an owl, but there! With a bit of glee glinting in your eyes."

"I do not feel glee, as you put it," he said, "due to the distress of others, if that's what you're saying."

"You know that's not what I'm saying. All I mean is you enjoy crises." Sibb softened her words with a smile. "There's nothing more you love than buckling on your sword and riding out the gates with your soldiers behind you."

"Perhaps," he admitted. "But if I'm out in the field, cold and tired and bruised, there's nothing I love more than riding home to you."

"Devnes Elloran!"

A strand of wool snapped in Sibb's fingers. She exclaimed in annoyance.

"That girl was a hussy if I ever saw one," she said. "She got what she had coming to her!"

"Sibb, Sibb—I wouldn't wish ogres on anyone. At any rate, the Farrow lad handily beat us there." Owain shook his head in wonder. "I still marvel at the story after all these years. He must've been the bravest fool in the land to have done what he did. Even with a column of men, I'd be wary of venturing into an ogre's lair."

"So what are you thinking of doing now?"

"Doing now?"

"Don't try that on me, Owain. I know when you've got something brewing in your head."

He smiled and kissed her, but then his face became serious.

"I've been wondering about our little foundling. To my knowledge, she's the only survivor of whatever's been murdering its way across Tormay."

"Murdering its way—what? There've been others?"

"I didn't want to trouble you, my dear," said her husband. "But there have been other incidents reported. Twice in Vo and three times in Vomaro. Mostly isolated farms. The news of them has been trickling in over the last few weeks. The same signs, the same methods of killing. Murder for no reason at all. No reason, at least, I can see."

"What are you going to do about it?"

"Do?" He picked up a ball of wool and turned it over and over in his hands. "I'm not sure yet. It doesn't affect Hearne, but the regency does have obligations. I can't just sit here and do nothing."

She touched his hand.

"No, you can't. No Gawinn would."

He smiled.

She said something else, but it was lost in the sudden shrieks and laughter that invaded the room as their four children burst through the door. Loy was scrambling about on all fours, mooing like a cow and chasing them about.

"Help, Father! Help!"

"My duties don't extend to defending the city against cows," said their father, laughing. But his smile faded when he looked up, for the girl was standing in the doorway. Her face was grave. Her eyes stared at the other children, but Owain had the distinct impression that she did not see them.

CHAPTER TWENTY-SIX
RONAN MEETS HIS MATCH

Some hot ale would do him good.

Ronan paused outside the Goose and Gold and considered. Even though night was approaching, the day still had time enough in it to accomplish what he had to do. Cypmann Galnes would be at his warehouse for at least another three hours. Plenty of time.

Any other inn would have been more to his liking, as the Goose and Gold was a dirty, run-down place, but he was chilled to the bone and the inn was conveniently on the way. A wave of warmth and noise met him, lit by lamplight and the roar of a fire burning on the hearth.

The boisterous chatter lulled as he walked through the door, and then it surged back. He recognized many of the people in the room. Guild members, mostly. Eyes slid toward him and then flicked away. Curiosity on some faces. Fear on others. He was used to it all. He sat down at the bar.

"Mulled ale," he said.

He drank and savored the heat flowing down his throat. He propped his elbows on the bar and shut his eyes. Oats and honey. A memory surfaced in his mind of his mother stirring porridge over a fire. The sun was not up yet and he remembered there had been a sound of horses nickering to someone nearby. Likely his father, bringing them something to whet their appetite before they ventured out onto the moor to crop the grasses. Oats as well, probably. His mother had turned to him and smiled, seeing him wake, and she had spooned honey into the porridge. Ronan took another sip of ale. The taste was like the memory of the taste. Porridge and honey. Oats and honey.

Someone slid onto the stool next to him.

"Go away," he said.

The Juggler tried to smile. He took a pull at his mug of ale and smacked his lips.

"Go away," repeated Ronan, not bothering to look at him.

"I was wondering," said the Juggler, "when I'd be compensated for the loss of my boy." Here, the Juggler almost managed to look sad but ruined the effect by rubbing his hands together.

"Your boy?" Ronan scowled at the fat man.

"Innkeeper, another ale! Ahh, that's more like it!" The Juggler took a gulp of his freshly filled mug. "We were family. Almost like father and son, we were. It pains me to have lost him. It pains me, lemme tell you! To have lost my son! Are you a family sort? I didn't think so. I can tell with most folks—I have a knack for it. You can't imagine the sorrow a father experiences when his son goes missing. A lamb from the fold! Ahh— someone's drunk my ale. Wuzzit you?"

"Innkeeper!" Ronan barked. "Get this man more ale!"

Another mug of ale appeared as if by magic. The Juggler blinked at it.

"Have a drink on me," said Ronan. "Drink and shut up. I don't want to hear another word."

The Juggler drank. He wiped his mouth.

"But where's my money?" he said. "Where's my—"

Ronan grabbed him by the collar and threw him headfirst into a nearby table. Plates and food went flying. The table collapsed in a tangle of legs and curses and spilled ale. The Knife had been moving so fast when he threw the fat man that it was doubtful anyone saw what he did, other than the innkeeper, who had been wiping the counter nearby. Ronan sat back down and took a drink of ale. Behind him, a joyous roar went up and the place descended into chaos.

A pitcher whizzed by Ronan's head and shattered against the wall behind the counter. He turned to survey the room. There was no logic to the brawl other than a willingness on most participants' part to fight whoever came within reach. The Juggler's face surfaced briefly in one spot, long enough for someone to break a plate over his head.

"No blades!" bawled the innkeeper.

A man staggered up against Ronan. The man took a swing at the Knife and then stepped back, aghast.

"Sorry," said the man. "Didn't recognize you."

"Don't mention it," said Ronan. He kicked the man's feet out from under him and sent him flying face-first into the thick of the fight. He sighed and mopped at his shirt. The man had spilled his ale.

"Can't a man drink in peace?" he said, glaring at the innkeeper.

The innkeeper scowled back at him.

Ronan closed the door of the Goose and Gold behind him. The street was quiet after the clamor inside the inn. It was raining. A lamp shone above the door of a pawnshop across the way, but the street was dark other than that. Time to visit the Galnes manor in Highneck Rise. He stepped out into the rain.

"Hey, mister."

The voice came from somewhere on his left. There, in the alley running back alongside the Goose and Gold. He saw some movement. Water streamed down from the eaves.

"Hey, mister."

He kept walking. He had a few hours before Cypmann Galnes would leave his warehouse down at the docks. A few hours to break into the Galnes manor. Time enough to find the missing ring.

"He's still alive, ain't he?"

That stopped him.

It was a young child's voice. High and taut with malice. There, just within the alley, he saw a face. A white blur of a face. He wiped the rain from his eyes.

"I saw him. You didn't kill him, cully."

"Kill who?" But he knew who the child was talking about.

Nothing personal, boy. We all have our jobs to do.

The boy was dead. When he killed people, they stayed dead. That was his job.

"You should know. You're the one knifing people."

But it hadn't been a knife. No. Poison. Enough of it to kill a horse.

Ronan stepped into the alley. The walls were close and high. The stones underfoot were slick with mud and garbage. There was no light at all, but he heard the scuffle of footsteps retreating before him. As quiet as a mouse, but enough for him. He'd tracked animals in the past that made less noise than mice. They were just as easy to kill.

"You saw him? Saw who?"

Abruptly, the alley angled around a corner. He strained his ears but all he could hear now was the rain pattering on the roof and dripping from the eaves.

"Who'd you see?"

The knife slid from his sleeve and into his hand without a sound.

"You know, cully, well as I do."

The voice was closer than where he thought it would be. It was a little girl's voice, he was sure of it. Brave. He had to give her that. Brave, like the boy had been. He paused. The knife felt heavy in his hand. But then he took a step closer and the night burst red with pain. A tremendous blow struck his head. Again and again. Something shattered on the cobblestones next to him. Wood splintered. He staggered, trying to duck and hide but there was nowhere to go. His body would not obey. The world spun. He caught a glimpse of the night sky above him. There were faces in it. No, not in the sky, but leaning out, peering down from above the eaves. Children's faces, wizened and evil, leering at him. A boy heaved over a wood barrel right on top of him.

The world went black.

It was still raining when he came to. He was laying face down in the mud. He tried to roll over and then immediately wished he hadn't.

At least it's still raining, he thought dizzily. I'll be able to wash this muck and blood off. Children. The Juggler's children.

I don't blame them.

Surprised they didn't cut my throat while they were at it.

"How you doing, cully?"

It was the little girl. He opened his eyes.

"Don't feel too good, do you?" she said.

She crouched down, hands folded around her knees, eyes intent on him. Just out of reach. Not that he was in any shape to try anything. The rain had plastered her brown hair against her head. She wore a shapeless brown dress several sizes too large for her, and the sleeves were bunched up in rolls around her arms. A scar lay like a hand slap across the side of her face.

"Felt better," he said. He could taste blood in his mouth. "Give me a few days."

He tried sitting up but he couldn't. The little girl did not move away, but he saw her tense. He heard feet shuffling around him in the darkness. Other children.

"You're the Knife," she said. "The big, bad Knife."

She flipped a blade in her hand, end over end and catching the haft. His knife.

"Jute," she said. "The boy who did the chimney job. He's my friend. The Juggler says he got snaffled by a fire-ward, but you can tell when he's talking rot. Besides, we saw you."

"You saw me?" he said stupidly. His head ached. This was almost as bad as when he got thrown and trampled breaking a yearling when he was a boy. Years ago. He could still remember his father's sudden yell, running toward the corral. Blacking out when the horse stomped on him. He hadn't been much older than this girl.

"Course we did," said the little girl scornfully. "Haro an' I climbed a house close by an' watched the whole thing. Jute went down the chimney, we saw that. An' then we saw you push him down when he tried to come out. We saw it all, cully."

Ronan closed his eyes and saw the boy's face again, staring up at him from within the chimney darkness. The girl stood up. She kicked him in the side. A rib grated against another and he almost blacked out from the pain of it. She crouched down next to his face.

"All that hurt like fallin' down a chimney, cully?" Her voice trembled. "I wish I could kill you, but I can't. I just can't. It ain't in me. I'd like to, for Jute. I'll be keepin' your knife. Maybe I'll grow up one day and change my mind."

He heard her footsteps fade away and then there was only the sound of raindrops dripping on cobblestones. He took a deep breath and pushed himself up to his knees.

Pain wasn't a bad thing altogether. It meant you were still alive.

He scooped up a handful of water from a puddle and tried to clean his face, but the water only ran through his fingers. His side was on fire. Broken rib, he though dully. More than one. He levered himself up to his feet, cursing the day. He was in no condition to attempt the Galnes manor. Maybe tomorrow. Maybe tomorrow would be a better day.

CHAPTER TWENTY-SEVEN
WARDS AND CARELESSNESS

Jute was a boy, and boys are best at forgetting, even if sometimes those things that they forget are important. And so, for a while, he forgot about the wihht and he forgot about Nio Secganon. If truth be told, he even forgot about the hawk, for the university ruins were so strange and marvelous they drove all else from his mind.

Emboldened by familiarity, he took to roaming the ruins. Ten minutes could not pass by without him encountering a ward of some sort, but he became adept at recognizing them, even if their warning was as unobtrusive as a single, warm stone underfoot in a cold hall or a shadow that fell slightly crooked while all others fell straight. Out of youthful curiosity—or simple foolishness—he experimented with wards at random, figuring out how to trip them by tossing stones or by sprinting madly through the danger spots.

This was not always the safest diversion, as Jute discovered a certain ward always produced large dogs that glimmered blue as if lit by strange fire. He also discovered that these dogs ran extremely fast and had sharp-looking teeth. They never barked; the only noise they made was the scuffle of paws on stone. Jute had a suspicion they were illusion, but he was not willing to gamble his flesh to test this.

The first time one such dog appeared, Jute had the luck to be standing near a wall made of roughly hewn stone, perfectly suited for climbing. And climb it he did, in a flash, for his heart nearly jumped up his throat when the dog appeared. The thing roamed about the foot of the wall for about an hour, glaring up at him with enormous blue eyes. And then it had vanished, disappearing like a blown-out candle flame. He stayed clinging high up on the wall with cramping fingers and toes for a good while after. One never knew.

In a hall that must have once been used for ceremonies and the like—for the ceiling, high above him, was festooned with hundreds of elegant chandeliers that he had never seen in any other part of the school – he discovered an unusual ward.

The floor of the hall was tiled with large squares of black and white marble arranged in whorls looping and weaving through each other with no apparent pattern. When Jute came to the center of the hall, he found a circle of blue stone set within the floor. He stood in the middle of it and admired the blue stone for a moment, for it had a lovely gleam and looked, to his eye, valuable and regretfully wasted as floor paving.

To his alarm, however, as soon as he stepped off the circle he discovered that he could not control his movement and marched stiff-legged all around the hall in a nonsensical pattern that would have done justice to a drunkard. At first, he was frightened, for he assumed that some sort of creature or fire or chasm was about to appear. Nothing of the sort happened, however, and he continued marching crazily about the hall, hopelessly caught by the compulsion of the ward.

After about an hour of this, he was cross and tired. By a stroke of luck, though, his wandering path brought him veering toward the blue circle, which had not happened yet in the last hour, so large was the hall. As he neared the blue stone, he felt the compulsion on him lessen and with a tremendous wrench he leapt into the safety of the circle. He sat there panting and mentally cursing all wizards, alive or dead.

Growing hungry, he attempted the floor again but was caught by the same compulsion. He could have wept, so tired was he. This time, however, his fatigue aided his escape, for with drooping head and eyes fixed on the floor he noticed that the compulsion marched him around only on the black stones. Not once was he allowed to step on a white stone.

The next time he neared the circle of blue stone in the center of the hall, he was ready. He leapt into its safety and then ventured back out, careful to step on a white stone. The compulsion did not seize him and he left the hall, stepping from white stone to white stone.

One afternoon, Jute wandered down a hallway lined with old mosaics. Many of them were missing stones, rendering faces eyeless and dragons toothless. A fool grinned at him with seven scarlet balls describing a circle around his patchwork body. A warrior leaned on a bloody sword under a bone-white moon. Horns mutely blaring, a hunt rode through a gaunt and ghostly wood. A fearsome dragon of black-scaled bulk curled its length about the base of a crumbling tower, eyes glinting red and a wisp of flame escaping from the massive mouth. The sun set on the horizon of an ocean that seemed to swell and surge with movement—but when he stepped closer, startled, to inspect the tiny stones of the mosaic, they were only that: tiny stones of varied shades of blue and green. Something stirred at the corner of his eye, and he whirled, fearing a ward. But nothing moved again. There were only long, sloping shadows from the setting sun and the dust motes that turned and glided within the light. For a moment, he thought he heard a voice whisper his name, but then there was only silence. He turned and walked quickly to the end of the hallway, the back of his neck prickling uncomfortably.

Through a door, Jute found himself standing in a high gallery that ran the length of one side of huge hall that was, perhaps, a staggering three stories in interior height. To his recollection, he had never been in this part of the university before. Tall, thin clerestory windows lined the walls, and the late sunlight streamed in, shining on the white stone walls and filling the place with a blinding radiance. Such was the reflective quality of the white stone that he could not see a single shadow cast anywhere in the room. Fragile pillars rose up from the floor below and swept up and up and up into an arched ceiling that seemed to float on the slender columns that lined the walls. At the far end of the gallery he found a winding stair that circled down and down until he stood on the hall floor. Faces were carved into the pillar facades—both men and women, old and young. He counted them as he walked along but soon lost track, for the pillars were not arranged in any particular order but were myriad and rose from the floor like the trunks of trees in some strange, unearthly forest. It was the oddest room he had been in yet, but there was a quiet peace to the place, and it seemed untouched by any of the ravages of the Midsummer War that had marred so much of the university.

CHAPTER TWENTY-EIGHT
A DISTURBING ENTRY ON SCEADUS

The night arrived as the sun slipped down into the ocean. The moon crept up into the sky, but no stars were visible yet. To the east, a dark bank of clouds rolled toward the city.

Nio sat in his library and stared out the window, a book open in his lap. Fynden Fram's *Endebyrdnes of Gesceaft*. The Order of Creatures. He knew the book by heart. There was not much point in reading it, but he was looking for reassurance. Vainly looking, of course.

When he had returned to the house after meeting the Juggler, he had found the wihht shambling about the rooms. It was unsettling, for his command over the thing should have kept it waiting in the basement. Somehow, his control was fraying. The thing had been unwilling or unable to give him much of a reason for its behavior, only mumbling that it was hungry. It needed food. Just some food. Just a taste. A bite. But wihhts didn't need food, like a man or an animal needs food to survive. Wihhts survived on the strength of their maker's will.

At least, that's what he had assumed.

The thing had lurched off to the basement without protest as soon as he snapped out the order. Still, it made him uneasy. There were definitely some things about wihhts he did not know yet.

But Fynden Fram, despite his genius, had nothing to say in his *Nokhoron Nozhan Endebyrdnes of Gesceaft* that Nio did not already know. Wihhts only ate on command of their master, and only then to bring about a modification their master willed. Nio thought uncomfortably about the wihht absorbing his blood. It had wanted to take more than he had wanted to give, hadn't it?—right at the end? That didn't line up with what old Fram had written. No matter. He would unmake the wihht soon. Besides, it would be good to have the thing unraveled and gone before Severan or one of the other old fools might come by the house and stumble on it.

The irritating thing about Fynden Fram's writing was that, despite the wealth of detail, his descriptions of creatures tended to be divorced from historical context. For example, if he wrote of giants, he had nearly nothing to say of their origins, or in what lands or wars they had been encountered. Rather, he provided terse descriptions of physiognomy, habits, and social customs. In addition, there were often details on how a creature interacted with magic or was affected by the same.

> The giant, or *oyrs*, can live to ages of over three hundred years, though they reach their full maturity at the first hundred. In death, they are laid out upon the ground where, in some curious interaction of the moonlight, they slowly turn to stone. In appearance, the giant resembles the race of man, though one must be a distance away from a giant in order to notice the similarity. If one gets too close, besides the hazard of proximity, one will find the giant's face so large that it cannot be viewed in entirety; rather, it must be looked on in part—here is the nose, here is a huge, staring eye, over there is a portion of mouth or cheekbone.

The scarcity of historical setting in the entries gave one the unpleasant feeling that all the creatures the old scholar wrote of were still alive.

Such as the sceadus.

A scant page in the book was devoted to details of the sceadus. It was the shortest entry among hundreds of other entries that ran from the next shortest—five pages about cobolds—to the longest—seventeen pages about dragons, a section that made for fascinating, but unsettling reading. Almost as unsettling as what Fram had written concerning sceadus.

> The sceadus were not created by Anue. Rather, they were made out of darkness, woven from the feorh of it into forms of their master's choosing. Legend tells that only three sceadus were ever brought into existence, though I am not certain of this claim. Some analogy exists between the making of a wihht and the making of a sceadu. An external will must be brought to bear upon the essence desired as the foundation material for the creature. There, the similarity between the two types ends. A wihht, of course, can be made from nearly anything, combinations of material such as earth, wood, water, fire, or stone. A sceadu, on the other hand, can only be made from darkness, and thus is a thing of pure evil. Certain histories indicate that the sceadus are close in power to the anbeorun themselves. While some have claimed the ability to fashion wihhts of all shapes and strengths, no man has ever had the power to fashion a sceadu. No man ever will—

thankfully. This begs the question: if not the gods, then who was powerful enough to have created the three sceadus?

That was the question. Perhaps one of the four wanderers, the anbeorun, could command enough will to shape darkness? But they would never have reason, for the creation of a sceadu meant a level of evil in the creator equal to the abomination created. That made no sense in light of what was known of the wanderers. According to history, the anbeorun existed to guard against the Dark. Yet the mosaic indicated a tie of some kind between the anbeorun of fire, Aeled, and a sceadu.

The entry in Fynden Fram's anthology continued.

A sceadu can take any shape it chooses: stone or shadow, the wind crossing the plain, animals, man, a tree growing in the forest. It mimics the shapes of things that already are, just as its power is merely a reflection of the strength of its maker and the darkness. There is no reliable way to determine the presence of a sceadu, though one account of the death of Allevian Tobry—

Who was Allevian Tobry? Nio had always wondered about that, for he had never come across any other mention of the name.

—records that a stranger appeared at his gates, cloaked and hooded despite the summer's heat, and so brought death to that lord with a touch of his hand. Everyone of his household felt an intense cold emanating in waves from the stranger, as ripples do spread out around a stone tossed into a pool. After the stranger had departed, all fell sick of a lingering fever. The wizard of the household claimed it had been no man, but a sceadu. I cannot vouch for the truth of this account, as there is little other firsthand knowledge of encounters with sceadus. There is no known way of killing the creatures, though they themselves feed on death and will kill for no reason at all. They need death in order to live. This is not surprising, as they are the oldest servants of the Dark.

CHAPTER TWENTY-NINE
LISS GALNES

The following day, Ronan made his way to the Street of Willows in the Highneck Rise district. It was still raining. It had not let up through the night. The gutters ran with water.

The worst of his injuries had faded to dull aches over night. Except for his ribs. He'd have to be careful there. He had always been a quick healer. His mother had said that came from her side of the family.

A sour smile crossed his face. He could only hope the children wouldn't breathe a word of what they'd done. If anyone found out about it, he'd be the laughingstock of the Guild. But those children would be thinking hard on what they'd done. Especially when they were alone. They'd be looking over their shoulders for a long time. He'd been the Silentman's Knife for seven years now, settling matters in alleys and in back rooms where his prey had nowhere left to run to, except into the tired arms of death.

Death. Like a shadow always on his heels, treading closer over the years until it was almost like his own shadow. But they weren't friends, even though he had handed over many souls into its embrace. No, it was a working relationship, begun in distaste and dulling over the years into numbness. He didn't dream anymore. His memories no longer troubled him, for they also had numbed.

But it would be different when he went to Flessoray. It was too late to go back home, but he could go to the islands. If he could get the Silentman to release him from his duties. Maybe he would have to sneak out of the city. The Flessoray Islands were north, off the coast of Harlech. They rose up out of the sea, made of stone and scrub pines. Folk lived apart there, content with their lives and having no interest in the outside world of Tormay. Life was measured by the patience of the sea and by the wind wearing away the days until stone and man alike were scraped clean to their bones. Perhaps then, there, things would be different, and he would let the wind blow through him until he was empty.

The Street of Willows was lined with manors, complacent behind their high walls. Gates were locked against the weather and thieves such as himself. The trees from which the street took its name stood in rows of drooping branches on either side of the cobblestones. He stood underneath one and considered the wall a few yards further down. Water dripped down from the leaves onto his head. Under normal circumstances, without broken ribs, the height of the wall would not have been a problem. He scowled. Children!

Ronan wasn't getting any warmer, or any drier for that matter, so he climbed the wall. Just as Arodilac had said, the tree outside the Galnes wall provided an easy ascent. He crept out onto a branch that reached toward the top of the wall and listened for a moment. But he heard no wards whispering, no rustle of invisible threads tightening, ready to snap around him. And then he was over and down, wincing as his ribs grated, a dark shape in the rain that melted into the darker shadows of the shrubbery.

It was a small garden, filled with bushes and trees that crowded about a patch of grass. The rain had stripped the flowers from the bushes, and everywhere the ground was dappled with white petals. Lights shone in the windows of the manor beyond. And there were the apple trees. He reached out and plucked one. Tart and sweet. Good, but certainly not good enough to warrant this mess. There were better apples to be bought in the city. Something tickled uneasily at the back of his mind, but then he thought no more of it. A job was a job, regardless of the client's reasons.

Ronan paused in the shadows against the manor wall and pressed his ear to the stone. He heard nothing. No wards muttering their hidden menace. Nothing at all. He shrugged and began to climb. The walls were made of granite and offered easy holds. His hands and feet were unerring in their instincts. His ribs twinged in protest but he ignored them.

He stopped at one window, just to the side of the casement. The glass was ajar, and he heard the sound of a lute. The notes bore a strange resonance in them that brought to mind the sea. They sounded singly. One like the wavering call of a seagull, others like wind plucking the rigging of a ship, still others that belled in the low tones of the buoy that swayed at the harbor mouth of Hearne.

He edged closer and peered inside. A girl sat upon a stool, her head drooping over the instrument. He could not see her entire face. But he could see enough. The angle of cheekbone, stark with shadow, a white brow and neck framed by a wing of hair, burnished blue-black like night on water. Her fingers wandered across the strings, slow and blind in their movement, for her eyes were closed. Silently, he eased away and resumed his climb.

A dormer window provided entrance to the house from the top of the roof. Ronan tripped the lock with a length of wire and slipped inside. Immediately within was a small room, dark except for light glowing from beneath a door. He took off his wet jacket and boots and then settled down in a corner.

Anyone can rob a house. But to do the job well takes more than just skill. It takes an instinct for places—being able to walk into a house and let your senses reach out and become aware of spaces, shapes, shifts in temperature, drafts betraying holes and hidden rooms, the creaks of old wood, of water dripping, mice mumbling within walls. No amount of teaching or practice can guarantee this; it's instinctive.

A few notes drifted up to Ronan's ears. The lute. He could smell bread baking—the old cook hardly ever left her kitchen, according to Arodilac. As he listened, he began to sense more: the tick of a grandfather clock, warmth from the kitchen stove rising up a chimney and exhaling into all the floors of the house, the contented creak of beams and boards complacent about the rain outside. There was a comfortable shabbiness to the place, as if many generations had been birthed and lived and died within its walls, leaving their marks in staircases worn smooth, faded paintings, and the ghosts of memories lingering in the place they loved.

Ronan eased open the door and found himself at the top of a staircase. The lute played faintly from several floors down. The steps were silent under his weight—good workmanship and heavy wood. He smiled complacently. He had no fear of discovery within the manor. It was a large place, with surely many hiding spots if someone approached. And he knew—he sensed—there were only two people within: the cook far below in her kitchen, and the girl still playing her lute. Two floors down was his guess. He could sense something else. A touch of power concentrated in a tiny place. The ring.

Far below him, he heard the lute stop.

Footsteps creaked up the stairs. The girl emerged up from the shadows, still carrying her lute. She stopped in front of him, an almost incurious look on her face. The lamplight brought her face alive. He tried to move, but could not.

"There are easier houses in Hearne to rob," she said. He could not answer.

She regarded him for a moment and then spoke again.

"I am mistress of this house." Her eyes turned on his, dark blue as a storm sky. Or gray. Yes—he was mistaken. They were gray. "My name is Liss Galnes."

Whatever held him vanished. He stumbled back and caught himself on the wall.

"It would only take the blink of an eye," he said, furious and shaky with fear at the same time, hand groping for the knife at his side.

"Not in this house," Liss said.

He believed her.

"Come," she said, turning away.

Liss led him downstairs, through room after room and more staircases. Faces stared down from paintings: knowing, secretive looks of men and women; children standing gravely with pet dogs; a mother holding a silk-swaddled infant who seemed to smile at him. Faded furniture, tall casement windows that reached up to the cobwebs of vaulted ceilings. Rain streaked against the glass. They crossed the polished wooden floor of a hall. Mirrors showed a girl who seemed to drift like a feather, followed by the grim-faced man moving heavily in her wake.

"Where are we going?" he said.

She smiled for the first time. "The kitchen. You're hungry."

He was about to deny it, more out of contrariness than anything else, but it was true. Besides the apple in the garden, he hadn't eaten anything that day.

The cook stood chopping parsley at a table in the center of the kitchen. She was an old woman with a face as brown and worn as a walnut. A fire burned on the hearth, pots bubbled, and kettles steamed. Iron pans and ladles hung from brackets on the wall, and a row of windows looked out onto an herb garden.

"Didja catch him?" said the cook, intent on her parsley and not turning her head.

"Him?" echoed Liss. She looked at Ronan. He had the distinct impression she already knew his name.

"My name's Ronan," he said. "Ronan of Aum."

"Sit, then—Ronan of Aum. His name," she said, turning to the cook, "is—"

"I know, I know," said the old woman. "I haven't gone deaf in my old age, though you think me feeble, with all your coddling, trying to do the cooking and whatnot. You'll be the death of me, girl."

Liss smiled.

Ronan sat down to soup, fresh bread, cheese, and a mug of red wine—tired, bemused, and not sure what to think. If anything, there was a pathetic humor in it all, in the fact that the revered Knife of the Guild could not defend himself against a handful of children. That the Knife could not even rob a house guarded by two women. But who would believe that? Certainly not the Silentman. He shook his head.

"What's that, then?" said the cook. "Don't like my soup?"

"No, no," he said. "It's good."

"Hush, Sanna," said Liss. "Leave him to his food. There'll be time enough to bother him later."

"Shaking his head like that," said the old woman, "with a face long enough for a horse. Who is he now, besides a name? Has he come to rob the house or is he another half-wit like young whatsisname, mooning about and eating all the cakes?"

"Hush."

132

"That's no way to eat the food. He'll sicken with that frown on him, no matter how good the fare. Why, what you'll get from this hearth is better than what even the regent sups on. Him and all his gold plates and—"

"Sanna."

The old woman shut her mouth, but began to clatter pots and pans about in the sink. Liss gazed at Ronan. He noticed that her eyes, even though he had thought them gray, seemed to shade blue or green at times, depending on how the light fell. He pushed his plate away, the bread uneaten. A sniff came from the vicinity of the sink.

"Why did you come here?" she asked.

"I think you already know," he said.

He was tired. None of it mattered anymore. Loyalty to the Guild. Serving the Silentman. Whether or not he could find the boy and prove his own innocence. The islands of Flessoray waiting for him. All the memories uneasy in his mind. The girl from Vomaro—how old would she be now?— surely graying and gone fat with bearing children. They could go to the shadows, every one of them, for all he cared. Besides, he hated the city. He always had. Sleep would be nice. That was what death would be. A dreamless sleep with no end.

"Perhaps," she said. "But I'd like to hear it from you."

Ronan shrugged, not caring anymore. "I work for the Thieves Guild. A job came through several days ago to recover the ring of Arodilac Bridd. You have the ring. Simple as that."

"Ooh, the Guild," broke in the cook. "I always thought if they were foolish enough to break in, they'd come for that sea-jade figurine in the drawing room—nice piece. Fetch a better price than that ring. I'm more inclined to a string of pearls myself. Pity the oysters are always so stubborn about giving 'em up, the grumpy little beggars. Here." She banged down a plate of cakes in front of him. They were tiny and sprinkled with chopped almonds. "Eat."

"Surely there's more to it than that," said Liss. She took a cake, as if to encourage him, and ate it in three neat bites.

Again, he shrugged.

"It doesn't matter if you know. I'm already ruined." He bit into a cake— apple—and almost found the strength to smile. "Nimman Botrell hired the Guild to recover the ring. He doesn't approve of you as wife of the next regent of Hearne. And that ring isn't just any old ring, it's—"

"The regent," said the old woman. "Doesn't approve of my Liss! Why, I'll give him what for, the wretched man! I hear he doesn't like fish at all."

"Of course," said Liss, ignoring the cook. "Of course it isn't just an old ring. Why else do you think I made him give it to me? I knew it wouldn't be long before you came looking for the thing. The tide always brings me what I need."

He almost choked on his apple cake.

"What? Me? Arodilac said that he gave you the ring impulsively. He climbed the wall, fell in love . . ."

Her eyes were unblinking and remote. He could not look away. The gray of them deepened to blue and then receded back to gray, like the surf of the sea washing up and away on a shore. Something ancient and serene gazed out at him, as patient as the tide. She blinked, once, and released him.

"Men can be impulsive. Particularly for love of a girl." She frowned, as if puzzled by the idea.

"It's an unusual ring."

He looked down, unwilling to meet her gaze. Somehow, he knew it would be better—much better—to tell her what he knew, rather than have it taken from him in some other way.

"It's his family's ring, passed from father to heir. It holds the key to the wards of the Bridd castle in Hull."

She waited patiently, displaying no interest in plundering the wealth of the Bridds, saying nothing. He took an apple cake and fumbled it to bits in his hands. It was the last part, of course. The regent didn't care about his nephew. Only a fool would believe that. But a ring that could open up the secret ways into the regent's castle—now that was something to care about. Why did she want him?

"The ring also . . ." Ronan trailed off in to silence. The tide turned within her eyes—gray to blue and back again. Infinitely patient. Water, wearing away the stone. The moon sailing over the sea to its dark, unseen horizon. Endless and inexorable.

"It holds the keys to wards in the regent's castle. Spells that guard his castle. Here, in Hearne." There. He'd said it. Now he could leave. Leave and tell the Silentman of his failure, and then wait for death, however it would be meted out.

She reached for the last apple cake, broke it in half and offered him a piece. She smiled and she was only a girl again. Behind them, scrubbing potatoes in the sink, the cook broke into wordless song.

"For a thief, you're an honest man."

"An honest dead man, mistress," he said. His voice was dull.

Ronan's thoughts drifted. He could creep out of the city at night. Over the south wall where it angled near that hostelry with the conveniently high roof. And then disappear. Forever. It would have to be north. The Guild never went there. There was nothing to steal except ice and snow and, farther north, the treasures of giants—and no one stole from them, even the Guild. Or perhaps he could go east, past Mizra and into the wastes.

"You needn't run," she said, frowning.

"You can read thoughts as well?"

"It's evident from your face." And she slid something across the table toward him. A ring. A gold ring fashioned in the shape of a hawk.

"Take it," she said.

"You'd just give it to me?" He reached out for the ring.

"No, of course not," she said. "Why else did the tide bring you here? You'll do something for me in return."

His hand hovered over the ring. "And that is?"

"In seven days' time, a ball is to be held at the regent's castle in honor of the Autumn Fair. I wish to attend, uninvited though I will be."

She smiled placidly, as if talking of a visit planned to the dressmaker's. "I'm afraid my good Cypmann Galnes has not noble enough blood to be asked to such an affair, else I'd lean on his graces. You will bring me into the castle, unseen, and shall keep me unseen through the evening. I've heard of your particular skills. In return, you may take the ring back to the boy." Her hand flicked in dismissal. "If I have you, then I have no need of the ring. I never intended to use it. That's all."

"That's all?" He gaped at her.

"Yes." Liss smiled at him. A girl with gray eyes. Her eyes were gray now.

"You don't just walk into the regent's castle!" said Ronan. "Do you know what you're asking? Particularly on a night as that. In all of Hearne, there isn't a more impossible place to enter unwanted."

"There is another place more perilous in this city," she said. The color of her eyes was shifting again. Gray washing into blue.

"Where?" He spoke without thinking.

"This house."

And it was back again. Someone—something—ancient looking through her eyes, examining him and weighing who he was. The ring was strangely cold in his hand, as if it had taken none of the warmth of her body. He knew he would not be able to deny her, even though what she asked might prove beyond him. The sea surged within her eyes and she sat before him, a wisp of a girl with her hands folded on the table. He suddenly realized he feared her more than the Silentman himself.

"You aren't Liss Galnes, are you," he said.

The girl said nothing.

"Sakes, dearie," said the cook, turning from the sink with her hands covered in suds. "Liss Galnes died near three years ago now. Caught the influenza and withered up like the flower she was. Just like her mother before her. Inconvenient for her, but timely for my mistress. She needed a place, like a hermit crab needs herself a new shell every now and again."

"Who are you?" His voice sounded hollow. "And how is it that Cypmann Galnes still calls this place home?"

But they said nothing to that. The girl and the old woman merely looked at him, the one with beady, black eyes and the other with eyes like the shifting sea.

CHAPTER THIRTY
TREATIES AND FOUL MOODS

"Enter!" barked Botrell.

The regent was sitting on the end of his bed and contemplating the floor. It didn't seem to be shimmering in such a sickening fashion anymore. He was in a filthy mood, for he had stayed up late with the envoy from the court of Oruso Oran IX in Damarkan. Who would have guessed that blue-eyed icicle would have had such a capacity for wine? But he'd shown him. The man had been scarcely coherent by the time his attendants had carried him off to his rooms.

The court chamberlain peeked in through the door.

"The Lord Captain of Hearne requests an audience, my lord."

"Tell him to come back another day! Next month!"

The chamberlain vanished for a moment and then reappeared.

"He says the matter is urgent and cannot wait another day. He says it involves the security of your people and Hearne and, consequently, the safety of your own lordship. He apologizes most humbly for bothering you in your bedchamber."

"Tell him to come back next year!"

The door closed and then reopened almost in the same instant.

"He says—"

"Good morning, my lord regent," drawled Owain Gawinn. He pushed past the chamberlain and stood smiling.

"Gawinn," gritted Botrell. "It's early. Don't you have a city to watch over? Aren't there soldiers to drill and horses to be galloped about?"

"Fear not, my lord. I watch over Hearne with a jealous and unsleeping eye. So have the Gawinns always served the regents of Hearne, and so do I. A danger has arisen, my lord. It requires your attention, even though, as you've pointed out, the hour is early. Nearly noon, isn't?"

There was ice in his voice and in his smile. Botrell stirred uneasily on the edge of his bed. When he was honest with himself, he had to admit that the Lord Captain of Hearne made him nervous. The man was much too serious about his job.

"Have the old scholars in the university uncovered something dangerous? Pirates threatening our sea trade again? Is the Thieves Guild overstepping their bounds?"

"Nothing like that," said Owain. "The university ruins contain nothing more dangerous than rats, in my estimation. The last pirate to plague our coast died on my sword three years ago. And the Guild? Bah! If you gave me a free hand with them, I'd hang the lot—but, as ever, I defer to your notion that they somehow encourage trade."

"Then what do you speak of?"

"I have reports of strange killings to the east of us. Isolated farms wiped out. Entire villages decimated. All in the last month."

"Old news," said the regent, yawning. "None of our business. The duchies can look after their own."

"The massacres happened in three different duchies as well as in northeastern Harth. Twice in Vo, thrice in Vomaro, once each in Harth and Dolan, and now just five or so days ago again in Vo. All the duchies have been in contact with me, as well as Damarkan's envoy. That was one of the reasons Damarkan sent their man north. According to the old treaty drawn up after the Midsummer War—a treaty, no doubt, you are conversant with, as it outlines the balance of power between Hearne and the duchies of Tormay—when danger threatens multiple duchies, leadership in such a situation is deferred to the regency in Hearne."

"The treaty says that?" Botrell was reasonably sure he had read the old document. Years ago, true, but he would have remembered such a ridiculous and imprudent provision. His head hurt.

"It does."

"Probably just bandits. Unfortunate, but merely part of life."

"No," said Owain. "Bandits steal, even if they sometimes will kill. Whoever is doing these killings isn't interested in gold. Nothing is ever stolen. Except for life. So I ask your permission, my lord, to scout in the east where the massacres happened. It would do us well to learn what we can of this new enemy. Besides the obligations of the treaty, who knows but there might come a day when the killers are within our walls?"

"I suppose there have been no witnesses," said Botrell, mentally cursing whichever addled ancestor had seen fit to sign such a treaty. An expedition of the sort Owain was intending would cost much gold.

"There is one. A girl of perhaps eight or nine years. She was found by a passing trader at the site of the last massacre in Vo."

"Aha! So she saw those involved!"

"Doubtlessly. However, the terror she has been through has struck her mute. She responds to little that is said to her. The only noise she makes is when she screams in her nightmares. I have hopes of her speaking someday—"

"Hmmph."

"—but for now she is in the care of my good lady. What do you say, my lord? Do I have your permission to undertake my duties? I'm confident that you, as ever, are eager to see our laws fulfilled."

Owain took a little of the sting out of his words by smiling, but it was a wintry smile at best. That was all he could manage for the regent. There was silence in the room. Both men thought their thoughts, one smiling and the other scowling, both despising the other.

"Oh, all right!" burst out Botrell. "Hunt and be damned! Just get out of my sight!"

"Thank you, my lord," said Owain, bowing. "As ever, you are a wise and able ruler."

"Just remember to leave someone behind to guard the city," said Botrell nastily.

"To be sure," said the other, and then he was gone.

"Chamberlain!" shouted the regent. "Bring me some wine!"

CHAPTER THIRTY-ONE
A MEMORY OF WOLVES

In the town of Andolan, near the castle, was a small church. It was a tumbledown building made of stone, weathered by the years and grown over with gray-green lichen. The church was older than the castle, even older than the walls of Andolan themselves. It had been built before Dolan Callas ever rode north to the Mearh Dun, when there had been only a hamlet where the town of Andolan now stood. The church was dedicated to the nearly forgotten sleeping god and was watched over by one old priest. He spent most of his days feeding the town cats who regarded the churchyard as their home. He also mumbled his way through mostly unattended vespers once a week and pottered about in the cemetery behind the church, tending the roses and weeding around the headstones.

It was midmorning when Levoreth walked around the side of the church. A rose bush grew at the back of the cemetery, where the oldest gravestones stood near the town wall. The bush had vines as thick as tree branches. They gripped the stones of the wall and climbed upward until they spilled over the top in scarlet blooms. Bees buzzed amidst the growth, and the air was heavy with perfume. The priest, armed with a rusty pair of shears, tottered around the perimeter of the bush, poking at some vines that curled out toward the nearest headstones. It was there, at the back of the cemetery, that the members of the Callas family were buried.

"Here," said Levoreth. "Let me get that for you."

"Thank you, my dear," said the priest, startled at the girl's appearance but happy to relinquish the shears. He blinked in admiration as she clipped the vines back.

"Eh," he said, mopping his brow, "Thought it might be the shears, but perhaps it's just my arms." He blinked at her some more. "Why, it's Lady Levoreth. I haven't set eyes on your pretty face in nigh on five years."

"Two years," said Levoreth. "You remember? I sat up with you for midwinter compline the evening the great snows started falling. No one else came."

"Ah," he said. "The great snows. What a winter that was. My poor cats refused to leave the church, even after they'd caught all the mice. Not that I blame them, with the wolves coming down out of the mountains. It was a wonder we didn't have them wandering about the streets."

"Aye," she said. "It's a wonder." She stepped back and looked up at the rosebush. "This old vine certainly has seen better days." A sparrow rustled its way through the leaves and trilled a burst of song down at her.

"That it has," said the old man. "That it has. Like us all." He sighed in contentment, sat down on a fallen headstone, and glanced about the cemetery. Sunlight lay on the headstones, on the mossed-over paths that ambled between the graves, the crooked back of the church hiding the cemetery from the rest of the town.

"What a pleasant place to sleep."

"I've always thought so," said Levoreth.

And sleep, the priest did—his head nodding forward until his chin was resting on his cassock.

It was remarkable how many Levoreths had been buried in the cemetery. One double headstone in particular drew her. It looked to be the oldest, and it was. Over six hundred years of sun and rain and snow had hollowed out the engravings until the letters were almost illegible. She knew them by heart, however. With one finger, she traced the stone: Dolan Callas. First Duke of Dolan. Levoreth Callas. Beloved Wife and Mother. Her namesake. Her own self. A smile crossed her face. She sat down upon the grass, the headstone at her back, and closed her eyes.

Two years ago. The coming of the wolves. That was why she had left Andolan for the solitude of the country manor in the east. At least, that was the practical reason. She would have left sooner or later, for she could never bear the town that long. Too many memories. The wolves had hurried her decision.

Two years ago, she had been woken in the night by the wind murmuring at her window in the castle. She had leaned against the sill to listen. Normally, she did not trust the wind, for she found it fickle, given to fits of whimsy and equally quick in turning to violence. It was not tamable, at least not by her hand. But that night had been different. She could not ignore the melancholy in the wind's voice. And in its murmur she heard news of an approaching winter, of shadows stirring on the far side of the mountains, and of wolves coming west.

The following night, midwinter's eve, she had heard the howl of a wolf lingering in the wind as she trudged back to the castle after compline. She had stopped, surprised, for there was fear in the wolf's voice. The snow drifted in her hair as she listened. Fear in a wolf was something rare.

And then the reports had started trickling in from the shepherds in the far reaches of the Mearh Dun. Huge timber wolves, the likes of which had never been seen west of the Mountains of Morn. Fierce beasts that terrorized the folds where the flocks were wintering, unafraid of dog and man alike. It had been only days later when the first one was sighted near the walls of Andolan. Children were no longer allowed outside the town. One day, the remains of a trader and his packhorses were found dead in the snow, three miles from the gate.

On that evening, she had wrapped herself in a cloak and slipped out of the town. A full moon was rising, and its light shone on the snow. Her breath steamed in the air. For half an hour she trudged through the snow before stopping. She stood on a hill, bare of anything except the snow and her footprints. In every direction there were only the rolling slopes of the Mearh Dun. There was not a cottage or tree in sight. She stood and listened to the land.

Then she had heard them, far to the north. She sent forth her thoughts and called. She subsided into silence, waiting in the cold, under the night and a scattering of stars like jewel shards and the moon with its pale eye.

They had come in a rush, shadows loping over the next hill, vanishing down into the divide and then hurtling up the hill she stood on. Snow flew through the air from their paws as the pack surged around her, a few daring to brush her hands with their cold noses. Tongues lolled and eyes flashed amber, blue, and polished as wet stone. They stilled their pacing and stood around her—near a hundred, she counted. A black wolf stalked forward. His eyes, gray as a winter sky, met hers, and then he dropped his head to nose at her palm.

Mistress of Mistresses.

"Drythen Wulf," she said. "The Mountains of Morn are the home of your folk, not the Mearh Dun."

Aye. You speak truth.

"What has brought you and yours west? Does your clan entire think to chase the sun?"

He had laughed at that, soundlessly, his yellowed teeth glistening and his eyes half closed. And then his head drooped, and a shiver ran through the watching pack.

Nay, Mistress. We have no heart for legends anymore. We have run away from our land.

We run, echoed the pack. Their voices were doleful.

"What follows after you?"

But his head had drooped lower at her question. She knelt in the snow and took his shaggy head between her hands.

"Drythen Wulf, what follows after you?"

A sceadu, Mistress. A cursed shadow out of our ancient legends. The home of our ancestors has become a haunt of shadows and dread. The mountains are no longer ours. The deer took herself away, and the rock hare vanishes since summer's sun. Our small ones dream of horrors and no longer wake, leaving us to chase the sun. He trembled with anger. His teeth snapped shut on the air.

"Are you sure of this? It has been many hundreds of years since such a one has been seen in this realm. There were three of them from days of old."

The wolf did not speak, but only gazed at her with his gray eyes. She nodded, then, in acceptance of his words. The pack waited in silence around her.

"The Mearh Dun cannot be your home. Your coming has brought great distress to its folk. They are a gentle people and unused to the ways of the wolf."

Are we not also your folk? Does the lady grow to love man more than her four-footed subjects? The nyten of mountain, hill, forest, and plain?

"Nay, nay," she had said, vexed under the eyes of the wolf.

Would have us south, then, into the crowded plains of man and the desert beyond? The north will not have us. Giants walk there in the fields of ice, beyond the realm of man, and they have never been friendly to our folk. Should we run west, into the great sea?

"I would not have you anywhere except the land that bears you love, the Mountains of Morn."

We cannot, Mistress. Unless—and here the wolf paused, unsure at his own daring—*unless we have your company to search out the sceadu and make it safe for our little ones.*

And so was struck the deal that brought Levoreth east from Andolan, bargained under the night sky and far from the sleeping town. The pack bore witness and the wolf brought forth a gawky-legged pup with his own black fur and eyes as silver as moonlight on the sea. It padded about her feet and licked her hand.

My own whelp, Mistress of Mistresses. I would have you name him, for someday he will lead the pack, after the sun has called me to the great chase.

She had named the pup Ehtan, after the great wolf that the Aro had bidden to hunt among the stars, tirelessly seeking after the Dark. She smiled and awoke in the stillness of the cemetery. The old priest was gone. The air was full of light and the sweetness of the rose bush.

"Aye," she said aloud. "This is a place well-suited for sleep." She stood up, somewhat stiffly, and lingered for a moment at the headstone of Dolan Callas before walking away.

CHAPTER THIRTY-TWO
A PLACE CALLED DAGHORON

Jute slept poorly that night.

He dreamt of the darkness. This is a dangerous thing to do, for such dreams are opportunities for the Dark. To dream of the Dark is to bring yourself to its attention. Who knows what may happen then?

It was a night without stars. Cold and breathless. A shadow stretched past Jute out into the expanse of space. If I turn, Jute thought, will I see this thing that casts such a shadow? Or what if it already stands before me, far on the other end of this darkness? For everything is shadow here, and the darkness stands everywhere. It does not need light to cast the shadow of itself.

The shadow gained form as he watched. Battlements rose up. Spires soaring above and below and on either side. Towers and walls that climbed ever upward, dizzying. Endless. The façade was pitted with windows that gaped without glass or light inside.

I could look for a lifetime and find no end to this. But I would find desolation. Who am I to stand here and live?

And in desperation he wished for a small place so he might creep away into it, close the door, and pretend his little room was the only world that was.

Light glimmered by his side.

The hawk.

Do you wish death upon yourself? What brings you to this place?

I do not know. Take me from here!

I cannot. We stand before the gates of Daghoron.

He felt the hawk's wing brush along his arm.

Know you not the words of Staer Gemyndes, with which he began the Gerecednes?"Deep within the darkness, further e'en the void, Nokhoron Nozhan built himself a fortress of night."

I am only a boy. I know nothing of such things.

If men forget such things, then all that is will surely pass away.

The shadow deepened. And moved, ever so slightly. As if that which cast it was beginning to wake. Nightmares stirring from their sleep. Shivering with hunger.

We must be away. Now!

I cannot! You said this yourself!

Not true. I only said I could not take you away by myself.

Then how?

Look down!

He looked down and could not breathe. There was nothing below him except the dizzying emptiness of sky. The hawk hovered next to him on outstretched wings. And he fell, plunging down into the nothingness, his mouth stretched wide in a scream and his arms flailing at the air. Darkness rushed past him like water.

Aye. There was satisfaction in the hawk's voice. *Fear serves its purpose at times.*

Jute awoke and rose from his bed. He opened the window and stood amazed. The university and the city were gone. Below, a plain lay gloomy under a moon colored ivory like bone. Far beneath the window, something gibbered. The thing turned and shambled alongside the tower. The boy rushed to the door and eased it open. Below him, up a winding stair, there came to him the creak of a turning handle. Footsteps shuffled up the stairs. A smell of decay and damp things assailed him and he stumbled away from the door. There was only the window.

He threw himself from it.

And awoke, again, in his bed. Sweating and shivering. A candle burned on the table. Severan sat there and watched him.

"You don't sleep well," he said.

"No," said the boy, but he was glad to see the old man, and he knew he dreamt no longer. There was bread and cheese on the table. Jute rose and ate.

"Have you ever heard of a place called Daghoron?" asked the boy.

Severan shook his head and helped himself to a hunk of bread. But it seemed to the boy that the old man avoided his gaze.

"Or someone named Staer Gemyndes?"

The old man froze.

"Where did you hear that name?"

"In my dream. Someone spoke it."

"Who?" said Severan.

"I don't know."

"Staer Gemyndes was the court wizard of Siglan Cynehad, the first king of Tormay. It is said that Staer Gemyndes wrote a book called the *Gerecednes* at the end of his life—a book that speaks of those events which brought Siglan Cynehad to Tormay, centuries ago. For the king did not come as a conqueror, as most scholars assume, or an adventurer out to win fame and glory for an older homeland. No, he came with his people—all those who are our own forefathers—fleeing some terrible doom. And in that book it is written of these matters. It's said that in the book are the answers to so many questions! But the book's been lost for hundreds of years, and we know only a little."

"And this book is one of the things you hope to find here in the ruins? You told me that before, didn't you?"

"Yes," said Severan. But he would not say anything more on the matter and did not ask again where the boy had heard such names.

CHAPTER THIRTY-THREE
THE WIHHT IS GIVEN A TASK

"The Guild," said Nio. "The Guild and this fellow they call the Knife. Ronan of Aum. Both of them made-up names that tell us nothing of the man, other than his vaunted position in the Guild and his own arrogance."

He was pacing back and forth in the library. The wihht stood silently. Only its eyes moved, slowly shifting back and forth to keep its gaze on Nio.

"I want you to find the Court of the Guild, the court of the so-called Silentman. It's somewhere in this city, that's obvious, and I've heard enough rumor to guess it's underground. A cellar, tunnels, something like that. Find one of these thieves and squeeze the truth out of him!"

"Is it permitted to then end his life?"

"What? Yes, yes—whatever you want. I don't care. Just keep it quiet, d'you hear? The last thing we need is the attention of the Lord Captain of Hearne and his men. And if you hear or see anything of the boy Jute, find him too."

"I remember his taste," said the wihht.

"If you catch him, bring the miserable rat to me. I'll wring his neck myself. Mind you, the Guild's more important now, not that guttersnipe. Find me a key that'll get us into the Guild, and I don't care how many bones you break along the way."

"Ah," said the wihht.

Nio stalked to the window and stared out. Water streaked down the glass. It was raining again. The street below was virtually empty. One solitary figure hurried by, shoulders bent and head hunched against the rain. It was a miserable day. Most of the city would be holed up like rats in their houses, Guild and non-Guild alike. The wihht would have a more difficult job of it.

"Concentrate on the inns," he said. "They'll be crowded, no doubt."

"And the man called the Knife?"

"I daresay you'll have an easier time finding the *Gerecednes* than that man. Find me my key. And I don't care if it's a key made of metal or one of flesh and bones."

The door closed silently behind the wihht.

Nio flung himself down in a chair and picked up a book. *A Concise History of Harlech*, written by some long-dead Thulian duke with aspirations

147

of being a scholar. It was a short and concise book. There was little to know about Harlech, for they did not give up their secrets easily and they were not fond of strangers.

> Travel in Harlech is not advisable in the winter due to the harshness of the climate, the frequency of wolves, and the peculiar fact that the roads and paths seem to rearrange themselves at will, particularly for the misfortune of visitors. The towns are few and the inns, while excellent and well-appointed, exist more for local traffic, rather than for travelers from afar. Furthermore, those who live in Harlech tend to be inhospitable unless some happy twist of fate has given one a reason to form an acquaintance, for if they give their friendship, they will remain so until death. If their enmity has been aroused, however, one would be advised to stay far away from Harlech, for they are implacable and feared in all of Tormay for their skill in battle.

Nio tossed the book aside. It made for dull reading. Particularly on a day like today. He got up and again went to the window. Rain. The drops ran down the glass and blurred his sight.

He still remembered her name. Cyrnel. Cyrnel, the farmer's daughter. For several years after he left the Stone Tower, he had purposed to return. To return once he had made a name and a fortune for himself. He would have rode up on a fine horse to the admiring glances of the students. The teachers would have invited him in to hear his tales. And then he would have ridden off south along the coast to the little valley and the farmer's daughter who lived there.

She was probably married and fat now. She probably even had grandchildren by now. He could not remember her face.

CHAPTER THIRTY-FOUR
STILL WAITING FOR GOLD

The Silentman received the return of Arodilac Bridd's ring with pleasure.

"Well done, Ronan," he said, tossing him a purse of coin. "Our client, the regent, will be pleased."

The Silentman was sitting on his stone throne, raised by a dais several steps up from the floor. As usual, his face was blurred and his voice muted by an obscuring charm. His form was shrouded by a cloak of black silk. Standing to one side was the short figure of Dreccan Gor, advisor to the Silentman. Dreccan was known for his wisdom and feared almost as much as the Silentman himself, though this was largely due to the fact that the advisor also served as chief steward to the regent of Hearne. Such an unusual association served the Guild well, as it allowed the Silentman to always stay one step ahead of the regent.

"Easiest job I've ever done, my lord," said Ronan.

The Silentman nodded and Ronan had the impression that the man was smiling. There was no way to tell through the blur. He had his suspicions about who the Silentman was, but no proof. Anyway, it was not healthy to voice such suspicions out loud.

"A question, my lord?" said Ronan.

The Silentman inclined his head.

"If I might step closer?"

Not that there was much chance of anyone overhearing them. The court was crowded and noisy with conversation and music. Besides, no one came near the Silentman unless bidden.

"Approach," said the Silentman. Ronan stepped up onto the dais and lowered his voice.

"Is our client pleased with the chimney job?"

"You want your money, don't you? The client is coming soon to collect. You know the rules of the Guild, Ronan. Satisfaction first for the client, and then you'll get your gold. Don't try my patience."

Ronan bowed and retreated back down the steps.

The court was busy that night—petitioners with grievances and jobs, thieves being given instructions, a trio of musicians jangling through the latest court tunes in one corner. The place was full of torchlight and shadow and the radiance of a fire burning on the hearth halfway down the room's length. A table sagged under the weight of its bounty: roast chicken, ham, breads and cheeses, cold sausage, kegs of ale, and baskets overflowing with fruit. All courtesy of the Silentman.

Ronan slouched against a pillar and chewed on a chicken leg. He fingered the purse in his pocket and added numbers in his head. He would have enough now, once the payment came through for the chimney job. Before the week was out, if the Silentman was to be trusted.

The chimney job.

The little girl. She had said the boy was alive. What had his name been? Jute. But that was impossible. No one survived a dose of lianol like that. Still, she had sounded certain.

Ronan shook his head. It was not possible.

We all have our jobs to do.

The boy stared up at him from within the chimney, falling backward. Vanishing down into darkness.

Just like himself.

Years and years of falling down into the darkness.

The stone ceiling seemed to be lowering. The lamplight swam in his eyes. The air was hot and stifling. Faces blurred by. Voices babbled around him. Ronan flung the half-eaten chicken away from him. His stomach clenched. Someone said something to him. He mumbled a reply, not knowing what the other had said or what he had said in return. He needed to get out.

The doors to the Court of the Guild swung shut behind him and he stood for a moment, breathing in and out and trying to quell the nausea inside. He looked up and down the stone passage. No one in sight. The place was silent. On the edge of his mind, however, he could hear the whisper of the ward that governed passage. It pushed its way into him, examined him, recognized him, and then retreated.

The first time Ronan had walked the underground passage as a novice member of the Guild, years ago, no one had bothered to explain the uniqueness of the ward guarding the passage. He had memorized the twists and turns and counted his steps. When he emerged once more into the sunlight, he retraced the way in his mind as he walked the streets of Hearne. But he found that the path only led him in a circle that meandered back to where he started. Later, it was explained to him that the ward guarding the passage was crafted to constantly manipulate the passage, forever shaping new routes beneath the city. It rearranged itself so that no one ever walked the same way to the Court of the Guild. The passage moved even as people walked within it, hurrying or slowing them on their way to the court. And for those who had no business with the Silentman?

Why, they never found their way out of the passage. Ronan had come across such intruders before, but the rats always found the bodies first.

It didn't matter what direction the passage chose. If you were walking away from the Court of the Guild, it would find an exit for you. The only trouble was, the ward spell was so powerful you could never be certain where you would find yourself when you exited. There were numerous places throughout Hearne the ward could choose from. It was irritating to emerge at the opposite end of the city from where you started.

Lamps burned on the wall every once in a while, but flames were so meager and the distances between them were always so great that most of the passage was plunged into gloom. Something scurried away in the shadows. A rat, most likely.

Scurrying away like himself.

Abruptly, the passage turned a corner and ended at some stairs.

"The stables on Willes Street," said Ronan to himself, guessing.

At the top of the stairs was a wooden door. He opened it and shrugged. He was not in the stables, not that he had expected to be. He had never guessed right before. He was in the cellar of the Goose and Gold. He stepped through a door concealed within a wine barrel.

Something crashed and he heard a gasp.

"Now look what I've done!"

It was one of the serving girls. She crouched down onto the floor to pick up some pottery shards.

"Just filled it with ale, too." She scowled at Ronan. "Gave me a turn, you did."

"Sorry," said Ronan. He shut the door behind him. It was built into a fake wine cask that sat at the end of a row of casks. If you didn't know what you were looking for, it was impossible to detect the lines of the door.

The sky was clear and cold when he emerged from the Goose and Gold. The first few stars were emerging in the east. He breathed deeply and smelled the salt of the sea. That steadied him and he strode off, collar flipped up against the cold. He slept well that night and did not dream, even of the girl with poor Liss Galnes's name.

CHAPTER THIRTY-FIVE
A DEATH, A DELAY, AND A WEASEL

They would have left that day for Hearne, but just after breakfast a horseman came clattering into the courtyard of the castle in Andolan. He was only a boy, but by the expression on his face, he bore sorry news.

"Stone and shadow," said the duke. "So that's why he didn't come." He stared down at the ground for a moment and then forced himself to smile—albeit grimly—at the boy.

"My thanks for your kindness. Get yourself to the kitchen and have them feed you there."

"Thank you, my lord," said the boy. The duke turned away, striding toward the castle steps.

"You, lad!" he yelled at a passing man-at-arms. "Find Willen and have him attend me immediately!"

Levoreth and the duchess were in the sunroom adjoining the duchess's rooms. It was a pleasant room suited for silence, and both women liked it for that reason. Melanor was knitting what looked like the beginnings of a blanket. Levoreth was curled up in a chair, intent on a book of poetry written by a long-dead Harlech lord. The door flew open with a crash.

"Hennen," said the duchess, dropping a stitch. "There's no need to be stamping about so."

"Ginan Bly is dead. He, his wife, and their babe. Torn apart by wolves— right inside their house."

"Wolves?" said Levoreth. Her voice was sharp.

"Oh, my dear," said the duchess. Her face whitened. "She was so happy to have borne a child."

"I'm riding north for Bly's farm. Willen and a score of his men will be with me as well. A couple of his lads are good trackers. If there's a trail to find, we'll hunt down the brutes. I don't know how long we'll be gone."

He turned to go.

"But what about Hearne?" said his wife. "We were to set out this afternoon."

"Hearne will have to wait."

"It was not wolves that did this," said Levoreth. But the door was already closing and the duke was gone.

152

She stared down blankly at the book in her lap. She flung her mind wide, ranging across the hills of the Mearh Dun toward the north and east. Earth and sky blurred through the speed of her thought. Dimly, she was aware of lives flickering by. Men, cattle, flocks of sheep scattered on the hills, dogs, rabbits in the heather, birds on the wing. Nowhere, however, could she sense wolves, even in the tangled weaving of old scents left from weeks past. Nothing. She pushed out farther, drifting up into the foothills of the Mountains of Morn.

"Levoreth!"

She blinked and looked up. Her aunt was looking at her.

"Are you all right? You had such an angry look on your face. I've never seen you so—"

"Ginan Bly was a good man," said Levoreth.

"Yes, yes he was." The duchess blinked back tears.

The duke and his men returned two days later, tired and gray-faced from the hard ride into the north. The duchess hurried down the castle steps to meet him, with Levoreth behind her. He swung down from the saddle and trudged over to his wife. Stubble covered his face and his eyes were bloodshot. His wife touched him gently, running a hand down his arm as if to reassure herself.

"It wasn't wolves, was it?" said Levoreth. It was more a statement than a question.

"No," said the duke. "No signs to track. Nothing at all. I'm half in mind not to go to Hearne now, but don't fret, love—we'll be going still. Ealu Fremman's six sons have promised to ride the borders and there are no better trackers in this duchy than those boys. The best of the men'll be staying on at the castle." He shook his head. "Dolan is in good hands with them, but this is poor timing. Poor timing indeed."

Dinner was a silent affair that night, although the duchess tried to make conversation. The duke hardly spoke at all and Levoreth was even quieter.

"I'm dreadfully sorry about the Blys," said the duchess, putting down her fork. "But they are gone and you do them no benefit by grinding your teeth like that, Hennen. My dears, we needn't go to Hearne. There'll be other times."

"We're going to Hearne," said her husband.

"I meant what I said," returned his wife. "It isn't as if the regent and his Autumn Fair cannot go on without us. After all, what are we to Botrell but uncouth country folk, smelling of horses and going about with straw in our hair?"

"We're going to Hearne!"

"Excuse me," said Levoreth, and she got up and left the table.

"And you're still coming, too!" said her uncle.

"I know that," said Levoreth. She glared at the duke and then slammed the door behind her.

Levoreth had not known the Blys well. She could not even recollect what Ginan Bly looked like, let alone his wife and child. But they were still her people. This was her land.

No.

She forced herself to unclench her fists.

No. All of Tormay was her land. Not just this sleepy little duchy of Dolan.

She locked the door of her room and blew out the candle. Outside, a sickle moon was rising in the east over the Mountains of Morn. The moon was so thin it looked like the sky's weight would snap it in two. There was something in the air. Something—she was not sure. She leaned out the window. Her nose twitched. Heather from the surrounding hills, woodsmoke, the scent of hay and horses in the stables, a guard in the courtyard below smoking a pipe. Apples rotting on the ground in the orchard behind the castle, the musk of a fox sniffing around the chicken coop.

A fox in the chicken coop. Teeth and feathers.

They kill for pleasure sometimes. But there are other things that kill for pleasure as well.

There was something else in the air. Her nose twitched again.

Definitely. Just the barest hint.

Something dark.

There was just enough time. She had to see for herself.

A cloak around her shoulders, Levoreth tiptoed through the hall. The castle was settling into evening. She could hear servants chatting and laughing down in the kitchen. Crockery clinked together. Somewhere on the floor above, her aunt was humming to herself. Levoreth tilted her head to one side and listened. The tune was an old Dolani love song. A smile crossed her face. She wondered if her uncle knew.

Mistress of Mistresses!

Levoreth looked down. A mouse scurried out from behind a chest and stood shyly before her.

"Sir Mouse," she said. "Well met."

Indeed, Mistress! Indeed!

"Can you do me a great favor?"

Aye! What is your wish? We mice will do anything in our power to aid you, even though it cost us our lives! Command us!

"I would have you and yours guard this castle and the town. Parley with the cats, with the hounds, with the horses, and with all that live hereby. Bid them my peace. Bid them that all must be my watch against the Dark."

The Dark!

The mouse squeaked in alarm and its whiskers quivered.

"Aye, Sir Mouse. Can you aid me?"

The mouse bobbed up and down. It reached out one tiny paw and patted the hem of her cloak.

We shall! We shall! Word shall come to you if we see aught!

The mouse scurried away.

The moon was rising high when she made her way from the castle grounds. A small gate in the gardens opened into the street behind the castle. Though, in truth, it was more of a cattle path than a street, full of ruts and mud puddles. Lights shone from the windows around her. A cow lowed in question from a shed nearby.

Hay.

Hay. And grass tomorrow?

She quieted the cow with a touch of her mind and passed on.

Steps were built into the wall here for the soldiers who walked the watches, but no one was in sight. She hurried up to the top of the wall and glanced at the moon. There would be just enough time. Barely enough, and she would be doubtlessly falling asleep in the saddle in the morning when they left for Hearne.

She took a deep breath and jumped off the wall.

Landed already running. She could hear the galloping of horses in her mind. Herself galloping.

The ground flowed away beneath her, earth and stone and trees blurring into one. The wind whipped through her hair and her cloak, tossing them back like a dark mane. She heard the river Ciele murmuring before her, and then she was past it, hurdling it in one stride. The moonlight flashed on the water, and the moon in the sky was the only thing that stayed motionless with her, watching her with the narrow curve of its unblinking eye. Hills rose and fell before her. The dew sprang from the grass at the strike of her feet. Her cloak was drenched in it. Time slowed, but she ran faster and faster.

Oh, Min!

Her heart was full and it seemed to her that if she turned her head she would see the great horse galloping next to her. She was up higher now, up on the plateau that rises in the northern portion of the Mearh Dun hills. She slowed her pace and felt sweat springing cold from her limbs.

The moonlight gleamed on the whitewashed stone walls of a cottage. A barn stood nearby. The ground was hard underfoot. She smelled the oily tang of sheep in the air. Sheep and hay and death.

And the other smell.

It was unforgettable. The Dark. Nausea twisted her stomach.

A memory struggled to life and for a moment she went blind to the cottage and the silent land around her. Shadows were falling from the sky. A mountain range rose like broken teeth into the night. Fires raged on the plain below. She heard the distant shouts and screams of the dying. The battle lines snaked across the plain. Iron clashed on iron. And the shadows fell from the sky.

They fell and they fell.

So long ago.

Long before we fled to Tormay.

But the stench was the same.

Levoreth forced her eyes open. Her head ached. The cottage sat waiting for her in silence. She swallowed and tasted bile.

In the little garden behind the cottage were two fresh graves. They were heaped over with stones and she touched them. The animals would respect her scent. They would not bother these graves. The lock on the cottage door was shattered. The smell was almost overpowering inside. She doubted, of course, that a normal human would be able to smell the scent. A wizard might be able to. Others would merely become uneasy, fearful, or sick to their stomachs, but they would not know why.

Animals, however, would smell it and know it for what it was.

The cottage was a single room that served as kitchen, living space, and bedroom. Just inside the door, moonlight slanted down onto the wood flooring. The wood was stained dark. Someone had kicked dirt over it, but the stain was apparent, ugly and dark red. Broken crockery, torn bedding, and splintered furniture had been piled up in one corner—all that was left of the Blys besides the two graves in the garden.

There was something else in the room. A thread of emotion fast fading away. Terror. And rage.

Ginan Bly had died fighting.

Levoreth nodded. She looked once around the cottage and then walked outside. The stench was all around. It clung to the stone walls and to the grass poking up from the ground. She stalked around the cottage, her head down.

There.

There it was.

The scent led away toward the north.

North. Yet she had no time to go north herself. Something in the city of Hearne was calling her. She cast her thoughts wide, searching across the surrounding land. Nothing. Not even a field mouse to be found. She pushed wider, but there was only a residue of fear. The animals had all fled. But there—there was something. A weasel skittering along the ground, nervous and hungry. She caught at its mind and pulled it toward her, but the animal shied away. She snared it again and soothed it with thoughts of fat mice and crickets. The weasel shivered.

Come.

The animal came, snarling and protesting, hardly able to talk for fear.

Afraid. Evil. Here! It is here! Run! Run away!

It popped its head out of a bush several yards away, its shiny black eyes darting every which way at once, and then it disappeared.

Come.

Run! Run away!

Come.

The bush quivered and then the weasel burst out from among the leaves and scurried across the ground to her. It wrapped itself around her ankles. She could feel the staccato of its heartbeat trembling against her skin.

Peace, little one.

Here! It is here! Everywhere!

Peace.

The weasel poked its head out from under her cloak and stared up at her. The moonlight glittered in its eyes. She felt the animal quiet down, but its thoughts still darted through her mind, tense and afraid.

Mistress of Mistresses. The Dark has been here. Not long ago. Can you not scent it? Humans lived here. They are dead. All dead.

Aye, the Dark has been here, but it is here no more. Peace, little one, and listen to what I shall say. Alone, there is none of you that can stand against the Dark. That is not your place, for it is the duty of those who have been given charge over you. Now, listen, for I would have you do a great thing for me.

Name your bidding, Mistress of Mistresses! Even if it be death, I shall do it!

Go now to all the nyten, all the four-footed folk who call these hills home. Go to the hares, the deer, the mice, and the foxes. In my name, put aside your enmities for a time and bid all to keep watch against the Dark. Do not stand and fight, but wait and watch.

I shall do so, Mistress. Even to the mice! The plump and tasty mice!

And one last thing, little one. A very important thing.

Aye?

157

Find me a fleet-footed deer and send her to the Mountains of Morn. Give her word for the wolves, that they must come to this place and track the scent of Dark as far as they dare. If the deer keep my name in her mouth, the wolves shall not harm her.

The weasel bobbed its head up and down in obedience. Then, without a backward glance, it scampered away and was soon lost in the night.

Levoreth sighed.

"I know this stink," she said to herself. "Damn you to your endless night, wherever you have gone! But my little ones shall keep watch, and the wolves shall track you to your doorstep, and then I shall unmake you, if it's the last thing I do. If my fate didn't bid me to Hearne, I would hunt with the wolves. I would hunt you to the ends of the earth. Even if it took me back east over the sea."

And with these words, she turned once again to the south. The moon gazed down upon her. The wind sprang up and the sky blazed with stars. As she ran, it seemed that the ghostly shape of a horse ran by her side.

They left the next morning for Hearne. The duke was quiet all that day, causing the duchess anxiety. However, the sunlight and the beauty of the late summer soon proved enough to wrest him from his mood into his usual cheerful self. Levoreth yawned and slumped in the saddle, such that her aunt thought her ill.

"You should've said something, my dear," said the duchess. There's a tea of willow bark and jona flowers I've had splendid success with."

"I'm fine," said Levoreth.

"You look dreadful."

"I'm fine," said Levoreth.

The road wound south, through hills thinly forested with pines. For a time, it followed the east bank of the Ciele, before the river swung toward the west and the great sea. Here, the hill country met the plain of Scarpe, which stretched from the Mearh Dun in the north to the cliffs far to the west that rose above the sea with their rocky heights. The plain of Scarpe extended a good five days' journey by horse to the forests of Lome standing on the western foothills and flanks of the Mountains of Morn. South was a hard week's ride before the plain met the river Rennet and Hearne, whose stone walls loomed over that course's mouth.

The plain of Scarpe was like an ocean of grasses, rippling in the wind toward an endless horizon. In the spring, it was patchworked with wildflowers—the different purples of the allium, the yellow-white spray of saxifrage, and the tiny blood-red poppies. By summer's end, however, the flowers were faded and gone, leaving only the grasses burnished into gold under the sun. Water was a chancy thing at best on the plain, but Willen, the old sergeant-at-arms, knew Scarpe like his own hand, having fought in the Errant Wars that had raged across that land thirty years earlier.

"Besides," he said to Levoreth as they rode along, "you give a horse a chance for his own notions, he'll find a waterhole soon enough. They're smart in that. There be other ways, too—the flight of bees and birds, the mixture of grasses, even the wind if you have the sense to smell it." And he chuckled and laid a finger alongside his own weathered beak of a nose.

Levoreth smiled at him, and the roan under her danced a few steps.

They were a day into the Scarpe when one of the outriders came galloping in toward the party. He reined up next to the duke, spoke with him, and then cantered away. The duke spurred his horse alongside his wife and Levoreth.

"Good news!" he said. "The Farrows! Just half an hour south of us!"

CHAPTER THIRTY-SIX
OWAIN GOES HUNTING

"It'll only be for a few weeks, Sibb. Not long at all."

The Lord Captain of Hearne was sitting with his wife in the garden behind the house. Sibb grew herbs for her kitchen there. The scent of sage and basil filled the air. Around them, the plants flourished in their tiny plots. Morning sunlight crept down the wall. The honeysuckle vines growing along the wall were covered in a profusion of yellow flowers.

Sibb picked up his hand, turning it over in her own. His palms were callused and his knuckles wealed with scars. A particularly large scar ran between his thumb and finger, reaching almost to his wrist. She ran her finger along the ridge, remembering. A frown crossed her face.

"Three weeks at most," he said.

She said nothing in reply, but only traced the scars on his hand.

"I'm leaving Bordeall in charge at the tower. He'll have near enough the entire strength to command, so Botrell can sleep soundly at night. Hearne will keep safe while I'm gone."

"It's not Hearne I worry about," she said, tracing the scar alongside his thumb. He laughed and kissed her.

"Don't fret, Sibb. With a sword and a good horse, I'll always have the luck to find my way home. Odds are we won't find hide or tail of them, so there'll be no need to worry on that account."

"Them," she repeated.

"Aye." He sighed. "I don't even know what we're looking for. Man, beast, or something in between. I have the feeling it's something in between. At any rate, we'll ride out to our foundling's village and see if we can find some tracks. How I wish she would regain her tongue. Without her knowledge, we'll be hunting blind. Even if we return with only stories of bones and an old slaughter gone cold, it'll be worthwhile, for I want Botrell thinking beyond this city. He's able as regent, I'll give him that, but he forgets that all the lands of Tormay look to Hearne. The other duchies are unsettled about these murders and, so far, Botrell ignores their unease."

"He's an odious man," said Sibb.

"Woman, you forget he is our regent. I'm sworn to protect his city and his personage. In pursuit of such office I'll have to—ouch!"

She punched him in the ribs and they were both silent for a moment. Bees drifted and settled among the honeysuckle vines.

"I'm worried about that girl. I fear she'll never be well."

He frowned. "Would any child who's lost their family at such an age ever become well?"

"I've held her while she sleeps. She's as fragile as a sparrow. Doubtless, she's older than our Magret, but less than half the weight. When she's taken by nightmares, her heart races and she pants as if she is running, as if there's some horror chasing her. I can't help but think the thing is chasing her still, sniffing along her trail. Perhaps, one day, it'll find its way here and so her nightmare and waking day will merge into one. Not just for her, but for all of us."

"Sibb."

She sighed and laced her fingers through his.

"I can't shake the thought from my mind, Owain. Such eyes she has. She's always staring and not noticing anything about her. Perhaps she sees things we cannot see. Sometimes she seems to focus on Loy—"

"Her devoted dog," he said, smiling.

"I can't help but think of our own in her stead."

Her hand tightened on his.

"Find them, Owain. Find them and kill them."

The Lord Captain of Hearne and his men rode out that afternoon. The troop was twenty strong—the best of Hearne. Some of the older ones had seen battle during the Errant Wars, when Owain Gawinn had been but a young sergeant and the forces of Hearne had been commanded by his father, Rann Gawinn.

Their saddles creaked with the weight of their gear and provisions. On their backs they bore spears and quivers bristling with arrows, muffled by their cloaks. They received scant notice from the folk in the streets going about their business—the vendors at their carts, the shoppers sniffing over turnips and fingering bolts of cloth, the drifting rabble, and the urchins—they made grudging way for the troop, action that stemmed more from the need for their own safety from the stamp of hooves rather than from any regard for the regent's men.

This lack of regard was due to no fault of the Lord Captain of Hearne. On the contrary, he had always been pleased by the blind eye the people turned to him and his men. He considered that his job was to allow folk to go about their lives while he dealt quickly and quietly with those who broke Hearne's laws. And he did that job well enough so that he had achieved a kind of facelessness for his men.

When the troop reached the city gates, however, a cheer went up from the soldiers standing watch. Owain reined in under the shadow of the tower, and a man strode forward. His hair was white but his back was as straight as a sapling. He held a spear in his hand.

"Bordeall," said Owain.

"My lord," said the other, touching the spear shaft to his forehead. His voice was deep and raspy.

"Hearne will be in good hands while we're gone."

"Thank you, my lord."

Another soldier came forward and both men turned in some annoyance.

"My lord Gawinn."

"Arodilac Bridd," said Owain. "You would do well to observe the propriety learned under the patience of my sergeants. Did they teach you nothing?"

Arodilac flushed red at the rebuke.

"Forgive me, my lord," he stammered. "I merely wished—is there no chance of—?"

"None," said Owain, cutting him off. "You will remain and serve here. Curb your patience, my young cub. Do not be so eager to rush into battle, though likely we'll see none on our hunt."

"It isn't because of my uncle wanting me kept from danger, is it?"

"No," said Owain, though it had been precisely for that reason. "Bordeall, I'd ask you to see that my household is well. My wife has some womanly fear concerning the foundling we took in. Perhaps send a man by, now and again, to have a word with my doorkeeper and see that the child is well enough."

"Assuredly, my lord," said Bordeall. "Might I not make that Arodilac's duty?"

"Certainly," said Owain, and looked sharply at the young man, for his mouth was opening. Arodilac shut his mouth with a painful click of teeth and backed away.

"The city is yours."

"Thank you, my lord. Good hunting." Bordeall turned away to bellow at the soldiers at the gate. "Present!"

Spears gleamed as they rose in a flourish. With a jingle of harness and the clop of horse hooves on stone, the troop rode out through the gates and onto the road that curved away east, over the bridge and across the river and then down through the long, green reaches of the Rennet valley. The sky was clouding over. It would be raining again soon.

CHAPTER THIRTY-SEVEN
THE JUGGLER'S MISTAKE

Nio tightened his cloak around his throat when he stepped out the front door. It was just past twilight and stars winked down from the dark sky. He was late, but it wouldn't hurt the Juggler to be kept waiting. A cold rain was falling. It had been a strange summer for weather, almost as if the earth was no longer sure of the seasons. He wondered what the fall would bring. An early snow, perhaps. The streets were nearly empty of people, and the only ones he passed hurried along with their heads down, intent on reaching their homes and the warmth and welcome and firelight waiting there.

Once, a long time ago, he had wanted the same kind of life.

Cyrnel. He had loved her—that much he was sure of. But when he tried to recall her face, there was only an impression of beauty and a blur in his memory. He remembered freckles on her arms and a low, laughing voice. She smelled of fresh bread and the sunlight on the wheat fields in the valley east of the Stone Tower in Thule. The school bought their milk and cheese and grain from her father, the farmer. Nio remembered the look of the cheese more clearly than the farmer's daughter: small, white rounds smelling of caraway. The cook had been stingy with that cheese. Nio almost smiled to himself at the thought.

Perhaps he had wanted to marry her. He would have had a home to hurry back to at night. Someone waiting for him, other than the old ghosts sleeping inside the books in his library. But he had chosen the ghosts. Or perhaps they had chosen him. Some days he wasn't sure.

It was dark by the time he reached the south market square—an ugly, cramped plaza hemmed in with shops shuttered against the night. The rain had turned into a mist heavy enough to blur the shapes of buildings and the lights shining from windows. The stars and the moon could not be seen at all. It seemed he was alone in the city, for the mist also had the effect of muffling noise. Even his boots on the cobblestones only whispered.

Nio smelled the butcher's place before he saw it. A cloying scent of offal and blood filled the air, and the mist felt greasy with it. The stones there were stained dark. He turned west and walked down the street called Forraedan. It was narrow enough to be more of an alley than a street. He fancied he could almost stretch out his hands and touch the houses on both sides as he walked. The mist thickened, and close by he heard water dripping.

Seventh house on the left, the Juggler had said. He passed the fourth. The street turned sharply to the right where the fifth house stood, though it was puzzling to make out where one house ended and one began. They were built right up against each other, sharing their walls and a common sweep of roof that loomed overhead. Perhaps he should have been counting doors instead of houses. Fancy a brothel being hidden away in this warren. But then he came to the sixth house and the street ended against a stone wall taller than the houses themselves. A door opened behind him, further back up the street. He turned.

"You're late," said the Juggler. The fat man was standing about twenty feet away. A lantern hung from his hand and cast a glow on the wet cobblestones.

"I was reading and lost track of the time."

"Ah," said the Juggler. "I've never gone in much for reading."

"There's no seventh house," said Nio. His voice was mild. "You did say come to the seventh house, didn't you?"

"I did," said the fat man.

"There's only this wall."

"Yes," said the other, nodding. "There're only six, and then this wall. It's not a house, as you see. It's the back wall of a warehouse where an old man makes candles, he and his family. Candles made of grease, boiled in cauldrons and poured into his molds. Nothing to steal inside. Only thousands and thousands of candles. We leave him alone, we do, and in return—well, he'll use just about anything to make his grease with. Just about anything. We keep 'em well supplied here. It's convenient for us."

"Where's the man called the Knife?" asked Nio.

"Ah, the Knife," said the fat man, laying one finger alongside his nose and looking concerned. "Well sir, I says to him, come on out tonight as there's a gent who wants to talk with you. But he says no, I've got better things to do than that—you go tell him I'll see his gold first before meeting. That's what he says to me. See now, sir, he's a difficult lad, the Knife is—always has been, always will. Won't come to heel when you call him, and even the Silentman knows that."

"That won't do. I'm afraid you've disappointed me."

"Aye, and I'm disappointed the same!" said the fat man. He shook his head sadly. "I begged the lad nicely. Just a few minutes' chat and then you'll have your gold. But he wouldn't have none of it. Tell you what we'll do, sir. Why don't you hand over your bag of gold and I'll see the Knife gets it. That'll put him in a better mood."

"No. I don't think so."

At the words, two shapes materialized out of the darkness behind the Juggler. They were both large men—the sort of brute that Nio had seen in the Goose and Gold. He sighed inwardly. The evening could have been spent in a more pleasant fashion, reading a book in his library and smoking a pipe.

"Tsk," said the fat man. "We'll just have to take it from you, then."

"I don't think so," said Nio.

This seemed to please the Juggler. He smiled, his teeth gleaming in the lamplight.

"Then we'll have to kill you."

The two men behind the Juggler moved forward. Knives appeared in their hands. The darkness and mist blurred their faces so their eyes were only gouges of shadow and their mouths black holes. Skulls, thought Nio. He sighed again. One of them reached for him, a big, bony hand. Moisture gleamed on the skin, and the lamplight picked out scars across the knuckles.

He whispered a word and time slowed. The air thickened around the two men approaching him so that they swam through it. Their limbs were ponderous and weighted. He stepped to one side. Their eyes could barely follow him. The Juggler stood frozen behind them, huddled against the stone wall of the building. The light cast by his lantern seemed to have congealed and turned a yellowish gray. Water dripped from an eave overhead, falling so slowly that he could have plucked them from the air, one by one, like jewels.

The darkness in the street behind the Juggler trembled, and then a wisp of it separated, clotting together to form the shape of the wihht. On unhurried legs, it started forward and reached for the fat man.

"*Na, hie aerest,*" said Nio. The thing obeyed, veering, and made for the closer of the two other men. Shadow closed on flesh and grew, flaring up like a flame leaping into life, but without light or heat—only darkness that surged with quick movements. A scream cut off into silence. The second man was turning, turning slowly until he saw the shadow reaching for him. His eyes widened, and then he was blotted out in a wave of darkness. Only seconds, perhaps, went by. Nio was not sure, for the spell of slowing still held sway within the confines of the cobblestones and walls and dark, shuttered windows that looked on in silence.

The mass of shadow receded until there was only the wihht standing there. The two men were gone, although a few damp rags of clothing fluttered to the ground around the wihht's feet. It turned toward Nio and seemed to smile. He could not rightly tell in the little light there was, but it seemed now that the features of the thing were finer and more human.

"And this other?" it said, voice still hoarse and awkward.

"*Bidan,*" he said. Wait. He bound it into patience with his will woven into the word. Yet, even though the word and his will held, the wihht walked at his heels as he advanced toward the Juggler. The lantern trembled in the fat man's hand, his fingers white-knuckled across the handle.

"You chose poorly," said Nio. The other only stared at him, eyes huge in their sockets. Behind them, the wihht chuckled.

"Though this night has proven disappointing," continued Nio, "as you have brought no Knife, we must talk, you and I. Perhaps you know nothing I would find valuable, but I must make sure. I hope you understand. Now, where is the Knife?"

But the fat man remained silent, frozen except for the lantern trembling in his clutch and his eyes flickering from Nio's face to the shadow waiting behind and then back.

"*Cweoan,*" said Nio. Speak.

"I don't know, my lord!" stammered the Juggler. His face shone with sweat. "He did a big job some nights back. A real big job! Did it with one of my boys. He owes me money now, but the Guild ain't paid up yet!"

"What was the job?"

The words came in a rush, but Nio knew the answer already.

"A box lifted from a rich merchant's house. Just a little box, but it had something valuable in it. It wouldna been so or the Knife wouldna run the job. Usually, those jobs are left to the burglars—and he ain't a burglar, he's the bleeding Knife! I saw the box myself, right after it was nicked. The Knife was carrying it when he entered the tunnel underneath the Goose and Gold—the inn where you and me first met."

Nio said nothing, though it was all he could do not to grind his teeth together.

"The tunnel—it goes to the Silentman's court," gabbled the fat man. "Through the labyrinth. Nice place, all old stone, but strange. I hate going there! The Silentman ain't paid up yet, which means the client ain't got the goods yet. That's standard Guild procedure."

"How many in this Guild of yours know about the box?"

"Er," gulped the Juggler, his eyes sliding past Nio toward what waited behind him, "prob'ly not many. The Silentman's real silent 'bout his jobs an' clients. That's why he's called the Silentman."

"How many?"

"Um, mebbe four at most. The Knife, the Silentman and his advisor fellow, and me."

"What of your boy?"

"Oh, well, he was—he was dead by the time the work was finished."

"Ah," said Nio. "Broke his neck in a fall, did he?"

"No, no! More a matter of tying up loose ends. Another sign of the importance of the job. No need for flapping lips about. The boy was poisoned."

"Poisoned?" said Nio. "What do you mean by that? A strange sort of business, this Guild of yours, if it kills off its employees as they work."

"Just a boy," babbled the fat man. "Nothing personal. As soon as he came up out of the chimney, handed the box over, the Knife jabbed him full of lianol. Out like a blown candle. He wouldn't have felt a thing."

"What?!"

The fat man gurgled like a water fountain, but Nio no longer heard him. Lianol. The poison was lethal. There was no way to reverse it. He had never heard or read of any way possible.

His mind froze. The box. If what he guessed about the box was true—if what he guessed about what was inside the box was true—then that was how the boy had cheated death. Nausea swept over him. The boy had opened the box. The boy had touched what was inside the box. Blood had been drawn.

Nio turned back to the Juggler. His voice shook with rage.

"Who contracted the Guild for this job?"

"I don't know," said the fat man.

Behind Nio, the wihht stirred to life and stepped forward. Out of the corner of his eye, Nio could see the pallid face and the light gleaming in the sockets.

"I don't know! I don't know!" shrieked the fat man. The lantern fell from his grasp and broke on the cobblestones, sending up a brief flare of flame over the pooled oil. Glass crunched underneath the wihht's boot and the flame was extinguished.

"No, no!" sobbed the Juggler. He shrank away and covered his face with his hands.

"I believe you," said Nio.

"You do?" faltered the fat man, peeping at him from between his fingers.

"Yes. By the way, it's nothing personal, but this will probably hurt a great deal."

Nio turned and stalked away down the dark street.

The boy was all that mattered now. Only the boy. But he would make the Guild and its client pay dearly for what they had done. First the boy, then he would see to everything else. Everything! He ground his teeth together in fury. He had been so close. The boy had been within his hands. He could have snapped his filthy little neck. The wihht would find him. It would find him, sniffing its way through the city until it caught the scent.

Behind Nio, a scream choked into a sort of bubbling noise, and then a sigh. The clouds in the sky had frayed away sometime in the last hour, and the moon stared down, pale and white and disapproving.

CHAPTER THIRTY-EIGHT
THE FARROWS

The Farrows had pitched camp within the shelter of a hollow containing a spring, a rarity on the plain of Scarpe. Groundwater was scarce on the plain. Creeks and rivers were nonexistent, apart from the Rennet River bordering the plain's southern edge. About a dozen wagons were drawn up in a semicircle near the spring, and a temporary corral had been put together for the colts. The older horses never wandered far; such was the bond between Farrow and horse.

There were upward of fifty Farrows, and they ranged the gamut from tiny Morn, the four-month-old grandnephew of Cullan Farrow, the patriarch of the clan, to old Sula Farrow, Cullan's widowed mother. Uncles, aunts, cousins, young, and old. The Farrows took their brides from all four corners of Tormay, and every hue of skin and hair could be found within their family, though the thin, hawkish face and gray eyes were seen everywhere.

The duke's party stayed with the Farrows for two days, even though this meant they would be late for the beginning of the Autumn Fair in Hearne. The duchess had words with her husband about this, but he was unrepentant, as there was nothing he loved more than talking horses with old Cullan Farrow. Though he was wise enough not to say this to her.

"My dear," said the duke, "there are two or three colts I'll have to see put through their paces. Cullan bought them in Harlech—bought them, of course—stealing a horse in Harlech! Why, you might as well cut your own throat on the spot. Best bloodlines in all Tormay. A positive gold mine for breeding."

"Imagine that," said his wife.

But she knew a lost cause when she saw one and contented herself with sitting in the shade of one of the wagons—for the Farrows had promptly cleared out of one their nicer covered wagons for the duke and duchess—where she spent hours knitting.

"It's not that I mind," she said to Levoreth. "It does seem to have taken Hennen's mind off the Blys. There's something restful about the Scarpe, the way the wind billows the grasses. It's like the waves on the sea. Even with these Farrows popping up everywhere like dandelions, it's peaceful here—which can never be said about a city like Hearne." And here she glared good-naturedly at several children who were peeping around the wagon wheel. They giggled and scampered away.

"However, I can't allow your uncle to have his way whenever he wants."

"Of course not," said Levoreth, smiling.

"You're laughing at me."

"Yes."

Cullan Farrow was a tall man and as lean and hard as a polished oak spear. His hair was white and cropped close to his skull. His eyes were gray, as cold and hard as a winter sky in Harlech. But he smiled easily, and then the gray warmed well enough.

"Botrell has a nice pair of colts now," he said to the duke. They stood at the edge of the camp, smoking their pipes and watching several yearlings being put through their paces.

"Foaled off of Riverrun's dam, no?" said the duke.

"Aye, so you've heard then."

"The traders have been talking of that line getting good hunters for him."

Cullan nodded.

"There's good blood there, and the newest colts should be proof if they're broken well. Botrell's got some wise lads in his stable."

They were both silent for a moment. The boys on the yearlings called cheerfully to each other as they galloped across the green sward. Sparrows dove and swooped overhead.

"You haven't come across any strange deaths lately, have you?" said the duke.

"What do you mean with that?"

"One of my farmers was killed recently. In the northeast of the Mearh Dun, just up under the foothills of the Morns. He and his family. I thought it wolves when I first heard, for we had trouble with them several years back. With the way you travel about, I figured you might have heard something of the sort."

"Can't mistake wolf," said Cullan. "They aren't shy in how they step."

"The manner of it's a cursed puzzle. They were torn by beasts, but the bites were huge. Bigger than any wolf I've ever heard of. If it had only been those marks, then I might still have been convinced of wolves, but there were cuts as well—thin, deep thrusts as if made with a slender sword. Beast and man killing together."

"Wolves never run with anything but wolves. No tracks for you to pick up?"

"A few signs, but we lost them quickly," admitted the duke. "I'd have given much to have had you there."

"Aye. Farrows don't lose tracks." Cullan smiled crookedly. "Though I wager you'd do as well if you were raised under the sky with no roof or walls withering your senses."

"Then have you heard of any such killings?"

"Not exactly. Though we passed through Vo two months past and heard talk about something odd in Vomaro. Something had the folk there worried. But I didn't bother for details."

"I'll have a word with Botrell when I get to Hearne. Perhaps he knows something. So you heard nothing of the matter in Vomaro itself?"

"We took the road to the east," said Cullan. He squinted up at the sky. When he looked back down, his gray eyes had gone cold. "Farrows don't go to Vomaro."

Levoreth loved the Scarpe. The plain stretched away in every direction. It billowed like the sea, as her aunt had said, with the wind rippling the grasses in waves that rolled on toward the horizon. A sweet, dry scent perfumed the air, wafting from the tiny jona flowers blooming in the grass. A robin trilled through the air, and she answered it absentmindedly, whistling in her thoughts. The bird sang in response, telling of worms and the bright, yellow eye of the sun in the sky that sees all, and three eggs warm in her nest.

Levoreth wandered away from the encampment until the only sign of it was a trail of smoke rising into the sky. The earth was peaceful here, slumbering under the passing of years and the faithful return of the sun. She lay down, with the grasses whispering around her, and fell asleep. The sun was high in the sky when she awoke. Sitting next to her was a girl. She was chewing on a stalk of grass and staring at Levoreth with curious gray eyes. Her face was narrow and browned by the sun. Tangled black hair waved across her brow in the breeze.

"Do you always cry in your sleep?" asked the girl.

"I don't think so," said Levoreth. She stared at the girl's face. Her heart ached, and she put her hand to her breast. "I'm not sure."

"You're the duke's niece—Lady Levoreth—aren't you? Mother said she dreamt about you."

"No need to 'lady' me. What did she dream?"

"She wouldn't tell," said the girl cheerfully. "When I dream, I'm never sure if I'm asleep or awake. Mother says my eyes glaze when she talks to me, that I do it on purpose so I don't remember what she's said. But maybe that's just me dreaming, or maybe that's just me forgetting—I'm good at that." She giggled and twirled the stalk of grass between her fingers.

"Have you forgotten your name also?"

"Oh." She grinned. "I'm Giverny Farrow, Cullan's daughter." Her hands rose and drifted through the air, palms up and fingers stained with earth. "How do you know if what you see is in a dream or in a waking moment?"

"There's more pain when you're awake. You'll learn that soon enough, if you haven't already."

"But you were crying in your sleep."

"Dreams hurt sometimes. But not compared to waking life." Levoreth sat up and plucked her own stalk of grass to chew.

"The wretched bay colt stood on my foot yesterday when I was brushing him. That hurt. Here, look." And Giverny kicked off her sandal to display her foot.

"Ouch," said Levoreth, admiring the blue-black bruise.

"He did it just to be spiteful," said the girl, "because I'd been spending too much time with his sister. Father had the pair from Duke Lannaslech in Harlech—who is terribly stern and scary, even though he gave me an apple and the horses all love him and follow him about like dogs. They're perfectly matched—twins, of course—but the filly is the sweetest colt you've ever seen."

She ran out of breath at this point and lapsed into silence. The sun was perfectly warm and the breeze had subsided to a murmur. Levoreth closed her eyes and felt the Scarpe stretching around her in leagues and leagues of grasses and the light, redolent with the scent of flowers and pollen, laying like gold over it all. The nearness of the girl stirred a memory in her of another girl from a long time ago. The same blithe heart, the same gray eyes, so clear and free of guile, those same fluttering hands expressing every nuance of word and heart. Long ago. Another time and another place. And now those hands were silent and unmoving in her lap.

"That's not what you meant, is it?" said Giverny.

"No. A colt can only kick you or step on you out of its foolishness. Or your own. That's not such a dreadful sort of pain. It's a thing that passes."

Giverny nodded. She inched a bit closer and propped her chin in her hands.

"My brother ran away when I was three years old. I don't remember what he looks like, though Mother says he looks like Father. She won't talk about it much, but everyone knows the story." Here, her voice fell into a sort of singsong tone, for she was telling a tale. Levoreth knew the story, had heard it sung by traveling bards more times than she could remember, but she did not stop the girl.

"Devnes Elloran, the only child of the duke of Vomaro, went riding with her attendants on the eastern shore of the lake. There, they were set upon by ogres. All were killed except for the lady, and she was carried off in great distress."

Here, Giverny made a face. "If it had been me on a horse, no ogre would've caught me. The stupid cow obviously didn't know how to ride."

"Ogres are cunning," said Levoreth. Her voice was mild. "Many wiser than Devnes Elloran have fallen into their hands before. Do not be so hard on her."

"No, maybe not for that," said the girl. "But for what she did later, she should've been boiled and eaten by those ogres!" She paused, frowning, and then continued. "The duke of Vomaro sent word throughout all the lands of Tormay, entreating men of valor to come to his castle at Lura. And they came there, from Hull and hilly Dolan, the coast of Thule, Vo, and Vomaro. Even the haughty lords of Harth came, though not a soul from Harlech—for they have never paid much attention to the rest of Tormay."

"Your Duke Lannaslech," said Levoreth.

"Yes," said Giverny, grinning. "I'd imagine he'd say if she were silly enough to get caught, then she might well deserve an ogre dragging her off. He has a terribly cold voice—all deep and hard. Father never steals horses in Harlech."

She sobered again. "My brother vanished one night, for the duke's proclamation promised the hand of his daughter in marriage for the man who brought her back. He stole Father's sword, so that he might walk with pride." Her chin lifted. "All Farrows take to horse and reading the signs of the earth. And Declan was the best of our family—so I've been told. But his hands lent themselves best to war, as had his father—our father—before him. The sword and the bow and all those other wretched things that take life."

Her own hands fluttered before her as if shaping the words.

"As the story goes, Declan found trace of the ogre trail on the moors south of Lome forest and tracked them through those woods for days. What he found there has never been told, for neither he nor the Lady Devnes Elloran ever spoke of it. On a cold, wet day in March, Declan rode out of Lome forest with the Lady Devnes. And then—and then . . . " Her voice trailed away.

"And then he was betrayed," said Levoreth.

"Yes!" burst out the girl angrily. "I hate it! I hate it all! Oh, he was brave and foolish to run away and think that he could make his way in such a world. I love him for that, for I sometimes feel the same thing inside myself—to see what's beyond the horizon and in far-off lands. I want to know more. I want to know more than just our wagons and our horses. But I hate him for leaving me not even a memory and Father and Mother growing old without him. Yet I hate that duke and his daughter even more for what they did. We Farrows no longer go to Vomaro, nor will we ever! May the Dark take them all!"

"Hush," said Levoreth. "No one should ever wish such a thing, for our lives here are only a breath. That which follows after endures. May we all come safely to the house of dreams and so escape the grasp of the Dark."

"Aye," said Giverny sulkily. "Save the house of Elloran."

"Child."

They sat in silence for a moment. Then, her face averted, the girl said, "That's what you meant about pain, yes?"

"Yes," said Levoreth.

The sun was lowering in the west, down toward the horizon and, past that, the far-off sea. Purple stained the sky in the east, and there a single star gleamed. Levoreth shivered in spite of the warmth left by the sunlight. It would be cold in the Mountains of Morn tonight. She reached out with her thoughts across the leagues, toward the peaks. The silence within her mind was broken by the howl of a wolf pack. It welled up like a lament, rising from the flanks of the range to the north, where the mountains climb high into the sky with their heights of stone and ice.

Mistress of Mistresses.

Drythen Wulf.

We have hunted along the scent of the Dark.

Where has it brought you?

We ran north from the hills of the Mearh Dun, north across the fields of snow and up into the heights. We found an eyrie, long cold, but the Dark did abide here a while, for the stink is rooted in the rocks and has crept down into the bones of the mountain.

And from there?

The scent did not end there, Mistress.

A hand touched her shoulder, and she opened her eyes to the fading afternoon of the Scarpe. Giverny drew back.

"Are you well, Lady Levoreth?" she asked anxiously. "You had such a look on your face."

"I'm fine. I was just thinking of an old friend." She forced a smile.

They walked back together. The girl skipped along beside her, humming an old Thulian song and darting away now and then to collect flowers that caught her fancy. Levoreth knew the song and she sang the words as she walked along.

"On the heathered downs of Davos bay
where the river meets the sea
the fishers mend their broken nets
upon the sandy lea."

"You know it," said Giverny, surprised, twirling around. She smiled in delight. "My grandmother taught me that one when I was little. She said 'The Girl of Davos Bay' was one of the forgotten treasures of Thule."

"Not yet forgotten," said Levoreth. "Some things are never forgotten. Delo of Thule was the finest bard Tormay has ever known. They say his songs wove themselves into the coast of Thule. If you walk the cliffs there, you can hear his music in the sounds of the wind and the sea, and in the call of the gulls." She continued singing.

"Blues and greens and shadows beneath—
the colors of the sea.
Breathe wind—blow the storm clouds hence
and bring my love home to me."

A brindled old hound loped out to meet them as they approached the camp. It licked at Levoreth's hand before pressing up against the girl's knees.

"Gala, my love," said Giverny, rubbing the dog's head. "That's Lady Levoreth Callas you just kissed. It isn't every day you're hobnobbing with the royalty of Tormay."

"Nay, girl," said Levoreth, laughing. "I darn my own socks."

Mistress of Mistresses.

Gala Gavrinsdaughter. The blood of the wolves flows in your veins. I knew your grandmother well.

Aye. There are days when I hear my mountain-kin calling. The hound turned sad, brown eyes on Levoreth. *Do you come for my little one?*

Levoreth caught her breath sharply. The hound nosed at her palm and whined. Giverny whirled away to pounce on a clump of blue bonnets.

What do you speak of?

Your mark is on her. All the nyten, even the sly jackal and the poisoned serpent, all things living cannot help but love her of instinct within them. The earth protects her, though she has ever been headstrong and foolhardy, even as a tiny whelp. Fate has not touched her for the life of her people. Do you have some design for her days?

Levoreth quickened her pace angrily.

I am not Anue that I would stand in the house of dreams and shape the futures of men. Would you assign to me more might than is my due? Listen well, Gavrinsdaughter! I did not seek my lot in life, for though I am the Mistress of Mistresses, there are powers beyond me that, unseen and unsought, move me to my fate, just as they do you. We are all borne upon the wind blowing from the house of dreams.

The hound padded alongside her, head hanging low. Behind them, Giverny trailed, deaf to their speech.

You speak of legends beyond legends, but you are the only legend we know to be true, for we see you with our own eyes and feel your touch upon the earth. You are our bulwark against the Dark. Do not judge me too harshly, Lady. You are the stillpoint of my people. Can we not help but think the skeins of our fate hang from your hands?

The encampment bustled with people: women washing clothes, children carrying buckets of water to a trough set up just beyond the wagons, where a string of horses was picketed. A fire crackled under an iron pot suspended from two crossed pikes. Levoreth could smell sage and onions and the sweet meat of the roebuck. She inhaled—dried rosemary, wild carrots that must have been plucked from the Scarpe itself, and a sprinkling of pepper all the way from Harth and worth its weight in gold. On the far side of the camp, the Dolani men-at-arms had their own cook fire burning. Night was coming. The hound lingered nearby for a moment and then slunk off among the wagons. Giverny brushed past her and Levoreth found a single blue bonnet in her hand.

The flames from the fire in the center of the encampment flickered sparks up into the darkness. In the east, the moon gleamed a yellow so feeble it seemed the night was about to swallow it up forever. But the stars overhead shone brilliantly within the black expanse. They were like the gleams of countless jewels—some tinged with the ruby's dark wine, others hinted at blue sapphire fire, yet even more gleamed with the incandescence of diamonds. As the darkness deepened, they burned all the brighter.

Someone handed Levoreth a bowl of stew and a hunk of bread. She sat down and leaned back against a wagon wheel. The bowl was warm in her hands. Across the way, she could see the duke talking with Cullan Farrow and several old men. Horses, no doubt. Smoke curled up from the pipes in their hands. She closed her eyes and let her mind drift, listening to the sounds of the night.

Children played at hide-and-seek among the tethered horses of the herd. Someone plucked a guitar, murmuring the words of an old Vornish love song. A mother crooned to her baby. The knitting needles of the duchess clacked quietly together. A young man-at-arms grumbled to the sergeant about having to eat their own food, as the old Farrow woman in charge of the cook pot had beckoned them over. The sergeant explained that their rations were good enough and that he'd break both his arms if he saw him laying a finger on the Farrow women.

Levoreth smiled. The Farrow women were famed through all the lands of Tormay for their beauty. But they were also renowned for their tempers and willingness to stick a knife in any who might offend. They wouldn't be needing any sergeants to defend their honor.

Lady.

Levoreth sighed. The hound lowered herself down beside her.

Gala Gavrinsdaughter.

The night is replete with sorrow. From three hearts it wells.

You would tell me, I think.

Aye. The mother of my little one. I have tasted her dreams ever since her firstborn went away. She is of the blood of Harlech, as you must know, Mistress of Mistresses. She dreams of shadows. Harlech dreams true, do they not?

And the second?

She is you, Lady. I can smell it in the change of season and the scent of the earth. I can—

You presume, hound.

The old dog flattened her head against the ground and was still.

And the third?

But the dog did not answer her and soon crept away into the darkness. Levoreth tasted the stew but it had gone cold. She got up, stiffly, and walked to the fire. Light flickered on the ring of wagons that encompassed it, gleaming on faces. A woman stooped over the cook pot. She straightened and turned. The promise of beauty and grace in the girl Giverny was fulfilled in her. A sheaf of silvering black hair was bound back from her head. Firelight pooled in her eyes.

"Lady Callas," she said.

"I'm only her niece," said Levoreth.

"Still a lady," said the woman. "There's old noble blood in your family line." Her head tilted to one side, her face impassive.

"My stew's gone cold."

The woman took the bowl from her and refilled it.

"I am Rumer Farrow," she said. "Giverny's mother."

"Yes, I know."

"Giverny is all we have left these days, Cullan and I. Ever since our son went away. As you know. As everyone, all of Tormay, knows." There was no bitterness in her voice, only resignation.

"She'll be a great lady someday."

Rumer touched her arm, as if to apologize. "But this I do not want for her. I would only wish her a quiet life, a man to love her just as mine loves me, children to grow up around her like young colts. This is all she needs. This is all anyone would ever need. Is not anything more than this only a burden and chasing of the wind?"

"You speak truly," returned Levoreth. She could not keep the harshness from her voice. "What more could anyone want? May all have such lives and find quiet deaths at their end, surrounded by loved ones and peace. Yet the Dark rises and men ride off to war. Lightning strikes where it will. Do we choose any of this? It chooses us and sweeps us along toward ends we can never see."

The woman bowed her head and, when she raised it, there were tears in her eyes. "I am from Harlech, Lady. We dream true there, for the veil of the sky wears thin in Harlech. I can't help but dream. I see my son's face, my young Declan, returning to me, but of my daughter I see nothing but darkness and the silent earth."

Giverny then appeared from the shadows and twined her arms around Rumer's waist. They stood and looked at Levoreth—the daughter smiling and the mother staring mutely. Levoreth did not dream her own dreams that night. The ground whispered to her of Rumer's sorrow, and she stirred uneasily on her pallet.

The duke of Dolan and his party stayed one more day with the Farrows and then left, with many plans voiced concerning colts and broodmares between Hennen and Cullan, until the duchess rolled her eyes and even Rumer laughed. The Farrows stood and waved goodbye until the vastness of the Scarpe swallowed them up in its horizon of grass, and they were gone.

"Fine people, fine people," said the duke happily.

"To be honest, my dear," remarked his wife, "they are pleasant. Rumer Farrow is a remarkable lady, and her father was the lord of Lannet in Harlech. I'd rather spend the next two weeks with them than having to survive Hearne and that insufferable sop Botrell."

The duke was pleased and startled at this. He suggested that perhaps they should return, as he was beginning to regret not buying a certain broodmare Cullan had shown him.

"Certainly not," said the duchess. "We're going to Hearne and the fair and Levoreth will fall in love, and I shall be polite to Botrell. We'll soon see the Farrows again, I'm sure. Perhaps they'll come through Andolan later in the fall."

"Oh, all right," said her husband.

"Duty, my dear."

"Hmmph."

CHAPTER THIRTY-NINE
FALLING FROM GREAT HEIGHTS

That day, Jute fell from the tower that stood in the center of the university grounds.

The tower stood by itself in the middle of a courtyard. He trudged up the stairs, hoping for a good view of the city from the top. The steps creaked under his feet, old oak worn to a dark, satiny sheen. Up and up they went, until his face was wet with sweat. The stairs ended beneath a trap door, which he pushed up, and he found himself standing on a platform. Hearne stretched around him in a patchwork of minarets, spires with their weathervanes pointing for the west wind, and flat-topped roofs, colorful and flapping with drying laundry. Sunlight shone on brick and stone, thatch and slate, and the green copper roofs of the regent's castle, perched on Highneck Rise. The castle rose up amidst the white stone villas of the nobility clustered on the heights. Its towers were the highest in Hearne, but the tower Jute stood upon was almost as high. Beyond the rooftops, the sea was a streak of blue under an even bluer sky.

A cloud drifted across the sun, and something creaked on the stairs far below him. At first, he thought he was imagining things. But then he heard it again. Wood creaking accompanied by an almost inaudible, wet sort of squish. The sounds came one after the other, climbing up the stairs. It was all he could do to clamp his chattering teeth together and remain silent. Hands trembling, he eased the trap door down and sat on it, thinking. Nothing at all came to mind except the desperate desire to jump up and down and scream.

"Hawk!" he said. "Please. Where are you?"

The cloud hiding the sun thickened and grew into a gray mass that obscured the entire sky. Rain began to fall. Jute scrambled over to the edge of the platform and looked down, hoping for ledges, handholds, anything. However, a master craftsman had his hand in the building. The stones of the tower had been fitted together with perfection. Jute leaned over and ran his fingers over the stone joints, and a groan of despair escaped his lips. They were impossibly smooth.

The trap door slammed open behind him. A stench of corruption filled the air, a stink of damp and rotting things. He had smelled the same odor before—in the cellar of Nio's house. He did not even turn to look but threw himself out into space.

This is going to hurt. Much worse than any beating the Juggler gave. For only a second. Maybe less. I hope.

The cobblestone court rushed up toward him.

A last thought floated by.

One more day would have been nice.

And then the wind caught him.

Softer than silk.

Silent.

Something—a door—eased open inside his mind for a moment, and then, just as gently, closed again. The wind left him standing, bewildered and mouth hanging open, in the middle of the cobblestone court. Around him rose the walls of the university and before him loomed the tower. A damp snarl floated down from high above. He turned and ran.

Jute had no clear thought except that he needed to hide. Somewhere quiet and still. A small space. Small spaces are always safer, but he shivered in doubt and thought about the open expanses of the sky. Hurtling around a corner, he started down a flight of steps. A man hurried into view at the bottom and looked up. Severan. They both stopped, staring at each other.

"What happened, boy?" said the old man. "Was it only a ward that set the air in this place quivering? I'm running out of explanations for my fellow scholars!"

"I don't know," said Jute, his voice cracking. "You tell me—you're a wizard, aren't you?"

"A scholar," said the old man. "Only a scholar. The true wizards all died many years ago. Come. We must talk."

The boy followed him to what was obviously the old man's rooms: a simple cell furnished with a writing desk, several cane chairs grouped around a banked brazier, and an iron-bound chest. Off to one side was a sleeping alcove. Severan stirred the brazier to glowing life.

"It's here," said the boy dully. "That thing. The wihht. It came for me. I was on top of the tower in the courtyard."

The old man's face turned pale. "And you escaped it for the second time? There's more than luck at play here. Who are you, boy? You must trust me."

"Why should I?" Jute's hands curled into fists.

"I was Nio's friend a very long time ago. He was a different man then. I don't know him now. Listen, Jute. I understand why you don't trust me completely. Hopefully in time you will. Perhaps if you understand more of what might happen. Scholars like myself are not just interested in the past. We're interested in the future, in what might happen. In what might become. I think there are other things that might become interested in you. Not just Nio and his wihht."

"What do you mean—other *things?*" asked the boy.

"When you broke into Nio's house, you stepped beyond the everyday world of Hearne. An entire life can be lived in this city without awareness of the larger world behind and beyond it. Anyone who can live this way should thank fortune for such happiness. They'll never face such a thing as you faced in Nio's cellar. But even a wihht pales in comparison to the ancient powers that serve the Dark."

"The Dark? Is there really such a thing as the Dark? I thought it was something made up, a bedtime story."

"Rest assured, it isn't a bedtime story." Severan smiled somewhat. "Unless, of course, you want to give children nightmares. You might laugh, but there's a great deal of truth to be found in bedtime stories and the like. You see, such tales don't just spring up out of nothing. They weave themselves into being out of truth. A whisper in the countryside became gossip in a nearby village. Details were added in the local inn, influenced by candlelight and winter boredom and too many tankards of ale. Traders passing through took the local tales and carried them away to the cities. And as years followed upon years, the stories worked their way into history, or into the delicious bedtime terrors mothers tell their children in hopes of securing their obedience. The very oldest of such stories, however, are as rare as pearls and, I think, even more valuable still."

"What are those stories about?" asked Jute. He drew his knees up to his chin and the old man noticed, for the first time, that the boy's eyes had a peculiar silvery sheen that gleamed in the light of the brazier.

"The very oldest ones are about four words and four mysterious creatures of immense power. Such power that the earth would shatter and reform itself at their bidding, that the wind and sea was theirs to command. The beasts and birds were their servants. They were the four *anbeorun*—the four stillpoints. It was said, though this has only been mentioned once in the single surviving copy of the Lurian Codex, that even the dragons would still their flame for them. The book that the wizard Staer Gemyndes wrote, the *Gerecednes*, surely contains even more knowledge of the anbeorun." He sighed and shook his head. "I'd happily spend the rest of my life looking for that book."

"There are no such things as dragons," said Jute.

"Don't be so quick to presume," said Severan. "There are more terrible things than dragons that walk this earth."

"I suppose so," said the boy doubtfully. "But what does all of that have to do with the four words?"

"Patience. We're coming to that. Most legends are rooted in fact, no matter how thin that fact might be when compared to the legend. Sometimes, the opposite is true. When the armies of Oruso Oran II sacked the city of Lascol, the plunder carried back to Harth included many books from the ducal library. Later, cataloguing the books, a court scribe discovered the memoirs of the wizard Sarcorlan."

"How do you know this?"

"That scribe went on to become one of the greatest historians that Harth has ever known. And if Harth is known for anything, it's known for a rigid attention to details, which has resulted in a highly efficient army, orderly cities, and marvelous historians. When I read the scribe's account of the discovery, I journeyed to Harth to see the memoir for myself."

Severan fumbled a ring of keys from his robe and unlocked the chest in the corner. He returned to his chair with a black book in his hands. He muttered a word over the thing and then opened it.

"Is that the memoir?" said Jute.

"Er, yes," said the old man.

"You're a thief?"

"Do you think thievery is the sole right of thieves?"

"No," said the boy, smiling. "It just seems a bit odd. Especially at your age."

"You shouldn't be so presumptuous. I, of course, don't mind. A dragon might." He turned over some pages. "Sarcorlan was never known for his humility, even on his deathbed. Listen to this, however, for his love of the truth was equal to his pride, as he remarks. 'What I am about to relate is true, for I am Sarcorlan of Vomaro, and all of Tormay has never known a greater wizard than I. My latter years were spent in peace, living in the mountains east of the great forest. A village nearby saw to my wants, which were few.'"

Severan paused in his reading. "I think he's referring to the Forest of Lome, which would have placed his village in the Morn Mountains east of Dolan, though I'm not completely certain. At any rate, there's no village there now." He turned back to the book and continued.

"In the spring after the fall of Ancalon, when the snows had melted in the mountain passes and the roads were open, a caravan of traders came east from Hull. I walked down to the village, as was my wont. The headman valued my presence when strangers came through, and thus we had a private agreement concerning such occasions. Three traders with their horses and pack-mules crested the ridge when I came to the inn. I cast a simple knowing on them, and they were as they appeared: tired traders and overworked, overloaded animals. Something else lingered in the knowing, however—a faint hint of power. Intrigued, I waited until they had arrived at the inn and set about unloading their goods. The whole village gathered around. There was the usual array of stock: knives, axe heads, Dolani wool, sea salt from Flessoray, spices, and a jumble of oddments spilling from a wooden chest.

"While the traders bickered with the villagers over the value of the local copper and opals, I cast a stronger knowing. This time, I felt a spark centered within the wooden chest. It was like nothing I had ever encountered before, and I am, mind you, Sarcorlan of Vomaro. At the bottom of the chest, tucked away in a small sack, I found the pearl. The trader to whom it belonged was reluctant to sell the thing, protesting that he would find a higher price in the markets of Mizra. I am not ashamed to say that I put a compulsion on him, for I gave him three fire opals for the stone, which was better than any price he would have received in Mizra. He did not know what he owned. I did him a favor to take it off his hands, for he was a fool to have been carrying such a thing.

"I did not ask him how he had obtained it, as the furtive look in his eyes proclaimed his association with the Thieves Guild. Still, to be sure, I probed his memory as he cheated Wan the Miller's wife out of several lengths of homespun cloth. There was nothing of import within his mind—just the usual, brutish thoughts typical of most men. As I suspected, he had bought the stone among an assortment of stolen goods from a member of the Guild in Damarkan. A certain Jaro Gossan. Perhaps I shall have to visit Damarkan someday and find this man?

"For thirty days and thirty nights, I studied the pearl. That is, I think it was a pearl. It resembled one, but it was harder and heavier than any pearl should have been. In color, it was dark blue with wisps of green in it that drifted upon the surface of the blue, but only if I were not gazing at the thing. Power lay bound within the pearl, bound in some strange fashion that kept it, I think, sleeping. The peculiar thing about the binding enchantment was that it seemed to be one and the same with that which it bound—a balance I had never encountered before. Despite all my skill, however, I was unable to unlock the enchantment.

"Had it not been for my leaky roof, I would have never discovered the secret of the pearl. A storm arose in the night, and water dripped down onto my table as I sat staring at the pearl. Several drops splashed on the pearl, and it was then I heard the sound of the sea. The surge of surf. The crash of waves on rock. At that moment a geas took hold of me, compelling me up from my chair. I could not muster the necessary strength to fight the compulsion. If truth be told, I was curious enough to see the matter out and where I would go. Pearl in hand, I left my abode and set off into the night in a westerly direction. At first, the geas was content enough to allow me to walk, but after several hours it grew so strong that I took to the winds in the form of a gray kestrel, pearl clutched in one claw.

"I did not wonder at the time why I chose the form of a kestrel, but it made sense after I thought on the whole affair, days later. Gray kestrels are lovers of the sea and do their hunting over the deep. I flew west for two days, over the mountains and across the plain of Scarpe. I crossed the hills of the Mearh Dun and then turned north, following the cliffs along the coast of Thule to the country of Harlech. It was at the bay of Flessoray that the geas pulled me out to sea, toward the islands. The waves were white with foam and the sea looked a cold gray, gray to match the sky and the feathers in my wings. On the barren rocks of Lesser Tor, I settled to the sand and retook my human form. The geas was gentle on my mind, bidding me stand and wait. In my hand, however, the pearl warmed.

"A wind sprang up and whipped the waves into a frenzy of spray. And out of the breakers the girl walked. She was formed of water and foam and shadows. Her skin was shell white, and seaweed twined within her dark hair in glistening strands of purple. A garment of water flowed about her limbs. Her eyes were a blue so dark that I could not discern a pupil within them. It was the unlined face of a child, one who has just woken from slumber and blinks sleepily in the sunlight. But I would not presume to guess her age, for her body was formed of the sea and the sea has existed from the earliest days. She was more beautiful than anything I had ever seen in my life, yet I feared her greatly. She smiled at me and the geas vanished from my mind.

"'Thank you for bringing back my name,' she said, and her voice was like the sighing of the waves. She reached out one pale, foam-colored hand and I placed the pearl within her grasp. I could do nothing else. She smiled again and turned to go, but I found my voice and desperately called after her to wait. At the edge of the waves, she looked back.

"'What is your name?' I said. A frown crossed her face and an ominous calm fell on the sea. Later, thinking back, I realize that the tide had stilled, but I did not recognize it then, so intent was I on her face. She spoke then, and the word was in a language I had never heard nor have ever heard since. I was almost unmade in the sound of that single word she voiced. For in the uttering was all the power and form of the sea itself. The sea roared back in response, waves rising and pounding in an exuberant fury of existence on the shoreline. At my feet, the rocks trembled and instantly became roiling sea. The island was melting away. She had vanished. And my body was dissolving into water. I flung myself skyward, taking the form of a hawk and frantic to escape. It was all I could do to keep that shape, for the word she had spoken still battered and grasped at my being. I strove onward, east, and so arrived on the coast of Harlech, exhausted and spent.

"Never in my life have I been so near death. And not just death. This was unmaking and a way of power long denied to those of us who are wizards, for we cannot tamper with the fabric of life. To unravel one small portion might mean the unraveling of all.

"I made my way back home, still in hawk's form. In my mind was the memory of the word she had spoken. I examined the remembrance. I was able to inscribe the barest hint of the word into good serviceable letters, but I soon discovered that if I delved into the memory deeper to retrieve the complete word, objects around me began to turn into water. Books, my furniture, my cooking pot, the clothes on my back, and, at one point, my entire left arm melted into a puddle of seawater before I was able to wrest it back into flesh.

"I resolved, then, to press the matter no further and sealed the memory with the strongest binding I could muster. I pray it does not reawaken some unexpected hour as I dream on my bed and so change me forever.

"The hint of the word I had already written, however, and this I set about studying. As summer faded into a rainy fall, I came to discover the ancient feorh of water woven within the word. As you know, there is a way to command the simple feorh, or essence, of what water is: *vatn*. This is known and used by most wizards. The girl's word (I only use the term "girl" because I am not sure what she was), however, was proof of a language older than existence itself. The word also indicated the existence of three additional words, as if the four together completed each other as do the sides of a square.

"At this point, I closed my books and stood in the doorway. It was a gloomy afternoon. Rain fell, blown by the wind from an iron-colored sky onto the soggy earth. Behind me, within the cottage, a fire burned on the hearth. Understanding bloomed in my mind. I had read the Lurian Codex when I was an apprentice, thinking it merely an entertaining collection of questionable history and quaint fables—the old tale of four words spoken in the darkness: wind, earth, sea, and fire. The four stillpoints that encompass existence. The four wanderers. The *anbeorun*. As I stood in my doorway, a sudden fear came to me. Fire, for example, is an amoral thing that can be used just as readily for good as it can for evil. A home can be warmed by fire or be destroyed by the same. The power I had seen unleashed at the isle of Lesser Tor could easily unmake the world. Her eyes, though, had been free of guile. They had been the serene eyes of a child. But if her power was turned toward evil, then there was no wizard, no creature in my knowledge, no army that would be able to stand against such might. Even worse, if there are four stillpoints that encompass all that is, then the danger is much greater. For though one might not turn to the shadow, there would still be three others that might fall.

"I am an old man as I set this ink to paper, but she still walks through my dreams."

Severan stopped reading and closed the book. The night sky outside the window was studded with stars. The boy stirred the brazier into flame. They were both silent for a while as they stared into the coals.

"Sometimes," said Jute, "I would run away from working the street and go down to the beach, sit on the rocks, and stare at the sea. I could sit there for hours. The waves going and coming back endlessly. She would have been out there all the time, wouldn't she?"

"If Sarcorlan is to be believed, and I think he is. I'd wager he encountered the anbeorun of the sea. Of water."

"And then the Juggler would beat me for not bringing in enough for the day." The boy shrugged and forced a laugh. "I'd always go back, sooner or later." He looked up. "But what has all of that, words and power and wizards, have to do with me doing my job?"

The old man sighed. "I'm afraid what was a simple job to you interfered with years of work done by Nio. He always was asking questions about the anbeorun. He told us some of his knowledge, grudgingly, for he needed our help in searching the university. We helped him, though we were all looking for different things. Books, words, bits of knowledge hidden in the ruins. He knew what he was looking for. A small wooden box. I daresay he spent years searching for it. I think he had some idea the box contained something to do with the anbeorun."

"You mean no one ever opened it?" the boy asked.

"No. When Nio found the box, he couldn't open it. The spell binding it shut was too strong. And he, mind you, is the strongest of us all. He didn't say anything at first. Later, though, he told us. Reluctantly. He thought, I suppose, that one of us might have some insight he had not divined. The thing's presence drove the servants mad and he's lived in that house, alone, for the past two years, with the box secreted in his tower. We lost interest in it after a while, for we all hoped to find the *Gerecednes* manuscript of Staer Gemyndes. That was always our real goal. Not an old box."

"But I don't understand," said Jute. "How could someone like him not be able to open a little box?"

"Just because someone's a wizard, it doesn't mean you can wave your hands and have pigs fly about. Though it would probably be simpler to sprout wings on a pig than to open that box."

"I'm sure someone'll figure it out someday," mumbled Jute.

Severan looked at him curiously, but the boy would not meet his glance. Outside, the wind rattled at the window, as if it wanted to get inside the room.

CHAPTER FORTY
THE CONTENTS OF THE BOX

"Tonight's the night, my good Dreccan."

The Silentman rubbed his hands together.

"Not until the gold's safely in our coffers," said Dreccan Gor.

"Always the cautious one," said the Silentman.

"I'm a Gor, and Gors are always cautious. I'd be that way even if you weren't paying me."

The Silentman and his advisor were hurrying along through the passage leading to the Guild court. Their shadows trailed behind them, for Dreccan was carrying a burning torch in his hand.

"The job's good as done," said the Silentman. "And there's nothing I like more than finishing a job. Unless it be gold. And the gold'll be plentiful for this job. Plenty for everyone. At least for you and me."

"Less a few coins here and there."

"How's that?" said the Silentman.

"Ronan will need his share, as will the Juggler. And Smede, of course."

"I don't grudge Ronan, he's a faithful dog, and we can't do without Smede to manage the books, curse his smelly little soul, but why's that fat oaf getting a cut?"

"Because," said Dreccan, trying to stay patient, "It was one of his boys that did the job in the first place. And then, of course, we had the little fellow done away with."

"Pity we can't do away with the Juggler as well. Why can't we do that? Have Ronan cut his throat."

"The Juggler, as you doubtlessly know, my lord, has proven to bring a consistent profit for us. His children sustain a steady stream of money into our coffers—"

"Then just have the children—"

"—and without his fatherly hand, I suspect that stream would dry up."

"Right, right," said the Silentman irritably. "This person needs that person to tell them what to do, and that other person needs someone else telling them how to do their job. Can't any of our people think for themselves? Perhaps we should have a few murdered, just to keep the rest of 'em on their toes."

They came to the end of the passage. An iron door was set in the wall. It bore a knocker fashioned in the likeness of a horse's head. There was no handle. Dreccan let the knocker fall. A deep bell-like tone rang out and echoed away. It sounded like a funeral knell. The door swung open for them.

"He should be here soon," said Dreccan.

The Court of the Guild was dark and empty, but the lamps high on the walls winked on, one by one, at their entrance. The light slanted across carvings etched into the stone walls and filled them with shadow. The footsteps of the two men were the only sound in the court. The Silentman shivered, and it seemed to Dreccan that the man's face trembled beneath the blur of his obscuring charm.

"Some days, old friend," said the Silentman, "I miss the sunlight. We spend too much time down here in the dark."

"Sunlight's nice," said Dreccan. "But gold is better."

The Silentman sat down in his stone chair on the dais and drew his cloak about his knees. "The cold in this place gets into my bones and aches. I'm getting old. Damn the man, where is he?"

"If our client is a man," said his advisor, frowning.

"What is he? A woman? An under-sized ogre? I don't care what he is, as long as his gold's good. Judging by the down payment, it's very good."

"I'd like to know," said Dreccan. "There was something unnerving about the fellow. Put me off my supper for days afterward."

"Who cares? Hand it to me." The Silentman turned the box over in his hands. "Strange, that such a little thing would command so much money. Have we ever gotten such a price, Dreccan? Never in my memory. It can't be the box itself our client is interested in. Look at this ugly carving. No, it's definitely what's in the box that matters. I wonder what it is? At that price, I can't imagine what it is."

"Magic," said Dreccan. "I'm sure of it. A book, or some object full of spells and power. These scholars and wizards, such as the old fools searching the university ruins, they'll spend their whole lives in search of one word from older days. Whatever's in that box is probably worth a lot more than just one word."

"Dreccan?"

"Yes?"

"You didn't try to open the thing, did you? Because this box won't open. See here? It won't open."

"My lord!"

"I can't help it. I had to try. Ever since I was a boy, I've never seen something locked that I didn't want to open. At any rate, no harm done because this thing won't open. Funny thing is, I can't sense anything magic about this box at all."

"It must have a locking spell on it. That's magic enough for me."

"Not necessarily so," said the Silentman. "Might be a lever built into the wood. Push on the hawk's beak or the like. Ingenious, some of these carpenter sorts. Though I'd have had the fellow whipped for making such ugly carvings."

At that moment, the knocker on the door tolled. Both men jumped. The tone echoed through the empty court and then died away into silence.

"Welcome to the Court of the Guild!" said the Silentman.

There was no answer. The lamps seemed to dim and the room grew even colder than it was. The Silentman shivered and pulled his cloak tightly around his shoulders. The little box was heavy in his lap. He strained his eyes but he could not see anything in the gloom. But then he blinked and there was the figure. Just like before. It stood in front of the dais. He could have sworn, a second before, nothing had been there. Damn Dreccan! The advisor's words had slipped into his mind and taken root. The figure was short and thin, shrouded in a cloak. The face was hooded and covered in shadow.

"Welcome to my court," said the Silentman.

The figure bowed its head but said nothing.

"I trust you've found your visit to Hearne profitable—that is, if you're not from our city? I hope you haven't minded the wait. These jobs can be difficult, you know, arranging all the details and—"

"No apologies are necessary," said the figure. The voice was low and muted. There was something peculiar about the sound, as if it were coming through water from a long way off. An obscuring charm, thought the Silentman to himself. A powerful one, too. Well, I won't grudge him that. After all, I use them myself.

"This is the appointed day," continued the figure. It paused and its head turned from the Silentman to Dreccan and then back. "Where's the box?"

"Right here," said the Silentman. "And our gold?"

"First the box. Was it found where I said it was?"

"Precisely," said Dreccan. "Right where you said."

The Silentman nodded. "A child could've waltzed in and lifted it."

"It took a great deal of skill," said Dreccan hastily, "our best men. And not without danger. Sadly, we lost one on the job."

The hooded face turned to him.

"Was the box opened?"

"Of course not," said the Silentman. "We followed your instructions to the letter. The Guild's about business, sir. When we accept a contract, we keep our word. We're known through all of Tormay for—"

"Put it on the steps."

Feeling somewhat disgruntled, the Silentman placed the box on the dais steps and then retreated back to his chair. The little fellow obviously did not trust them. The figure crouched over the box but did not touch it.

The hood lowered until it was almost touching the carved hawk's head on the lid. And then, the figure sniffed sharply. It straightened up.

"What have you done?!" said the figure.

"What do you mean?" said the Silentman. "We've got you your box, haven't we? Where's our gold now?"

"Your gold?" said the figure. "Curse your gold! You've opened the box!"

"You must be mistaken," said the Silentman. "No one's opened the blasted thing."

"The box has been opened, and what was once within is now gone. You'll not get your gold!"

"Here now," said the Silentman. "How do I know you're telling the truth and not just trying to swindle us out of our gold, hey? What about that? I wasn't born yesterday!"

"Fool! I would happily give you the wealth of the entire world for what was once in this box. I would have filled this court with gold. But you have brought your doom upon you. You and this accursed city!"

"Doom?" said the Silentman, alarmed at these words. "What do you mean by that?"

"Death," said the figure. "Death, and something worse. Unless you can do one thing."

"What's that?"

"Bring the person who opened the box. Bring them alive and you yourself shall live."

The Silentman gulped and mopped his forehead. The person who opened the box?

"Certainly," he said. "Anything you want. Anything at all."

"It isn't what I want. My wants are nothing. It's what my master wants. And he is coming."

"Oh, he is? And when do you think—"

"Find the person who opened the box. Quickly, for you do not know what you have done. The power that was inside the box is beyond your imagining, the power to destroy, the power to bring to life in a single breath. The power to preserve. Do you not know that all of Tormay is as dross in comparison to what that box held? Find the person who opened it. My master is coming soon!"

The Silentman opened his mouth to say something—he was not sure what—but the figure was gone. The lamplight flared and the shadows in the court retreated.

"Ronan," said Dreccan, after what seemed like a long silence.

"Find him!" The Silentman pounded his fist on his chair. "Find him now!"

"And what of the boy?" said Dreccan.

"What do you mean?" said the Silentman. "The boy's dead. Ronan killed him."

"But you heard what he said."

"What are you babbling about? I want that gold!"

"The power to destroy." Dreccan's face was pale in the lamplight. "The power to destroy, the power to bring to life in a single breath. The power to preserve."

When the Silentman spoke. His voice was slow and tired.

"Then maybe it isn't just Ronan we need to find."

CHAPTER FORTY-ONE
THE VIEW TO THE EAST

The hawk angled through the night sky on his outstretched wings. The city of Hearne lay far beneath him, pricked with light here and there, but mostly sleeping in darkness on the edge of the sea. The night sky above the hawk had more light to offer than the city, blazing and sparkling with stars in a perfectly clear expanse. The stars seemed impossibly close, and they bent their gaze down to the world and to the hawk flying alone in the night.

There were, perhaps, only four people in all of Tormay, save the hawk, who would have had the wisdom to hear the speech of stars, but they all were asleep. Only the hawk heard.

The stars hastened lower, growing in brilliance and deepening in the colors of their fire. Ruby, emerald, diamond and amethyst, the night grew darker and blacker around them as they burned ever brighter with their gem-like fire.

Hast thou seen? whispered one star.

Hast thou seen and hast thou not heard?

There is one who dreams in the darkness.

But he sleeps still, said another star.

Thankfully, he sleeps.

And thou, little wing, thou must watch and wait.

Watch and wait.

Look ye to the east.

Fly well, little wing, murmured another star.

Aye, fly well, for the house of dreams sleeps not.

Never sleeps but doth watch over all.

Even the stars, added another stars.

Even the stars!

Rejoice!

And with this word echoing in the sky, the voices of the stars grew and rose in liquid song, thrilling through the dark and the bitter cold and the unfathomable distances of space. The sky trembled with the sound. The beauty of it was so sharp and sudden that the hawk faltered in his flight. But then the chorus died away and the stars withdrew to their appointed courses, shining in comfort and sorrow. The two will ever go hand-in-hand, for that is the balance of wisdom. The hawk knew it well, knew it to his own comfort and sorrow.

As he flew, the hawk considered carefully what he had heard. His gaze until this moment had ever been on the city of Hearne, particularly on the dark ruins of the university where the boy Jute slept. Now, however, he turned his beak to the east and looked there. There was no one in all of Tormay, no person, animal, or bird, who had as keen eyesight as the hawk. But even he could not pierce the night with his vision. All he could make out, far across the miles and distance, was the vague, jagged outlines of the Morn Mountains in the east, their snowy peaks touched here and there with starlight and moonlight.

With a shrug of his wings, the hawk turned and spiraled down toward the city. Hearne slept in an uneasy quiet below him. He could hear the surge and crash of the waves on the beach beneath the wharves. He could smell bread baking as a baker went about his lonely morning duties. His sharp eyes caught a hint of movement in an alley as three cats strolled along, careless and casual in their pursuit of rodents. Despite these tiny signs of life, the city lay in darkness. A deep darkness.

The hawk alighted on top of the tallest tower in the university ruins. He furled his wings. He could feel the whispering of the wards guarding the university. Down and away to his right, in one of the larger and better preserved wings of the complex, he sensed Jute. Sleeping, safe and sound. The hawk nodded in satisfaction at this. The wind blowing past the tower seemed to sigh in agreement.

The hawk turned and gazed to the east. There was nothing to see there except for the night, of course. But that did not matter to the hawk. He waited and watched and he did not sleep. He spent the remainder of the night there, perched in silence on the tower roof. And even when the first faint blush of sunrise crept up into the eastern sky, the hawk was still watching.

This story continues in
The Shadow at the Gate.

AUTHOR NOTE

Thank you for taking the time to read *The Hawk and His Boy*. I began writing The Tormay Trilogy ten years ago, back in the year 2000, during a snowy Chicago winter. It was a labor of love, inspired by all the reading and dreaming I'd done, ever since I was a child. I hope some of my own enjoyment in the creation of the story shines through. *The Hawk and His Boy*, however, is merely the beginning of the tale of Jute and the land of Tormay. It was never intended to be read on its own, but should be followed up with *The Shadow at the Gate* and *The Wicked Day*. I hope you have the chance to read those two books as well.

A great many thanks are in order: Jen Ballinger for copy-editing, Alex Aparin and Ron Eddy for the cover design, and Jared Blando for illustrating the map. Also, a heartfelt thanks to my many test-readers: Rob and Sandra Kammerzell, Daniel White, Frank Troya, Jaemen Kennedy, Susanne McLarty, Scott Mathias, Dave Palshaw, Wayne and Jessica Collingwood, and the many, long-suffering members of the Bunn Clan (David, Michael, Jodi, Ben, Micha, Megan and, of course, Jessica).

Anyway, if you enjoyed *The Hawk and His Boy*, please take the time to tell a friend or leave a review on Amazon (or wherever you found my writing). I greatly depend on such kindness from readers to help spread the word about my stories. Please feel free to contact me with questions or concerns at my website: www.christopherbunn.com.

Sincerely,
Christopher Bunn

ABOUT THE AUTHOR

Christopher Bunn was born and raised in California. After serving his required sentence in school, he spent some years wandering around the world. He has worked in six of the seven continents, holding jobs in construction, television production, relief and development, and shoe-making. Currently, he lives and works on a farm in California with his wife and children.

Made in the USA
Charleston, SC
11 November 2013